Another Woman's Man

Also by Shelly Ellis

Can't Stand the Heat

The Player & the Game

Published by Dafina Books

Another Woman's Man

SHELLY ELLIS

KENSINGTON PUBLISHING CORP.
www.kensingtonbooks.com

DAFINA BOOKS are published by

Kensington Publishing Corp.
119 West 40th Street
New York, NY 10018

All Kensington titles, imprints, and distributed lines are available at special quantity discounts for bulk purchases for sales promotion, premiums, fund-raising, and educational or institutional use.

Special book excerpts or customized printings can also be created to fit specific needs. For details, write or phone the office of the Kensington Special Sales Manager: Kensington Publishing Corp., 119 West 40th Street, New York, NY 10018. Attn. Special Sales Department. Phone: 1-800-221-2647.

Dafina and the D logo Reg. U.S. Pat. & TM Off.

ISBN-13: 978-0-7582-9038-0
ISBN-10: 0-7582-9038-1
First Trade Paperback Printing: May 2014

eISBN-13: 978-0-7582-9099-1
eISBN-10: 0-7582-9099-3
First Electronic Edition: May 2014

10 9 8 7 6 5 4 3 2 1

Printed in the United States of America

To Chloe:
I walk a little taller knowing I'm your mommy.

To Andrew:
My load's a lot lighter because you are my hubby.

Acknowledgments

With each book it becomes harder and harder to write my acknowledgments page because the list of people whom I should thank gets longer. Inevitably, I'm going to forget someone, but I will try my best!

First and foremost, I'd like to thank my husband, Andrew. You were there long before the first book in the Gibbons Gold Digger series was ever written. You've listened to me lament or held me during a good cry after every rejection letter. You did the happy dance with me whenever I got good news. Even though you prefer to just skip to the sex scenes, you believe in me and my work, and I will be forever grateful for that. Now that we have our little girl, my writing time is even more compressed (and coveted), so I appreciate you watching her while I type away. Your love and assistance is invaluable, Andrew.

Thanks to my editor, Mercedes, for taking a chance on me. You've gone the additional step by believing I can actually have a career in this industry and you're willing to support it. I'm happy my submission made it into your inbox (and you responded!). You chose me out of many. I'm a very lucky girl.

Thanks to my parents; you were my earliest supporters and critics. Mom, I don't know where I would be now if you hadn't lent me the first book in the MacGregor Series, which made me *really* want to be a romance writer. Dad, thanks for patiently waiting for me at the library desk when I couldn't decide between copies of the Sweet Valley Twins.

Thanks to Aunt Rachel, Great-Grandma, and Grand-daddy for knowing how to tell a good story.

Thanks to the blerds and blerdettes of Black Girl Nerds for giving me a platform to share my literary work, my nerdiness, and my thoughts. I've met so many of you guys through the site and Twitter. Jamie Broadnax, I have no doubt that you will build your Black Girl Nerds media empire one day. At least I can say I was there at the beginning!

Thanks to fellow authors Samara King, Alexandra Caselle, Stacy-Deanne, Jill Archer, Sezoni Whitfield, and Deatri King-Bey for hosting me on your websites. And thanks to DJ Kimberly Kaye for hosting me on the radio!

Thanks to Romance Novels in Color, Teresa Beasley, KC Girlfriends Book Club, African Americans on the Move Book Club, and Romance in Color for your glowing and *honest* reviews. Thanks to Black Expressions for selecting my book to sell to your readers.

Thanks to the readers who have reached out to me to say they like my books.

Finally, thanks to the family members and friends who I didn't mention by name but who have supported me and my writing.

Chapter 1

(Unwritten) Rule No. 5 of the Gibbons Family Handbook: Family always comes first—while men come somewhere between shoes and handbags.

"He's amazing!"

"I know! Isn't he brilliant?"

"The show is wonderful! Just wonderful!"

If they only knew, Dawn Gibbons thought as she glanced around the crowded gallery.

She looked at the people strolling throughout the exhibition space, at the couples who stared at the canvases on the exposed brick walls and nodded in appreciation, and she wanted to give herself a toast. She hadn't thought she would be able to pull this off, considering the limited amount of time she had to organize this exhibition, considering how much arm twisting she had to do to get tonight's featured artist to just pick up a paintbrush and *paint something!* But she had done it. Despite all the obstacles she had faced, tonight had been a resounding success. Dawn didn't toast herself, but she downed what was left of her Moët & Chandon and smiled.

"Great work, darling!" said Percy, the gallery's owner, in his British accent as he sailed toward her.

He was wearing a leather jacket and faded jeans today—an outfit that was much too young for a man his age. His thinning gray hair was pulled back with a rubber band, leaving a knobby stub of hair at the end. The three top buttons of his silk shirt were open, revealing the wiry hairs on his pale chest. He wrapped a skinny arm around Dawn's waist and gave her an affectionate squeeze.

"Thanks, Percy." She wrinkled her nose at the overpowering smell of his cologne and nodded. "It did turn out well, didn't it?"

"We should go somewhere after the show and celebrate, darling," he whispered warmly as he leaned toward her ear. The smell of his cologne became five times stronger. The heat of his breath on her cheek almost singed her. "Maybe you'll finally let me take you out to dinner." His hand descended from her waist to her ass. He petted it gently—like he would a purring kitten—and winked one of his blue eyes at her. "What do you say?"

"Oh, you don't have to do that." She slowly removed Percy's hand from her bottom. "But thank you for the offer."

Percy was one of the few rich men in Dawn's social circle whom she hadn't dated, and quite frankly, she didn't have any plans to ever date him. He was her boss! Her art and her work as gallery director were more important to her. Unfortunately, Percy wasn't accustomed to women turning him down, which probably made him even more eager to get her to dinner and finally get into her pants. She was a challenge to him now, the Mt. Everest that he had yet to climb. But she desperately wished he would take his mountain boots and pick and climb somewhere else.

"I should go around the room and mingle." Dawn

patted his arm soothingly, hoping to soften the blow of her rejection. "You know, make sure everyone is enjoying themselves and—more importantly—buying the artwork."

"Yes. Yes, of course, darling." His smile tightened, barely masking his disappointment. "Mingle! Mingle! Don't let me keep you."

She turned and walked away, handing off her empty glass to one of the waiters who strolled around the room with Lucite trays covered with hors d'oeuvres and champagne glasses.

Her sister Lauren's restaurant, Le Bayou Bleu, was catering the event with Southern-style, high-end cuisine that all the patrons couldn't seem to get enough of. In fact, she heard whispers from the staff that they were dangerously close to running out of food.

Lauren couldn't be here tonight herself to supervise. She was still on maternity leave and was at home with her infant son, Crisanto Jr., but Dawn's other two sisters had shown their support by coming to the event. Her very pregnant sister, Stephanie, had waddled through an hour ago. She had purchased one of the smaller pieces on display before leaving the gallery with a mouthful of shrimp. Dawn's eldest sister Cynthia had left fifteen minutes later. She said she had a date with a very wealthy construction company owner and had to run home to change clothes.

"He's handsome, charming, and he pulled in seven figures last year, girl. You never know," Cynthia had remarked. "He could be *the* one!"

By "*the* one" Dawn assumed Cynthia really meant number three, since this would be Cynthia's *third* husband if she managed to get this one down the aisle. Though, truth be told, Dawn had little room to talk herself. She had been married twice before also, continuing the long tradition in her family of women who married often and divorced just as frequently. But unlike Cynthia, Dawn had little interest in finding a third husband.

Dawn had been doing some soul-searching and self-examination lately with all the changes that were going on around her. Two of her sisters had fallen in love. One had recently had a baby and the other had one on the way. Dawn felt like she had reached a point in her life when obtaining a rich husband wasn't as important to her anymore. Besides, rich men were a lot like the temperamental artists whose work she featured at her gallery. They both required coddling and their egos had to be constantly fed. She didn't have time to cater to both right now.

Dawn continued her path across the gallery, adjusting the cowl neck of her maroon top and the hem of her asymmetrical wool skirt as she went.

"Congratulations, dearest," said Madison McGuire, a small-town girl who made good by marrying one of the most powerful lobbyists in Washington, D.C. Now the wealthy D.C. socialite patronized the local art scene.

"Thank you for coming, Maddie!" Dawn said, leaning forward and lightly kissing the air beside Maddie's rouged cheek.

"Oh, I wouldn't miss it for the world!" Maddie exclaimed. She took a sip from the champagne glass. "The exhibit is fascinating . . . and of course, I have to do my research!"

"*Research?* You know, a little birdie told me that you're thinking about buying Sawyer Gallery, but I wasn't sure if that was just a rumor."

Maddie laughed. "Oh, it's not a rumor. I can assure

you of that! Martin Sawyer is ready to move on to a new venture, and I told him I'd happily take the gallery off his hands. We signed the paperwork a month ago. I plan to hold our grand opening sometime in the spring." She leaned toward Dawn and whispered, "Do you think you would be interested in changing venues? I'd love to have you at the helm of my gallery."

Dawn glanced across the room at Percy, who was idly groping some bouncy young blonde as he stood among a circle of friends.

Maddie's offer was certainly tempting. Unlike with Percy, Dawn wouldn't have to worry about Maddie patting her ass and trying to seduce her on a weekly basis. Plus, Dawn had always admired Maddie. If there was nothing a Gibbons girl loved more, it was a fellow woman who used her wiles and her wits to climb the socioeconomic ladder, a woman who knew how to "get her hustle on" but to do it with grace and style.

But Dawn liked the control Percy gave her over the gallery. She loved her staff. She was comfortable here.

Dawn sighed. "I don't think I would, Maddie, but thank you for the offer."

Maddie glanced in Percy's direction. He and the blonde were now making kissy faces at each other, making Dawn cringe.

"Are you *sure?*" Maddie asked again. "I heard Percy can be quite the handful."

You have no idea, Dawn thought. She hesitated then nodded. "I'm sure."

"Oh, well. It was worth a try." Maddie waved her hand. "Always good to see you, Dawn."

"You too," Dawn replied, continuing to make her way across the cavernous space. She stopped now and then to talk to and kiss the cheeks of a few patrons, but she soon noticed two men she hadn't seen before. They were standing near one of the floor-to-ceiling canvases on the far side of the gallery. They drew her attention because their staid business attire made them stand out like sore thumbs from the rest of the flamboyantly dressed art crowd.

The shorter of the two stood in front of one of the paintings, gazing at it admiringly. The elderly gentleman was dark-skinned and very distinguished looking with his navy blazer, tan slacks, white dress shirt, and penny loafers. He leaned his weight against a bamboo cane as he bent forward to read the plaque near the painting.

Beside him was a man who was almost a foot taller and was several decades younger. He was less engrossed in the artwork than his companion. Instead, he stared in amazement at the people in the gallery as if he were watching circus performers. His honey-colored skin and short dark hair was in striking contrast to his pale gray eyes that she could see distinctly even at this distance. He was handsome, though a little too straitlaced for her taste.

Accountant? she thought as she scanned his perfect black suit, sensible blue tie, and starched white shirt. *No, he's probably an actuary, I bet. Any person who dresses that boring has to be in insurance.*

She slowly walked toward them. Boring or not, they could be prospective buyers—wealthy suburbanites with a lot of cash to spend who wanted to impress their friends with the discovery of a hot new artist.

"Hello," Dawn said. She extended her hand. "My name is Dawn Gibbons. Is this your first time at our gallery?"

She offered her hand to the older gentleman first. He hesitated before taking it.

"Hello," he said softly, finally shaking her hand. His

wrinkled face filled with warmth. "It's a . . . a pleasure to finally meet you, Dawn," he began nervously. "I-I had debated on coming here tonight. I couldn't work up the nerve at first until my friend Xavier, here"—he nodded toward the younger man who stood silently at his side—"agreed to come with me. But I really wanted to . . . Oh, listen to me ramble. I should introduce myself first." He cleared his throat. "My . . . My name is Herbert Allen."

"Pleased to meet you, Mr. Allen." She nodded in greeting. "Thank you for coming to our gallery." She pointed toward the painting. "So tell me, are you interested in this piece?"

He paused and gazed at her quizzically. "You've . . . you've never heard of me before?"

Dawn's smile faded. She shook her head. "No, I'm sorry. I haven't."

He looked deflated.

Now put on the spot, Dawn quickly flipped through her mental Rolodex, trying to recall the name, Herbert Allen, but she came up with a blank. She hoped he wasn't someone important. Percy would be royally PO'd if he found out she had offended one of his friends.

Suddenly, something came to mind. She snapped her fingers. "Oh, I remember now! I'm so sorry. Tonight has been so crazy and I've been so frazzled!" She laughed and patted his shoulder, turning back on the charm. "Herbert Allen. Yes, I remember. We met at the spring benefit last year, didn't we?"

He and the younger man exchanged a look. He then shook his head. "No, we didn't meet at a spring benefit. In fact, we've never met before. I had . . . I had hoped your mother had mentioned me, at least." He shrugged. "But I guess not."

Dawn frowned. "My mother?"

He took a deep breath and gazed into her eyes. "I'm your father, Dawn."

"*What?*" Her gaze shifted between the two men. "I'm sorry. Is . . . is this some kind of a joke?"

"No, it's not a joke. I really am your father."

He took a step toward her and she took a hesitant step back, trying desperately to process what she was hearing.

"Dawn, I wanted to have a chance to—"

"Wait. Wait! Stop! Back up!" She held up her hands. Her heart thudded like a snare drum in her chest. "What are you talking about? What do you mean you're my father? I . . ." She took a deep breath, fighting to regain her calm. "I haven't seen or heard from my father in thirty-seven years and you . . . you just show up out of the blue like this! You just blurt this out!"

His eyes lowered to the hardwood floor. "I know and I'm sorry. I didn't want to do it this way, but I don't have—"

"No!" She furiously shook her head. "No, I'm not . . . I'm not doing this."

Dawn turned around and walked away from him. She angrily strode toward the gallery's revolving glass doors, ignoring the curious stares that followed her as she passed. She felt as if she had been ambushed. Was he really her father? If so, why did he choose tonight of all nights to announce himself? Why hadn't he picked up a phone and called? Couldn't he have sent a letter? This was ridiculous! She was practically trembling with anger and confusion. She had to get out of there.

"Darling, where are you going?" Percy called after her, but she ignored him.

Dawn stepped into the gallery's foyer. It was decorated for the holiday season with garlands, holly, and twinkling Christmas lights, but she certainly wasn't in the holiday mood right now. Just before she reached the doors, she felt a strong hand clamp around her wrist. She whipped her head around and looked up. When she did, she was staring into the gray eyes of the wannabe actuary. His warm touch and gaze instantly made her tingle, catching her by surprise. It was a feeling she didn't want right now. She yanked her wrist out of his grasp.

"Can you hear him out?" he asked. "It took a lot of courage for him to come here tonight!"

"Courage?" She glared up at him. "Is that what you call it? Why didn't he find that same damn courage ten or twenty years ago? Where the hell has he been all this time? Why is he doing this here? Why *now?"*

His stern expression softened and once again she was struck by how handsome he was.

"Look, Herb knows that he hasn't been the best father to you. Believe me. But your mother didn't exactly make it easy for him these past years."

Dawn narrowed her eyes at the mention of her mother. She crossed her arms over her chest. *"Excuse me?"*

"Look, all that it'll take is ten minutes of your time. He came all this way. Just . . . just let him explain himself. Please? He has a lot that he would like to get off his chest and he doesn't have much time left to do it."

"What? What do you mean?"

"Your father is sick, Dawn. He has cancer . . . and the prognosis isn't good."

Dawn's arms dropped to her sides. She stared at him in disbelief.

God, this was a lot to take in! Here she was in the middle of an exhibition and her apparent long-lost father had suddenly popped up out of nowhere, and now she had the added shock of finding out he was dying from cancer. What was she going to find out next? That a spaceship had landed outside the gallery? Dawn closed her eyes and raised her hands to her now-throbbing temples. She desperately wished her sisters were here. She could use one of their shoulders to lean on right now.

"Will you give him a chance?" wannabe actuary asked quietly. "Hear what he has to say?"

Dawn opened her eyes. She was still furious, but part of her worried that she would regret this moment if she walked out of the gallery and didn't come back.

"Fine."

She then walked back across the gallery with wannabe actuary trailing behind her.

As she crossed the room, she examined the older man more closely. He had skin the same shade as her own and large dark eyes she could have easily inherited. Those dark eyes now gazed at her worriedly.

Her mother had never talked about her father—or any of Dawn's sisters' fathers, for that matter.

"As long as he takes care of his financial obligations to you, what difference does it make whether you see him?" Yolanda Gibbons would ask when her daughters were younger and they openly wondered why they had not received so much as a birthday card or telephone call from any their fathers. "*We're* important," Yolanda would insist. "Not a man who knows absolutely nothing about you."

Though Dawn had longed for her father in her younger years, she had gradually accepted her mother's opinion on the issue as she got older. If Dawn's father really had cared, he would have tried to contact her. He would have moved heaven and earth to let her know he wanted her and loved her. Now as she watched the man claiming to be her father take uncertain steps toward her, she knew there was no real explanation he could offer for his absence all these years. But she would listen. She would give him his ten minutes, then send him on his way.

"Thank you for coming back," he said gently. He leaned most of his weight on his cane. "I apologize for how I did this. I didn't want to tell you this over the phone, and I didn't know how to—"

"Not here," she said firmly, cutting him off. "We can talk in my office."

She walked around him and led him toward a corridor filled with a series of rooms at the back of the gallery. She paused at her office door and turned. "In here," she said, motioning toward the doorway.

He glanced up at the younger man.

"I'll take it from here, Xavier," he said. "Thank you."

Xavier looked at Herbert, then at Dawn. Their eyes met. She cocked her eyebrow in challenge. Was he going to insist he come along?

After some time, Xavier finally nodded. "Okay, I'll . . . I'll wait here."

Herbert continued down the corridor.

"But call me if you need me!" Xavier shouted out to him.

Herbert nodded and waved him away. "Don't worry. I'll be fine."

"Is he your bodyguard or something?" she whispered when Herbert stood next to her.

She still eyed the actuary guardedly. He equally scrutinized her from the other end of the hall.

"Close," Herbert said with a soft chuckle. "He's my lawyer . . . well, corporate counsel for my company."

Lawyer, huh?

Well, she guessed he wasn't an actuary after all.

Dawn ushered Herbert into her small eight- by eight-foot office and shut the door behind him. She had kept the space simple in its décor with an industrial design desk and leather chairs. A bookshelf was on the right wall. The only adornment in the office was the several paintings by the gallery's many artists and a few works of hers.

"Have a seat," she said, gesturing to one of the chairs opposite her desk.

She sat down in her rollaway desk chair and watched as he carefully lowered himself into his. When he sat down, he let out a barely stifled groan.

He does look sick, she thought as she looked at his slightly ashen face.

"Dawn," he began, "I understand that you're angry with me, but I didn't want to put this off another day. I've been putting off coming to see you for weeks now."

"Why?"

He lowered his eyes. "Because I know it's something I should have done years ago and I feel like such a . . . such a bastard for taking so long to do it, sweetheart."

Sweetheart? It was odd hearing a stranger call her that.

He hesitated. "When you were a little girl, I had thought about seeing you. But your mother and I did not part amicably, to be honest. I allowed my feelings toward your mother to taint whatever possibility we had of developing a relationship. I was . . . I was wrong for doing that."

Dawn didn't say anything in response. What was there to say?

"I didn't find out about you until after you were born," he continued. "My lawyer at the time got a letter from your mother stating that she had a baby and that she was seeking child support. I was . . ." He paused again. "I was very shocked . . . and angry. You see, Yolanda and I hadn't dated for very long."

"Long enough to make a baby, though," Dawn interjected, leaning back in her chair.

"That is true. I'm not denying that. But again, we had dated only briefly. We were together for only a month or so and then I was transferred to my company's satellite office in Europe. I never got the chance to really know her. Then my lawyer found out a bit more about her . . . her background. The marriages . . . How she dated wealthy men almost exclusively. When I found out, I felt . . . manipulated . . . *duped,* in a way. Like she had used my affections and—"

"Trapped you?" Dawn finished for him. She rolled her eyes. "Look, if you're here to talk shit about my mom, we can end this conversation right now." She began to rise from her chair. "Thank you, Mr. Allen, for your visit, but—"

"No, no! That's not what I intended. I just . . ." He took a deep breath. "I just wanted you to know why I did what I did. There's no excuse for it, but that was my thinking at the time. Please, Dawn. Please sit down."

Her nostrils flared. She slowly lowered herself to her seat, crossed her legs, and adjusted the hem of her skirt.

"Sweetheart, I didn't come here to insult your mother or to make you angry. I came here to try to make amends. I'm not well. I have . . . I have prostate cancer, and despite my doctors' best efforts, it's . . . it's spread."

"I'm sorry to hear that," she said quietly, and she meant it.

He cleared his throat. "When you're faced with an illness, you start to reexamine your life and the mistakes you've made. Not building a relationship with you was one of my biggest mistakes, and I would like to rectify that if I can."

"How?"

"I'd like to get to know you, Dawn, and to spend time with you, if you will allow it. Maybe we can have dinner together or spend a day or two together. Whatever you would like to do, I'm willing to do it."

Dawn closed her eyes again. She didn't want to be cruel, but this was too much, *way* too much. She hadn't even known this man existed until fifteen minutes ago. Now he wanted to build a relationship. She opened her eyes.

"Maybe. But can I . . . can I take some time to think about this?"

He gazed at her for a long time then finally nodded. "Sure, I understand."

But he didn't look like he understood. He looked disappointed.

Dawn rose from her chair and he followed suit. She walked him to her office door. When she opened the door, he turned and looked at her.

"Even . . . even if we don't see one another again, Dawn, it was a pleasure to finally meet you," he said, offering her his hand.

She shook it. "It was a pleasure to meet you too, Mr. Allen."

He gave a small smile. "Please, you don't have to call me Dad, but at least call me Herb."

"It was a pleasure to meet you, Herb."

He opened his jacket and handed her a business card. "If you do wish to meet again, here is my number. I do hope . . . I do hope to hear from you, Dawn. I sincerely do."

"Thank you," she said, taking his card.

She watched as he stepped into the corridor. He was still gazing at her as she shut the door behind him. When the lock clicked, she fell against the wooden slab and let out a pent-up breath she didn't know she had been holding all this time.

Chapter 2

"So he just showed up at the gallery?" Cynthia exclaimed.

"*Shh!*" Dawn said, raising her finger to her lips and silencing her sister. She glanced at their mother, Yolanda, who was smiling and chatting with the salesgirl on the other side of the bridal shop. The older woman pointed to an off-white, off-the-shoulder wedding gown on display on one of the mannequins in the shop window. The eager salesgirl nodded, climbed on the dress platform, and began to undo the buttons and zipper at the back of the gown.

Their mother was picking out the wedding gown she planned to wear when she married a widower and her *sixth* husband, Reginald Whitfield III, two and a half months from now. Her daughters were helping her with the selection, though Yolanda could have easily chosen the dress by herself. She certainly had enough practice at it.

Dawn, Cynthia, Stephanie, and Lauren sat on the plush velvet chairs near the shop's three-way mirrors and dressing rooms while their mother flitted around the front of the store, pointing at dresses, floating in a sea of satin, organza, and tulle. Cynthia was nursing a complimentary glass of champagne. Stephanie was stuffing her face with the box of mint chocolate cookies she had stashed in her leather purse. Lauren was leaning over her infant son Crisanto Jr., who was sleeping in his carrier, and Dawn was recounting the story of meeting her long-lost father.

"Try to keep it down!" Dawn whispered shrilly at Cynthia. "Mama might hear you."

Dawn didn't want to ruin her mother's day by bringing up one of her exes. She didn't know when she would approach the topic with her mother, but now certainly didn't seem like the best time.

Cynthia rolled her hazel eyes heavenward. "Fine." She dropped her voice to a whisper so that she could barely be heard over the harp music tinkling in the background on the bridal shop's hidden speakers. "So he came to the show after we left?"

Dawn shrugged. "He could have been in the gallery when you guys were there, for all I know. He and his lawyer looked like they had been there for a while."

"He came with *his lawyer?*" Stephanie asked between munches of cookies. She pushed her long hair over her shoulder then slowly rubbed her ample pregnant belly. "Who the hell brings their lawyer with them to meet their daughter for the first time?"

"I don't think he was, you know, a regular lawyer. He called him his friend. And he seemed like a friend. He was very . . . very protective of him. Besides, I think he was only there for moral support."

Suddenly, the image of her father's lawyer Xavier came to mind: his firmly set jaw, those pale gray eyes, and that sculpted mouth. He didn't look very old, in his early thirties, maybe. A handsome brother like that probably had women clamoring for him. She hadn't noticed a wedding ring, but she bet Mr. Prim and Proper was already taken. He practically had "wife, dog, and two kids in a sensible two-story colonial home" written all over him.

Dawn shook her head, pushing thoughts of Xavier aside. He wasn't the focus right now. Her father was.

Cynthia placed her champagne glass on the end table beside her. "Well, what are you going to do? You said he left you his business card. So are you going to call him?"

"I don't know. I haven't decided yet," Dawn admitted.

"What do you mean you haven't decided?" Lauren asked. She adjusted the yellow baby blanket over her son and turned to look at her sisters. "Dawn, honey, I would jump on this one. This could be a once-in-a-lifetime opportunity. You said yourself that he has cancer. You have no idea how much time he has left."

"But that's the thing," Dawn said, throwing up her hands. "He finds out that he's dying and he suddenly decides he wants to look me up! What was he doing? Checking me off his bucket list? *Goal Number Four: Contact the daughter you deserted thirty-seven years ago and suck up to her.* I suddenly mean something to him now that he gets a bad prognosis from his doctor? I mean, come on! I'm sorry if I sound selfish, but I'm a little pissed off!"

"Maybe it's the season," Lauren suggested. "Christmas and the holidays tend to make people more reflective. Maybe that's another reason why he contacted you."

"Oh, that's even better! So if he got his prognosis in August he wouldn't have even bothered," Dawn said.

"I can't imagine walking away from my little girl," Stephanie confessed suddenly with a frown, rubbing her belly again. She stopped eating her cookie. "It would be like ripping my heart out of my chest."

"I couldn't do that to my little one either, Steph, but think about it," Lauren said. "If Keith and you were to break up and the baby never got a chance to know him, wouldn't that break your heart too?"

Keith was Stephanie's man—a rugged private detective whom no one would have pegged as Stephanie's type. The two had a whirlwind romance that began nine months ago when she hired him to find her ex-fiancé, a con man named Isaac who had swindled her out of her money. The couple now lived in Stephanie's townhouse in Chesterton, Virginia, and they were expecting their first child.

Stephanie scowled at Lauren's question. "Of course it would break my heart! I love Keith! I'd want the baby to love him too."

"Soooo," Lauren said slowly, "if your baby got older and she got the opportunity to finally meet her father, you'd encourage her to do it, right?"

Stephanie thought for a minute. "Well, yeah."

"Exactly!" Lauren exclaimed. "I rest my case."

"What do you mean? You rest *what case?*" Cynthia asked. "My little girl Clarissa—"

"Cindy, Clarissa is almost nineteen years old. I think you can stop calling her your 'little girl' now," Lauren muttered sarcastically.

"*My baby,*" Cynthia insisted, "has only seen her father six times after he and I divorced, and if you ask me that was six times too many."

"But you hate your ex's guts," Dawn argued.

"For a good reason—he's an asshole!" Cynthia shouted, drawing the salesgirl's and their mother's attention.

The salesgirl lowered the tulle veil she had been holding. Yolanda glared in her daughters' direction. "What are you girls talking about?"

"Nothing!" they answered in unison. They all forced smiles.

Yolanda stared at them warily for several seconds before returning her attention to one of the wedding gowns.

"But not everybody's ex is an asshole like yours, Cindy," Lauren whispered, continuing their conversation. "Dawn's father actually could be a nice guy, and the only way she'll ever find that out is if she agrees to see him again."

"Well, I'll be honest with you, Dawn," Stephanie said, nibbling at another cookie. She clutched the half-empty cellophane package in her other hand. "I'm a little jealous that he came looking for you."

"Me too," Lauren concurred with a nod.

"I'm not!" Cynthia loudly proclaimed.

"I mean, my father didn't come looking for me. I've always wondered what he was like. Unless I track him down, I'll never know." Stephanie turned and gazed into Dawn's eyes. "You don't have to do that. He came to you. Now all those nagging little questions you've ever had about him will be answered."

Dawn stared at her sister in surprise. Stephanie wasn't usually the most insightful person. In fact, Dawn had always considered Stephanie to be the most self-involved sister in their little family, but today Stephanie was making a damned good argument. Like her sisters, Dawn had always wondered about her father. Where did he grow up? What was his family like? What traits might she have inherited from him? It was as if there was an entire side of herself that she knew absolutely nothing about. Her father had now offered her the opportunity to find the answers to all of those lingering questions. Whatever time she spent with him, she knew instinctively that he would treasure it. He saw this as a chance to right past wrongs. Meanwhile, it could be a chance for her to discover new things—perhaps even new things about herself.

"All right," Dawn muttered. "I guess I'll give him a call."

"Good decision!" Lauren clapped her hands and beamed. "Honey, I am so proud of you!"

Just then Crisanto Jr. opened his eyes and began to whimper. His tiny face formed into a tight ball of irritation at being woken up. Lauren quickly leaned forward and gave him his pacifier before gently rocking his carrier.

"So how does this work?" Dawn asked, glancing at her sisters. "Where exactly do you go on a first date with your father?"

The three women sat and contemplated Dawn's question for several seconds.

"Well, the few times Clarissa met her dad, they always went to Chuck E. Cheese's," Cynthia volunteered. "That seemed to be his thing. I always saw lots of fathers there with their kids."

"Considering that I'm thirty-seven and not six years old, I don't think Chuck E. Cheese's will work in this case, Cindy, but thanks for the helpful suggestion," Dawn said with a droll roll of her big brown eyes.

"Take him to a place where you feel comfortable," Stephanie suggested, wiping away cookie crumbs from the front of her silk blouse. "Where's your favorite place to go?"

Dawn thought for a minute. "I know just the place."

Chapter 3

Xavier Hughes was used to his fiancée, Constance, looking bored. Whenever they were at dinner parties or when he talked about his busy day at work as general counsel at Allen Enterprises, her eyes would glaze over. She'd glance at her nails and mutter something about needing a manicure, then she'd get up and walk away minutes later. That's just the type of girl she was. Despite her name, concentration and consistency weren't Constance's strong points.

But Xavier wasn't too happy seeing her looking bored now while they were in bed together, particularly while they were in the middle of foreplay and he was trying his very damn best to make her moan and her toes curl. Instead, Constance gazed at the ceiling above her, absently twirling a brown lock of hair around her finger and staring at the blades of his ceiling fan like they were the most fascinating objects in the world.

Xavier raised his mouth from her breast, leaned back on his elbows, and grimaced. "So I guess this isn't working for you?"

She tore her eyes from the ceiling fan and looked down at him. "Huh? Oh, no, pumpkin, I like it. It feels ... nice."

"*Nice?*"

A word you used to describe the weather, but not a word that a man wanted to hear while he was sucking on your nipples.

She must have realized that this wasn't the response he was hoping for.

"I mean *very* nice, pumpkin." She pushed herself up and lay back against the pillows stacked behind her. "I-I mean . . ."

Xavier grumbled as he climbed back to the head of the bed. He rolled onto his side and looked down at her, his hard-on now fading faster than the dying embers in his bedroom fireplace. "What's wrong?"

She pushed her hair out of her eyes. "Why do you think something's wrong?"

"Because you're lying there . . ."

Like a corpse, he wanted to say, but he caught himself.

He didn't want to start an argument. They had argued before about her being unresponsive in bed. The last time they did, she had stalked out of his bedroom in a huff—buck-naked. He had to chase her down as she threw open his front door and walked into the hallway. She had been mere milliseconds away from giving all his reserved, elderly neighbors a free peep show. Constance had even threatened to call off the wedding. Xavier had to apologize and beg her to calm down and come back.

He certainly didn't want to repeat that little episode.

"You're obviously not into it tonight," he said diplomatically. "Something's on your mind. What's wrong?"

She pursed her lips and he gazed at her profile. His eyes scanned the outline of her perfect button nose, perfect pouty lips, and perfect dark eyes in the shadows of his darkened bedroom. Constance Allen had always been a head turner. At least, Xavier had always thought so, ever since that first day he met her when she was thirteen years old and he was fourteen, and her father, Herb Allen, had introduced them at one of his soirées.

"I wonder what she's like," Constance finally said, her eyes returning to the ceiling fan.

"What who's like?"

"Dawn . . . my half sister. I wish I was there when he met her."

So that's what's eating at her, Xavier thought.

Constance and her mother, Raquel, were surprised to hear about the existence of Herb's other daughter, Dawn. The two women had found out about Dawn only a few days ago, after Herb announced that he and Xavier had gone to her gallery in Washington, D.C. Since then, Constance had been bugging Xavier for details about her half sister, though Xavier admitted there wasn't much to tell. He had only met her for a few minutes.

Constance tugged the bed sheets over her bare breasts and pouted. "He invited you! He invited *you* to go and not Mom or me!"

"But I'm his lawyer."

"*So what?* Daddy's company has a *team* of lawyers, Xavier. You're the only one he took with him to meet her. You know your relationship is different. He trusts you! You don't have to pretend with me."

Xavier couldn't argue with her.

His relationship with Herb was different. Xavier's father, Malcolm, had once been part of Herb's legal team—the top legal counsel at Herb's software company. His father and Herb had become friends, going on golfing trips together and taking their families on group vacations. But Malcolm died suddenly from a heart attack when Xavier was seventeen years old. Herb took the young man under his wing, seeing Xavier as the son he never had. By the time Xavier graduated from law school and passed the bar, he had a corporate legal job waiting for him at Herb's company, and his friendship with Herb only grew stronger. Now he was Herbert's lawyer *and* confidant, offering him a listening ear when Herbert needed it.

"I came to the gallery with him because he asked me to . . . but they talked alone," Xavier explained, though Constance still pouted. "I was there to keep him from changing his mind and leaving."

And it hadn't been easy. On the drive to the gallery, Herb had waffled back and forth over whether he should see Dawn. Xavier had never seen his mentor riddled with so much anxiety or self-doubt. He hadn't been sure if Herb was going to tell him to throw his Audi into reverse and drive him back home.

"But one of us should have been there, pumpkin! *We're* his family!" Constance continued to rant. "He's an old man dying of cancer! I mean what if . . . what if she's some horrible bitch, you know? What if she's some user who wants Daddy for his money? Maybe she expects him to foot the bill for her from now on!"

Xavier squinted at his fiancée in disbelief. This from a woman whom Herb had indulged almost her entire life?

Even the indoor heated tennis court at Herb's estate had been for Constance. Herb had built it six years ago when Constance decided to take up tennis as a new hobby. Of course, this was after Herb had built the private dance studio for her when she decided to become a ballerina, and then changed her mind again and decided to become a champion swimmer. For that, he had an Olympic-sized swimming pool built on the property in the effort to help her train. Then there were the purebreds he purchased and horse stalls he had built two acres from the estate because Constance decided to become an equestrian. But she deserted that aspiration two years later. Needless to say, Herb was happy to spoil Constance, regardless of the cost. He had done it for years, doting on her and adoring her tirelessly. But now Constance wasn't the only child anymore.

Xavier was starting to suspect that Constance found the prospect of no longer being the only crowned princess in Herb Allen's heart a little intimidating.

"Baby, I'm sure she's nice. She seemed like a good person who wouldn't take advantage of him," Xavier reassured Constance softly, running a finger along her nutmeg-colored cheek. "Don't assume the worst."

Constance turned onto her side and faced him. "Why do you think that?"

"Why do I think what? That you shouldn't assume the worst? Well, because it's—"

"No, you said she seemed nice, that she's a 'good person.' I thought you told me you barely spoke to her."

Constance was narrowing her eyes at him, waiting for his reply.

"I *did* barely speak to her. Dawn and I only spoke for a few minutes."

"And you got *all* of that from talking with her for a few minutes? It sounds like she made quite the impression on you, pumpkin."

Constance was smiling, though he could tell she was far from happy. He had seen that smile before. The last time she had smiled this much, it was seconds before she stomped toward his bedroom door in her birthday suit.

Her syrupy-sweet smile tightened. "*Did* she make an impression on you?"

He thought back to Dawn Gibbons and when he first spotted her in the gallery. She had been chatting with another woman on the other side of the room before she had turned, noticed him and Herb, and walked toward them.

No, she didn't walk, Xavier thought, correcting himself. *She glided.*

Where Constance had the traditional, perky beauty of any Miss USA, her half sister Dawn's beauty was more mature, exotic, and almost regal. She had looked around the room like an African queen surveying her kingdom. He thought her dark skin shone under the gallery's overhead lights like she was lit from the inside, and her large, dark brown eyes were expressive and alluring. She didn't have a bad figure either: round hips, long legs, and pert breasts that pushed against the front of her maroon sweater. When he and Herb followed her to her office, he saw that the back of Dawn looked just as good as the front. He had to remind himself that it was an emotional moment for her and Herb. He shouldn't be ogling her but respecting the gravity of the situation. Besides, it wouldn't look good if he was caught staring at his future sister-in-law's ass.

So did Dawn make an impression on him? If Constance wanted the honest answer: Yes, of course she did . . . to the point that the image of Dawn was still firmly implanted in his brain. But Constance didn't want the honest answer tonight. He knew that.

"She was okay," Xavier lied with a forced casual shrug.

Constance must have accepted his answer. Her painted-on smile disappeared and she flopped back onto her pillow again.

"I wonder when Daddy has plans to see her again," she mused.

"I heard next week."

Constance's mouth fell open.

"They're supposed to meet at some—"

"You knew that and you didn't tell me!" Constance cried. She crossed her arms over her chest and glowered at the ceiling, now fuming.

Damn! This was going downhill fast. There had to be a way to salvage their romantic evening.

"Baby, look . . ." He took a deep breath. "I don't know why you're obsessing about this." He leaned down and lightly kissed her shoulder. "Just let it go."

"I can't let it go! She's my half sister, pumpkin! How can I not obsess about it? Of course I want to know everything I can about her! Mom wants to know everything she can too, but Daddy's keeping us in the dark for some reason!"

"Maybe he's being vague on details because he's getting to know her. He only met her about a week ago. He probably knows only a little more about her than you do. Let him do it in his own time."

She didn't say anything for a very long time after that, making Xavier grumble to himself in frustration. He punched the pillows behind his head and adjusted them before reaching for the remote control on his night table. If they weren't going to have sex, then he was going to watch the game replays and catch the scores on *SportsCenter*. He certainly wasn't about to endure another minute of her angry silence.

Xavier pressed one of the remote buttons and the flat-screen television over the fireplace turned on. He lost himself in the anchors' banter.

"Can *you* do it?" Constance suddenly asked minutes later.

"Can I do what, baby?" he answered distractedly, frowning at the basketball play onscreen. "Damn, he should have made that shot," he mumbled.

"Can you find out more about Dawn for us?"

At that, his interest in the game recap abruptly dissolved. He turned around to face Constance again. She was gazing at him innocently, making him wonder if she realized exactly what she had just asked him.

"You want me to do a background check on your sister?"

"Half sister!" she corrected him, like the designation made much of a difference. She trailed her index finger over the dark curly hairs on his chest. "You said yourself that you're Daddy's lawyer. It's only right that you protect his interests. And he's going to be your father-in-law pretty soon. You're practically family now, pumpkin!"

"Baby, I can't spy on her!"

She rolled her eyes. "It's not 'spying'! I wouldn't put it that way! It's . . . it's . . ." She paused and considered the right words. ". . . doing research."

Research? Yeah, right!

Xavier was getting more and more wary of this conversation. How had a night of lovemaking turned into a discussion about how to find out information on Dawn Gibbons?

"Please, pumpkin," Constance begged, lightly kissing his lips. "Do it for me?"

He shook his head. "Just think about it. *Think* about what you're asking me to do. Don't you think it's a little . . ."

His words trailed off when she threw back the bed sheets and climbed on top of him. Xavier sucked in a shaky breath, seeing his beautiful fiancée in all her tempting, naked glory.

Constance slid down the length of his thighs, lowered her head, and kissed his chest. "But Mommy and I would be ever so grateful, Xavier." She kissed his navel before giving it an enticing lick. "Ever so grateful," she whispered, sending a blast of warm air against his stomach, making the muscles clench.

Damn! She was playing dirty, and he could see he was quickly losing this battle.

"Look, I'm not going to spy on her, but maybe I . . ." His eyes lowered as he watched her kiss a trail down his stomach to his groin. "Maybe I can find out a little bit about her . . . if it'll . . ." He stifled a moan as her mouth descended even lower. "If it'll make you feel better."

"Thank you, pumpkin."

Once her deliciously warm, wet mouth closed around his manhood and started to suck, Xavier lost all coherent thought. He knew he had agreed to do something, but he couldn't remember what. But why bother to remember? It was better to lie back and enjoy the ride.

Chapter 4

Dawn paused underneath the green awning and glanced at her reflection in the glass door. She adjusted her purple beret and smoothed her bangs before tugging the door open.

She had taken her sister Stephanie's advice and chosen for her first "date" with her father a place where she felt most comfortable. It was one of her favorite D.C. haunts—Big Ben's, a small tea shop on the outskirts of Georgetown. She had come here often during her undergrad days at Georgetown University and still visited every now and then when she had a hankering for one of her favorite scones and some Earl Grey tea, or when she wanted to escape the sometimes-claustrophobic atmosphere of Chesterton, Virginia, where she and the rest of her family lived.

Dawn looked around the shop in search of her father.

The owners of Big Ben's took the name literally. More than two dozen replicas of the iconic Big Ben clock were sprinkled around the room in the form of figurines, statues, and posters. Several Union Jacks were hanging from the walls and ceiling. A red telephone box was in a corner. Even the floor mat at the front door was emblazoned with the words "Keep Calm and Carry

On" with the British royal crown above it. Dawn had always gotten a kick out of the place because of how quirky it was.

She did another sweep of the room and finally spotted her father. While most of the customers in the shop were wearing casual clothes—jeans, cable-knit sweaters, boots, and wool coats—her father was the only man wearing a suit and tie.

Overdressed like the day I met him, she thought with a small smile.

He sat at a table in one of the far corners, sipping from a porcelain teacup. As she drew closer she noticed a biscuit sat on the paper napkin in front of him. Beside it was a leather-bound photo album.

He still looked sickly, but she could tell he was a man who would not allow illness to make him neglect his appearance. Everything on him from his tie to his calfskin shoes was impeccable.

Her father slowly looked up. When he saw her, he reached for his bamboo cane and started to rise from his chair.

"Please, no! Don't get up," Dawn said, waving him back to his seat. She removed her coat and pulled out the chair across from him. She tossed her coat over the back of the chair and sat down. "Thank you for coming."

"No, thank *you* for inviting me. I was hoping you would agree to see me again."

Dawn clasped her hands in her lap. Father and daughter fell into an awkward silence. Her eyes scanned over him while he continued to stare at her eagerly. Again, she was taken aback by the idea that *this* was her father. He had made her. She shared DNA with him, and yet he was barely more than a stranger to her.

"So," Dawn said, after clearing her throat, "I see that you didn't bring your bodyguard this time."

"*My bodyguard?*" Her father squinted in confusion then his face brightened. "Oh, you . . . you mean Xavier! No, I didn't think it was necessary for him to be here this time."

"Oh, well, that's . . . that's good. I'm glad he doesn't feel like he has to protect you from me anymore," she said with a forced laugh.

Dawn didn't know why, but she was a little disappointed that Xavier hadn't come this time. She had been thinking about the stuffy handsome lawyer off and on for the past week.

Well, maybe a little more than off and on, she thought, correcting herself. Actually, Dawn had thought about him more than she cared to admit. Again, she didn't know why. He wasn't her type and she had already resolved that men were too complicated to try to pursue anything with them right now. But still, he lingered in her memory like a fish bone stuck between her molars; she couldn't get him out of her mind.

"The usual, Dawn?" a waitress asked as she walked past their table.

Dawn snapped out of her thoughts. She looked up and nodded. "Yes, thanks, Tracey."

"So they know you by name. Do you come here often?" her father asked.

"For the past twenty years or so. But I came here a lot more when I went to Georgetown."

"You went to *Georgetown?*" He shook his head in bewilderment. "You *are* a very smart woman, aren't you?"

She looked up from the teacup and blueberry scone that the waitress sat in front of her. Dawn cocked an eyebrow as she shook out a napkin and tossed it across her lap. "Did you expect me not to be?"

"Well, frankly, I didn't know what to expect. I would hope that any child of mine would be as accomplished as you are and as intelligent. And might I add, as beautiful," he said softly, making her cheeks warm at his compliment. "That's what any father would dream of. But I . . ." He hesitated. "I wondered if your mother would encourage such things, or if she would—"

"Focus more on catching a rich husband and popping out babies?" Dawn said, finishing the sentence for him. She took a bite of her scone.

He shifted uncomfortably in his chair. "I don't wish to insult your mother, Dawn. That isn't why I'm here."

Too late, she thought flippantly as she chewed. Though the truth was, her father wasn't far from the mark on this one. Yolanda Gibbons considered lessons on how to ensnare a wealthy man as important as any algebra class Dawn had taken. She expected the same level of excellence in both endeavors.

"How is your mother, by the way?" he asked.

She appreciated his attempt to be polite. "She's fine . . . very busy, actually. She's getting married in a few months."

Her father gaped. "Married? *Again?*"

Dawn nodded.

"When I met her, she had already been married twice."

"Oh, she's had a few more since then. This will be her fifth . . . no . . ." Dawn paused, closed her eyes and counted off the long list of her mother's ex-husbands. "I think this is her sixth husband."

"*Sixth* husband?"

"Don't look so shocked," Dawn quipped as she sipped her orange-scented herbal tea. "It happens. I've been married twice myself."

"*Twice?*" She could see him struggling to control his features, struggling not to judge her. "Well, perhaps number three will be Mr. Right."

Dawn shook her head and chuckled, setting down her teacup. "I highly doubt that."

"Why?"

"Because I don't believe there *is* such a thing as Mr. Right, and frankly I don't have time to find out. I certainly don't have time for a third husband."

When it looked like her father was about to mount an argument in reply, she held up her hand. "Anyway, enough about me and my love life. Tell me something about yourself, Herb. I'd like to know more about the man who made me."

"What would you like to know?"

"Where did you grow up, for one? What were my grandparents like? What were you like as a teenager? Are you married? Do I have brothers and sisters?"

He smiled. "Well, I've been married for thirty-one years to a lovely woman. Her name is Raquel. We have a daughter named Constance."

Constance and Raquel . . . Dawn didn't like the sound of those names. They sounded better fit for the villains in soap operas than extended family that she might meet in the future.

"What are they like?"

"Oh, Raquel is wonderful, just wonderful! When I met her at a country club thirty-two years ago, I knew she was the woman for me. She used to be a television correspondent before she retired. She's very poised, yet very direct. Constance didn't fall far from the tree. She's a beautiful, delightful girl." He laughed. "I'm afraid I spoil my Connie mercilessly. I have since she was little. But I love to give to the ones that I love, and she's my only child, so . . ."

Dawn flinched. Her father paused at her reaction, suddenly realizing what he had said. He looked horrified.

"I'm so sorry, Dawn!" He reached across the small bistro table and placed his wrinkled, dry hand on top of one of hers. "Sweetheart, I didn't mean that. I know I have *two* daughters. I really meant—"

"That's all right, Herb." She shook her head and pulled her hand away. "I get it."

She got that she had been pushed to the back of his mind for the last thirty-seven years while he lived his life and built a family of his own. She was trying to be adult about it, but part of her envied Constance, and she hadn't even met the woman.

It wasn't that Dawn felt neglected. She had her own very sheltered childhood. Her mother had made sure that she and her sisters got everything they needed and mostly everything they wanted, but Dawn had always felt the emptiness of not having her father around. She had once wanted the affection and protection of a father that money couldn't buy. Meanwhile, her *real* father had been doting on Constance, showering his "only" daughter with his adoration and attention.

Dawn shoved aside her hurt for now. *What's done is done. The past is in the past,* she reminded herself.

"Please keep going. Tell me more," she insisted.

He wavered, looking as if he wasn't sure if he should continue.

"Where did you grow up?" she asked, trying again to draw him out.

"Well, I'm . . . I'm a boy from Detroit who made good. I grew up poor in this little run-down . . ."

Herb then began to tell Dawn the story of his life. She found out that the album he brought with him contained pictures of dozens and dozens of relatives. They hunched over the pages together, examining the pictures and laughing at the stories he told. She found out that he was a man who had pulled himself up out of poverty. He had worked his way through college and grad school and eventually started a multimillion-dollar software company back when most people didn't own computers. And she was shocked to find he dabbled in art back in the day.

"My work was nothing compared to the ones you sell in your gallery," he admitted humbly, "but I've handled a paintbrush or two in my day."

He told her more about Raquel and Constance. She wished she could say the more she heard about them, the more she looked forward to one day meeting them, but in actuality, she felt the opposite. His wife sounded overbearing and his daughter sounded like a pampered princess who was accustomed to getting her way. He added that Constance was getting married in the spring, and when he started to rave about how beautiful the wedding and bride were going to be, Dawn had to quickly change the subject. She just couldn't take it anymore.

Dawn told him a bit more about herself and her family. She avoided talking about her mother, since it seemed to be a touchy subject. She regaled him with stories about her sisters and their antics that made him almost delirious with laughter.

"Would you look at that sunset?" he said softly after she finished one of her stories. His gaze was focused over her shoulder at the shop's floor-to-ceiling windows.

Dawn turned in surprise to see a bright orange sun descending behind the darkened city landscape. "*Sunset?* We haven't been sitting here that long, have we?"

Her father pulled back one of his shirt cuffs and glanced at his Rolex. He raised his gray eyebrows in surprise. "We've been here for three hours and fifteen minutes, to be exact. I didn't know it was that late either."

"Oh, I'm sorry!" She pushed herself away from the table. "I didn't meant to—"

"No! No, please don't apologize. I enjoyed myself." He grabbed his cane and bit by bit rose to his feet. "But I really must be going." He grinned. "Dawn, I had a wonderful time today."

She tugged on her coat. "So did I."

And she meant it. She did have a good time speaking with him and learning more about him. She thought he was a fascinating man and very humble, despite his many accomplishments. He also had a great sense of humor. She was glad she had come to meet him.

"We should do this again," he said, leaning on his cane and gazing up at her.

"We should."

They began to walk toward Big Ben's glass door, stepping aside for a couple who had walked into the tea shop.

"Why not next weekend?" her father asked.

"Why not what next weekend?" Dawn answered distractedly. She tugged on her calfskin gloves then buttoned her coat. She pulled out her cell phone.

"You should come to Windhill Downs!"

She looked up from the messages on her phone screen. "What's Windhill Downs?"

"My property . . . my estate . . . that's what we call it. You should come there! In fact, why don't you come next weekend and have dinner with the rest of the family? We throw a Christmas Eve bash every year, but we try to also have an intimate dinner—family only—the night before that."

Dawn stopped midmotion. Her slender fingers hovered over her phone. She gaped. "An *intimate dinner?*" she choked. "Next . . . next weekend?"

He nodded eagerly.

Oh, hell, Dawn thought. It was one thing agreeing to meet her long-lost father. It was a completely different matter having dinner with her father, stepmother, and sister at "Windhill Downs." Shouldn't she be slowly eased into this? She wasn't sure if she was ready to take on the whole family right now.

Dawn stared down at her father, trying to find a delicate way to decline his invitation.

"I'd be honored to have you there, sweetheart," he said softly.

Dawn grimaced. *Damn it,* she thought. How could she possibly say no?

"Sure, uh . . . give me the address and the time and I'll be there."

"Wonderful!" her father exclaimed.

Dawn lowered her phone back into her purse. She wished she could be equally excited. She wondered what her sisters would think when she told them about this one.

Chapter 5

"Now, we can hold the wedding ceremony here," Cynthia Gibbons said as she pointed to the front hall and walked swiftly across the marble-tiled floor. Her voice and the sound of her high heels echoed off the front hall's coffered ceilings and forest green walls. "Mama, you can enter the ceremony this way, down the left wing staircase. It would definitely be dramatic."

"It would, wouldn't it?" Yolanda said before turning to the squat man who stood beside her. Her arm was looped through his. "What do you think, honey? Does the staircase sound nice?"

A smile creased his dark, bulldog-like face as he warmly patted Yolanda's hand. "Whatever you want, baby."

Whatever you want, baby. . . . Those seemed to be the only words that came out of Reginald Whitfield's mouth since Cynthia started giving him and her mother the grand tour of the recently restored historic mansion, Glenn Dale. Cynthia had spearheaded the renovation of the mansion herself as head of the historic preservation association in Chesterton. Yolanda and Reginald planned to hold their nuptials there in March. Reginald didn't seem to have any opinions on the venue, the ceremony, the reception, or the décor. He was leaving all the decision making to Yolanda.

Which is just as well, Cynthia thought wryly. Her mother was marrying him for his willingness to write checks, not for his opinions.

"Another thing you two may want to consider is where you'll hold the cocktail hour for the reception," Cynthia said as she walked across the front hall and pointed to the adjacent rooms. "You can hold it either in the front parlor or one of the sitting rooms."

"Hmm, I don't know." Yolanda turned to Reginald expectantly again. "Any preference, sweetheart? One of the sitting rooms or the parlor?"

Yolanda was in her mid-sixties, but she looked several years younger and was still a very beautiful woman. Her salt-and-pepper hair was upswept today, though soft curls fell around her face. She wore a trim tan Michael Kors suit and a simple string of pearls.

Reginald looked out of place standing next to her. Though his clothes were just as expensive, they didn't complement his rotund frame quite as well. The buttons of his single-breasted suit were pulling so tightly they looked as if they could pop off at any second. He kept tugging uncomfortably at the starched white collar of his dress shirt.

He stuck his finger in his collar even now and tugged at it again as he shook his head. "Whatever you think is best, baby."

Cynthia stifled a groan. If neither of them made a decision soon, they would be wandering around this mansion forever.

"Well," Cynthia ventured, "if neither of those options work, you could even—"

Cynthia stopped when she suddenly heard a light melody tinkling, letting her know her cell phone was ringing. She glanced down at her phone screen and saw that Dawn was calling her. Considering that Dawn was probably calling to talk about yesterday's meeting with her father, Cynthia guessed it would be better to answer this one without their mother around.

"Mama, I have to take this call," Cynthia said, pasting on a smile. "Would you guys excuse me?"

Yolanda and Reginald were just walking into one of the sitting rooms. At Cynthia's words, Yolanda turned away from her fiancé.

"Is everything all right, honey?" Yolanda asked.

"Oh, everything is fine. Just fine! Why don't you guys continue to look around? I'll be right back." Cynthia then walked toward the front hall, tossing her sun-kissed locks over her shoulder.

"Hey," she whispered after pressing a button on the glass screen.

"Hey! Sorry I didn't call you yesterday, girl. I got home a little late," Dawn answered.

"Yeah, I was wondering why I didn't hear from you." Cynthia walked farther away, hoping their mother couldn't hear her in the echoing, vacant rooms.

Though Dawn knew Cynthia didn't approve of her clandestine meeting with her father, they both knew Cynthia still counted on being the first person Dawn called after the meeting. The two oldest siblings in the Gibbons clan had always been the closest: best friends as well as lifelong rivals.

"So how'd your 'date' with Daddy go?" Cynthia asked.

"Well, it was . . . Wait. Why are you whispering?"

"To cover your ass." Cynthia took a cautious glance over her shoulder. "Mama and Reginald are nearby. I'm giving them a tour of Glenn Dale today. Mama's thinking about holding the wedding ceremony and reception here. Remember?"

"Oh, yeah! Totally forgot. Well, anyway, the 'date' went pretty good, I guess."

"*You guess?*" Cynthia paused. "Why? What happened? He didn't turn out to be an asshole, did he?" Cynthia slowly shook her head and sucked her teeth. "I knew it! I told you that it was a bad idea to agree to meet him again. There was something about that—"

"Calm down, Cindy! He's not an asshole. He's nothing like that. He seems . . . amazing, actually. It's just . . ."

"Just what?"

"It's just . . . weird, you know? I mean, this person was a total stranger to me a couple of weeks ago and now he's my dad! *My dad!* He has all this history and his own family. He has a wife and a daughter. And listen to this, Cindy—he wants me to *meet* them!"

"Say what now?"

"Yeah, I know, right? We're supposed to have dinner together around Christmas Eve."

A dinner at Christmas Eve? Cynthia leaned against the foyer wall. She pulled back the thick velvet curtains and peered out the window at the mansion's snow-dappled front lawn and pebbled driveway.

Though one part of Cynthia had worried that Dawn meeting her father would only lead to heartache, the other part of her had worried that it would lead to something much different: Dawn building a relationship with another family. Within the past year or so, Cynthia had already felt the strong bond between her and her sisters being tested. It was no longer just the Gibbons girls laughing over mani-pedis or conspiring over Saturday brunch how to seduce rich men. Now Lauren and Stephanie were madly in love, involved in their own relationships, and wrapped up in their budding families. They had little time for their sisters anymore. It was just Cynthia and Dawn left, and now it looked like Dawn was going to drift away too.

"A holiday dinner, huh?" Cynthia mumbled sullenly. "So I guess you got a good package deal out of this, then . . . an 'amazing' father, a whole new family, and a new sister too."

"I don't *need* a new sister. Believe me, honey, I've got enough!"

"You're damn right about that."

"Look, Cindy, don't worry," her sister reassured her, reading her mind. "*You're* my sisters—you, Steph, and Lauren—and always will be. I love you guys. Having dinner with my father and his family isn't going to change that."

"I know, I know," Cynthia said, though it warmed her heart to hear those words. She could breathe a little easier now. "So tell me more about the new relatives. What're their names?"

Dawn sighed. "Constance and Raquel," she answered flatly.

"Oh, Good Lord, girl! Are you serious? *Constance and Raquel?* It's like an episode of *Dynasty!*"

"I know. I feel like I should show up in a sequined gown and shoulder pads," Dawn drawled sarcastically.

Cynthia cracked up laughing, then she quickly quieted. She made another hasty glance over her shoulder to make sure their mother hadn't heard her.

"I'm the long-lost sister from the wrong side of the tracks!" Dawn exclaimed.

"Pardon me? *Wrong side of the tracks?* We didn't exactly grow up in the projects."

"Yeah, but we come from gold-digger money. You

know people see it differently. They always look down on it."

"Well," Cynthia said, casually waving her hand and glancing at her nails, "I've never given a damn either way. You know what Mama always says, 'A hundred dollar bill is a hundred dollar bill, whether it comes from your paycheck or your ex-husband's wallet.' "

"True. Very true."

"So, next question: When are you going to tell Mama about all this?"

Dawn moaned. "Oh, God, do I *have* to?"

"You're the one who's getting chummy-chummy with them! You can't keep it a secret forever, and the longer you do, the more pissed she's going to be when she finally finds out."

"Please! Mama is more focused on getting married to Daddy Warbucks over there than she is on anything else. Hearing about my father would just be a distraction for her."

"Yeah, right." Cynthia chuckled. "Coward!"

"Call me what you want, but I think this way is best. And you *will* continue to keep it a secret until I say not to do so, won't you, Cindy?"

Cynthia dropped a hand to her hip and rolled her eyes.

"*Cindy?*" Dawn repeated tersely on the other end of the line. "Promise me you'll keep it a secret!"

"All right! All right! I promise. I just think it's silly. You act like you're having an affair with him or something."

"Your opinion is appreciated, but I'll follow my own opinion for now." Dawn paused again. "Look, I've got to go. I've got a meeting with the gallery staff. I'll talk to you later, okay?"

"Okay, talk to you later," Cynthia said before hanging up her phone.

She was just about to turn away from the foyer window and head back toward the sitting room where she could hear—even from here—Reginald answer with yet another, "Whatever you want, baby," when something caught her eye. She pulled back the curtain panel again and squinted at an unfamiliar car parked in the driveway.

A woman sat in a tan Grand Marquis, staring out the windshield. Her car was parked behind Yolanda's. The woman had a pen in her hand and was furiously scribbling on a sheet of paper perched on the steering wheel.

"I wonder who that is," Cynthia muttered.

She slowly opened the front door, stepped onto the limestone, and stood underneath the archway of the loggia. She rubbed her arms and shoulders against the chill in the air, walked down the steps, and waved at the mysterious woman.

"Hello! Welcome to Glenn Dale!" Cynthia called. "May I help you?"

The woman froze and suddenly looked up from her sheet of paper. Her brown face was slightly obscured by the oversized faux fur hat she was wearing, but Cynthia could see the woman's panicked expression instantly. The woman pushed back her hat and gazed up at Cynthia.

Her plump face was covered in about two tons of makeup. She wore false eyelashes that fluttered like window shades as she blinked. With the press of a button, she lowered her car window.

"I-I just wondered if you knew whose car that is," the woman asked hesitantly, pointing at Yolanda's Mercedes.

"Yes, I do, but . . ." Cynthia narrowed her eyes suspiciously. "Why do you want to know?"

The woman's panicked expression abruptly disappeared. She pushed back her shoulders. Her face became stern. "Because I saw whoever was driving that car," she said, jabbing her stubby finger at Yolanda's Mercedes again, "walk in with *my* Reggie, and I wanna know who the hell she is!"

My Reggie? Oh hell, Cynthia thought. It seemed that Yolanda might not be the only woman in homely Reginald's life. But that was neither here nor there. Yolanda was the one who was sporting the engagement ring. This chick would just have to accept defeat and step aside.

"Ma'am, this is private property. Unless you would like to schedule a tour of the mansion or the grounds, I'm going to have to ask you to—"

"Well, if you won't tell me who the hell she is, can you at least tell me *why* they're here?" the woman exclaimed.

Cynthia loudly cleared her throat. "What Mr. Whitfield and his fiancée are doing here today is, frankly, none of your business."

The woman gaped. Her drawn-on eyebrows shot up an inch. "His . . . his fiancée?"

"Yes," Cynthia said with a mocking grin and a nod, "*his fiancée*. Now again, if you aren't scheduling a tour, would you kindly leave?"

The woman's expression darkened. She raised the car window, turned on the engine, and threw the car into reverse. Cynthia had to jump out of the way to keep from getting hit by the car's bumper as the vehicle suddenly lurched backward. The woman then did a three-point turn before speeding off, sending up a spew of gravel, dirt, and day-old snow.

Chapter 6

Xavier rushed from the glass-enclosed conference room, making quick business of getting back to his office. The early-morning meeting had run long, and the list of things he still had to do today was even longer.

"Hey, Xavier! Xavier, wait up!" someone shouted behind him.

He turned slightly to see Byron Lattisaw, another member of the Allen Enterprises corporate counsel team, smiling and jogging to catch up with him.

Xavier stifled a grumble.

Though he had known Byron for more than a decade, the fellow corporate climber wasn't one of Xavier's favorite people. Byron was much better at schmoozing and ass kissing than he was at his actual job, which meant he passed the burden for most of his work onto his overwhelmed underlings.

Byron had a similar wealthy background to Xavier's fiancée, Constance. The Lattisaws and Allens belonged to the same country club. Constance and Byron went to the same prep schools and similar Ivy League colleges. They got the same lavish gifts for their birthdays and graduations. But while growing up with a silver spoon

in her mouth had made Constance innocent and sheltered, Byron came off to Xavier as the most pretentious
asshole that ever was.

"What's up?" Xavier asked, not breaking his stride
as he walked toward the elevators. "I'm in a bit of a
hurry."

"Yeah, I can see that," Byron said. His smile widened
into a grin. He thumped Xavier on his broad shoulder.
"Look, I just wanted to let you know that if you need
any help—I mean *any* help at all with that whole
Spencer debacle, I'm more than happy to offer you my
assistance."

Xavier did a double take. *Wait!* Was Byron actually
volunteering to help do something? Xavier glanced out
the floor-to-ceiling windows along the seventh-floor
corridor, making sure pigs weren't actually flying past
the city landscape. He then glanced at Byron warily.
Byron volunteering to do work instantly made Xavier
suspicious.

"Why do you want to help?" Xavier asked as he
pressed the up elevator button.

Byron shrugged. The smug grin didn't leave his
brown face. "This Spencer thing is an important matter
to Herb, the board, and the credibility of the company.
Of course I want to help! It should be taken care of as
soon as possible!"

The "Spencer thing" was a reference to Monique
Spencer, a former Allen Enterprises accountant who was
now threatening to sue the company for the "pain and
mental anguish" she endured as a result of sexual harassment by one of the company's upper-level managers.
But prior to being let go for poor work performance five
months ago, Spencer hadn't breathed a word to anyone
about the harassment—not her direct boss, Human

Resources, or even her coworkers. She hadn't shared in her legal claim the identity of the upper-level manager that harassed her either.

The lawyer Spencer hired was willing to go through arbitration for now, but he had been pushing for a sizeable settlement: a whopping two million dollars. Because the matter was so delicate, Herb had asked Xavier to be the go-to guy on this one. He trusted Xavier to make the right decision.

The stainless steel elevator doors opened and Xavier and Byron stepped inside.

"I suggest we push for a quick settlement," Byron said, unbuttoning his suit jacket and shoving his hands into his pockets. "Take care of it quickly. No need to drag this out and mar the company's reputation."

"But her claim is ridiculous!" Xavier argued as the elevator car traveled to the twenty-second floor where his and Byron's offices were located. A continuous beep filled the car, marking their ascent. "She's claiming sexual harassment, but she has no proof. This is obviously just a shakedown. She refuses to name the guy who harassed her, so we can't hear his side of the story or make sure he's terminated so that we can distance ourselves from him. She doesn't want him punished for mistreatment. She isn't trying to take a stand against sexual harassment. She's made it pretty damn clear that all she wants is money."

"Which is why we should give her what she wants," Byron insisted. "It'll make her go away!"

The doors opened and both men stepped onto the plush carpet. They were greeted instantly by the receptionist, who sat behind a large lacquer desk. The stainless steel Allen Enterprises sign sat four feet behind her.

"Hi, Mr. Hughes, Mr. Lattisaw," the young woman said perkily, shifting aside the mouthpiece of her headset.

Xavier gave her a polite nod. "Good morning, Jen."

"Morning, lovely," Byron echoed. "That's a sexy dress you're wearing." He winked at her, making her giggle.

Xavier was taken aback. Here they were having a conversation about sexual harassment and Byron was flirting with the receptionist. Not to mention Byron was married. His wife Kelly probably wouldn't appreciate that little compliment he had given Jennifer.

Now Xavier knew even more why he didn't like this guy.

"But what about the pregnancy," Byron continued as they walked down the hall, returning to their discussion. "That's proof enough, isn't it? If we give her the money, then make her sign a—"

"Yes, she's pregnant, but that still doesn't prove anything. From what I understand, she isn't that far along. She could have gotten pregnant *after* she was fired." Xavier shook his head. "Look, I'm sympathetic to her plight. The guy who got her pregnant—even if he is an employee of Allen Enterprises—should be held accountable for what he did. But that doesn't mean the company itself should foot the bill. She should go after him, not us! Make him stand up and accept his responsibilities."

They reached the end of the corridor and rounded a corner.

"That's a noble sentiment, Xavier," Byron said dryly, "but wouldn't it be better to—"

"Oh, Xavier! There you are!" his office assistant, Ramona, exclaimed as they walked toward her desk. The middle-aged woman let out a deep breath and frantically waved a note in the air. "Thank God! You've got three messages. I tried to patch into the meeting to let you know, but the secretary down there said that machine isn't working today."

"*Three messages?*" Xavier frowned. "Were they that urgent? The person couldn't just leave a voicemail?"

"No, *she* could not," Ramona said through tightened wrinkled lips as she peered at him over the top of her glasses.

Xavier took the slips of paper, wondering if maybe something was up with his mother. He hoped not. Leslie Ann Hughes was a widow who lived alone in Columbia, Maryland, with her two beloved sheepdogs, Lenny and Squiggy. The two dogs were named after the characters on one of his mother's favorite old TV shows, *Laverne & Shirley*, and the pooches were as screwy as their namesakes. Leslie Ann wasn't old but Xavier still worried about something bad happening to her all alone in that big house.

But when he read the messages, he realized they weren't from his mom, but from Constance. Xavier rolled his eyes at one of the messages' multiple exclamation points, "Updates on Dawn, PLEASE!!!"

Constance had been badgering him for almost a week about the promise he had made to her in bed to do more fact finding on Dawn Gibbons. He had agreed under duress. (Seduction counted as a form of duress, *right?*) He didn't think Constance would actually hold him to it. But obviously he had thought wrong. She was growing impatient, and though he had finally managed to track down more information on Gibbons and had even scheduled a meeting with one of Dawn's ex-husbands for later that day, Constance still felt he wasn't moving fast enough.

"Wow, Connie's really cracking the whip, huh?" Byron chuckled as he read the messages over Xavier's shoulder. "So do you get your nuts back *after* the wedding, or is she going to hold on to them permanently?"

In response, Xavier bestowed Byron with a withering glare.

"You know," Byron continued, "if you need some lessons on how to get her to chill out, I can help you. Remember, I've known her a lot longer."

Xavier gritted his teeth. "Byron, why don't we talk later? Like I mentioned before, I'm a little busy right now."

"Yeah, busy," Byron said sarcastically with a snort. "Sure, I'll catch you later."

"Asshole," Xavier muttered as he watched Byron leave. He then turned to Ramona. "Thanks for taking these." He gave an apologetic smile as he held up the messages.

"Oh, it's no problem, Xavier! That's my job! I only hope everything's OK. She seemed really anxious."

Xavier walked into his office a few seconds later, balled up the messages, and tossed them into the waste bin. He had another meeting with the company auditor in about twenty minutes, but he figured he should take the time to call Constance back lest Ramona have to deal with another deluge of messages. He shut his office door and dialed his fiancée's cell number.

"Pumpkin!" Constance cried with relief after the first ring. "I thought you'd never call me back!"

He fell back into his desk chair. "I was in a meeting. Did you really have to leave three urgent messages with Ramona?"

"Well, if you had called me back this morning when I—"

"I told you that I was in a meeting, Connie."

"So are you making progress on the Dawn thing?"

He sighed. "Yes, I am."

"So don't be so tight-lipped, pumpkin! What did you find out?"

"Besides the fact that she's a gallery director, I know she has no children, has been married twice, and lives alone in a small town called Chesterton. She's never gone to jail and hasn't had anything more than a traffic ticket, so she has no criminal history."

"*That's it?*" Constance cried. "That's all you found out?"

Xavier was tempted to remind his fiancée that he wasn't getting paid to do this. Also, it wasn't like he found it completely ethical to conduct a background check on Herb's other daughter. But he bit his tongue.

"That's all I've found out for now. But I'm supposed to talk to one of her ex-husbands today. Maybe he'll tell me more about her."

"I hope so, pumpkin. Like I said, I don't want Daddy to get too close to this woman if she's just going to take advantage of him."

"I understand, baby." He glanced at the clock on his desk. "Look, I've got to go. I've got another meeting I have to run to."

"OK, just call me when—"

"Don't worry. I'll call you this evening to tell you everything. Talk to you later. Oh, and, uh, love you. Bye," he said hastily before hanging up the line.

Xavier stood from his chair and grimaced. He hated rushing Constance off the phone, but her anxiousness was starting to get really irritating. He just hoped whatever he learned today would finally alleviate her fears.

"Clinton Parks?" Xavier asked as he walked toward the restaurant table.

The man slowly lowered his drink, looked up from

his menu, and nodded. He stood and extended his hand to Xavier. "Yes, and you must be Xavier Hughes."

Xavier firmly shook his hand and pulled out a chair. "Pleased to meet you."

They both sat down.

Funny, Xavier thought. Dawn's ex-husband wasn't quite what he had pictured. A sophisticated, beautiful woman like her seemed like she could have just about any man she wanted, but in front of him sat a so-so-looking black man of average height who had to be almost Herb's age. In fact, Clinton Parks's only distinguishing characteristic was the wealth he emanated. It radiated from his Armani suit and his Gucci watch, from his leather shoes and his diamond pinkie ring. Xavier had grown up on the periphery of men like this. Some rich men like Herb were kind and humble. Others like Byron Lattisaw were true assholes. He wondered which one Clinton Parks was.

"Thank you for agreeing to meet me today," Xavier said. "I know my invitation came out of the blue."

"Oh, no problem. I was intrigued by the invitation more than anything else. Found it hard to say no."

A sultry-looking waitress suddenly appeared behind Parks.

"Hello, gentlemen," she said. "Are you ready to order lunch? I could tell you about today's specials."

Parks reached up and grabbed the waitress's hand, catching Xavier off guard. The woman's polite smile tightened, but she didn't tug her hand away though Xavier could tell she was uncomfortable.

"Give us a few more minutes, honey," Parks said softly, rubbing her wrist with his thumb. "My friend here hasn't had a chance to look at the menu yet."

She nodded. Her pale cheeks flushed bright red.

"S-s-sure. There's, uh . . . no rush. Take your time." She pulled her hand away.

Parks's eyes stayed riveted on her ass as she walked off. He finally turned back around to face Xavier and chuckled.

"Cute girl. She reminds me a lot of my third wife."

"You don't say," Xavier mumbled, instantly disliking the man.

"I'll ask for her phone number before I leave." Parks raised his chilled glass to his lips. "Always on the lookout for wife number five."

Xavier clenched his jaw. Well, he guessed he knew what category of rich men Parks fell into.

"So you want to know about Dawn?" Parks asked with a sly grin.

Xavier nodded, grateful for the subject change. "Sure. Whatever information about her you're willing to share."

"You aren't marrying her, are you?"

Xavier frowned.

" 'Cuz if you are, make sure you get a prenup. Learn from my mistake! That girl can get *pretty* expensive. She cost me damn near a quarter of a million dollars before all was said and done. But she taught me a lesson." He tapped his index finger on the table. "All my wives after that, I made them sign on the dotted line before I said any vows. I don't care how much they *claimed* they loved me."

"No, I'm not marrying her. I'm just on a-a fact-finding mission for a client of mine." He cleared his throat. "So Dawn was wife number . . ."

"Number two. I started dating her around the time I was divorcing my first wife." Parks smirked. "She was quite the beauty back then."

She still is, Xavier was about to say, but stopped himself. He knew that comment was inappropriate coming from someone who was supposed to be strictly on a "fact-finding mission."

"She was on staff at a museum . . . one of the assistants. We met at a party one night in D.C. I thought I had spotted her across the room first, but it turns out, she spotted me *long* before that." He laughed. "I didn't find out that important fact until much later—*too* late, if you want to know the truth."

"What do you mean?"

"I mean that she had already tracked me down before I met her. She knew who I was. I think she might have even planned to meet me that night. She came with a mission and she accomplished it."

Xavier's brows furrowed in confusion. "Which was?"

"To get me to marry her and for her to take most of my money," Parks declared bluntly before finishing the last of his drink. "I wasn't anywhere near as wealthy back then as I am now, but . . . my wallet definitely took a hit when she filed for divorce."

Xavier was taken aback. "How do you know all of this was her intention from the beginning?"

"Because I had my lawyer dig up stuff on her for the divorce proceedings. He found out about her background, about her family. How her mother and all her sisters were a bunch of merciless, conniving gold diggers. I also found out that Dawn had been married before to another rich man." Parks shook the ice in his glass. "She hadn't mentioned anything about that in the eight years we were married."

"So your lawyer shared all this in court?"

Parks nodded. "He did. But it didn't make a bit of damn difference."

"Why not?"

"Well," Parks evaded Xavier's gaze, "her lawyer introduced some . . . some evidence in court that didn't . . . show me in the best light."

Xavier sat silently, waiting for Parks to elaborate.

"Before Dawn and I divorced, you see, I had . . . I had already started dating my third wife. Dawn caught wind of it. She and that son-of-a-bitch lawyer of hers got . . . they got pictures of us . . . together. The judge ruled in her favor."

"I see," Xavier said quietly.

As the lunch wore on, the more Parks rambled, the more uneasy Xavier felt. He had no pity for a man like Parks, who seemed to see women as sexual conquests or merely objects to collect. Dawn had taken advantage of Parks's shallowness and robbed him blind. So what? But did Dawn see all rich men as potential marks? Maybe Constance's fears about Dawn taking advantage of Herb to gain his money weren't so far-fetched after all.

Xavier left the restaurant that afternoon in a quandary over what to do next. He could tell Constance exactly what he'd found out, but it would only further raise his fiancée's alarm. He didn't want her to judge Dawn simply on the word of a bitter ex-husband. No, when he talked to Constance tonight, he would stay vague. Before he broke the news to her about her half sister, he wanted to talk to Dawn Gibbons first.

Chapter 7

The first thing Dawn noticed when she entered her father's mansion in Windhill Downs was the giant family portrait in the foyer.

Dawn had debated back at her apartment whether she should go to the Allen family dinner. She considered calling and making some half-assed excuse for why she couldn't attend. Finally, guilt over disappointing the man who seemed to be so eager to build a relationship with her tipped the scales. She put on her big-girl panties and arrived at her father's home fashionably late.

When Dawn was escorted through the doorway by one of the servants, who asked to take her coat and gloves, she looked around her. The two-story foyer was decked out in a colonial-style Christmas décor with real garlands that had a zesty smell that burned her nose, pinecones, a cornucopia of dried apples and oranges, and so many candles that the room was filled with their hazy glow. An eight-foot-tall Christmas tree sat near the staircase that led to a west and an east wing.

Her eyes instantly gravitated to the six-foot portrait hanging over the stone mantel where a wood fire crack-led. In it was her father, Herb, who sat in a leather wingback chair, smiling. He looked younger and healthier and quite handsome in the painting. He even had some hair on his head. Behind the chair stood a tall, light-skinned redhead—even lighter than Dawn's eldest sister, Cynthia—who wore a strapless blue gown. Dawn assumed the woman was her stepmother, Raquel. Raquel was certainly as beautiful as Herb had described, but her green eyes and expression looked cold. Beside Raquel was a young woman in her late teens who Dawn could only surmise was Constance. Constance seemed to favor Raquel in looks, but was closer to Herbert in skin tone. Her smile was perky. Her long hair looked bouncy. She wore a flouncy pink taffeta dress with a bow at the waist.

Dear God, Dawn thought wryly as she gazed at the portrait, *it's black Malibu Barbie.*

"Well, this is a surprise," Dawn heard a deep voice say behind her. "I didn't expect to see you here."

Dawn turned to find Xavier standing on the other side of the foyer. He had just handed off his wool coat and gloves to the same servant who had taken hers. He quietly thanked the man. Xavier was wearing another suit and tie today, but he quickly undid the button at his collar and loosened the tie knot at his throat.

At the sight of him, her heart skidded to a halt then picked up again.

He was as good-looking as she remembered—maybe even better. He confidently strode across the room toward her. She was sucked in by his striking features and the pale gray eyes that were framed by long lashes. Dawn usually found men like Xavier way too pretty, but there was something about him that she couldn't put a finger on, that she couldn't resist.

"Same here," she finally said breathlessly. "I wasn't

expecting to see you here either. I didn't know corporate counsel made house calls."

"We don't, generally, but I make an exception for the Allen family." He turned to the man standing a few feet behind him. "Carl, don't worry about escorting Miss Gibbons to the dining room. I'll show her there myself."

Carl nodded and silently walked away with Xavier's coat in hand.

"So you're on a first-name basis with the help," Dawn remarked as Xavier led her out of the foyer and down a dimly lit hallway, "*and* you know where the dining room is? You must come around here often."

"You've got me there. I'm probably here more than I am at my own home. Luckily, Herb hasn't kicked me out yet or changed the locks on the doors."

"You guys really are close, aren't you?"

"Since I was seventeen," he remarked before turning a corner and leading her down another corridor.

They had been close since he was seventeen years old? That was a long damn time. She eyed Xavier more discerningly. Was something romantic going on between him and her father? Were they secret lovers?

Nah, she thought, inwardly shaking her head at that one.

Though it wasn't unheard of for powerful old men to get young boy toys and put them on the payroll, she didn't think that was the case with her father and Xavier. Her father seemed crazy in love with his wife, and Xavier seemed totally straight. But she still found their relationship confusing. What could Xavier and her father possibly have in common to warrant such a strong connection between the two?

"So you got an invite to the family's annual preChristmas dinner?" Xavier asked casually.

"Looks like it. Makes sense since I'm family now. Guess Herb wanted to officially welcome me to the Allen clan."

Xavier suddenly paused. He turned to her. "You know, Herb is a very special guy. He's very compassionate . . . very kind."

"I know. He seems very kind."

"Some people see that kindness as a weakness, as something they can take advantage of." His face suddenly became stern. "But they're wrong. Herb's no pushover. He can see through people. He'll know whether they have good intentions."

Good intentions? What the hell is this about?

"Is there a reason for this speech?"

"No reason. I just wanted to let you know what type of man Herb is. That if he's reaching out to you, take it as a gift . . . and appreciate it."

"I do. Why else would I be here tonight? Why else would I have agreed to have dinner with them?"

Xavier tilted his head. "I don't know. Some people can have different motivations for what they do. I don't claim to be a mind reader."

"Here goes those 'some people' again." She crossed her arms over her chest. "Look, why don't you just come out and say whatever the hell you want to say."

"Fine." He took another step toward her so that they were merely inches apart.

She glared up at him, meeting his gaze.

"I'm very protective of Herb and his family," he began, "and when I get wind that someone isn't what they claim to be, that that person *may* take advantage of them, I'm no pushover either. I'll see that it doesn't happen again. So just make sure your intentions are good here."

"Duly noted," she said tightly. "But you can save

your warnings. No one has to protect my own father from me—including his lawyer slash bodyguard!"

Xavier nodded. "I guess I'll have to take your word on that." He abruptly turned and continued to walk down the hallway.

She followed him, but for a fleeting moment she contemplated going back to the foyer, getting her coat, and going home. She didn't need a warning or a lecture from Xavier. And to think, she had been finding herself attracted to his anal-retentive, sanctimonious ass. But she reminded herself that she had told her father she would come to dinner tonight, and she was already here. Plus, she didn't want to give Xavier the satisfaction of high-tailing it out of there. He'd only think his suspicions about her were right. She might as well see this through.

A few seconds later, she and Xavier stepped through a doorway and into a cavernous dining room.

"Pumpkin!" a woman suddenly cried, startling Dawn. "I wondered when you'd finally show up! I was worried about you!"

The woman, who looked to be in her mid to late twenties, then bounded in her stilettos across the room toward Xavier. She closely resembled the girl in the foyer portrait, so Dawn guessed she was Constance.

Constance leapt into Xavier's arms and planted a warm kiss on his lips. She draped her arms around his neck and grinned. "You bad boy!" Constance cooed, gazing into Xavier's eyes. "Where were you? Why didn't you call to say you'd be late?"

Xavier slowly tugged Constance's arms from around his neck.

"Sometimes I have to work late, baby," Xavier said softly to Constance. "You know that."

"I told her that you were probably busy and time got away from you, Xavier," Dawn's father called from across the room with a laugh. He grabbed his cane as he slowly rose from his chair at the head of the dining table. He walked toward them. "But you know how your fiancée is."

Fiancée? So that explained why Xavier was so protective of the Allen family.

Dawn had rightly guessed that Xavier was already taken, but she had no idea he'd be taken by her half sister. She hadn't recalled during their "date" at the tea shop her father saying anything about the two getting married.

"But you cut him off. Remember?" a voice in her head reminded her. "Every time he tried to talk about the wedding, you'd change the subject."

That was true. She had tired of hearing about darling Constance's nuptials. But sharing the name of the groom seemed like an important detail that her father shouldn't have left out.

"So you two are engaged?" Dawn said, feigning a smile. "Congratulations!"

Constance turned toward Dawn, finally acknowledging her presence. She leaned her head against Xavier's shoulder. "Yes, we are! We're getting married in early May!" Constance showed off her princess-cut diamond ring, extending a hand toward Dawn. "It's a custom design. *Three* carats!"

"Well, it's . . . it's lovely," Dawn murmured, glancing at the engagement band.

"I'm Constance!" the woman said. "You must be Dawn."

"Yes, I am." Dawn shook Constance's hand awkwardly since the younger woman kept her fingers dangled like Dawn should curtsy and kiss her ring instead. "It's great to meet you. Herb has told me so much about—"

"We were wondering if you had gotten lost," a woman said, breaking into the conversation.

She was sitting to the right side of the head of the table with a glass of red wine in her hand.

"Dawn, let me introduce my wife, Raquel," her father said, gesturing toward the woman.

But her father didn't have to make introductions. Dawn knew instantly that she was Raquel. The auburn hair in the family portrait was a lot grayer now, but the cold green eyes were the same.

"Did you have trouble finding the property?" Raquel asked. She glanced at the watch on her thin wrist. "You're a bit late."

"No, I just got held up at the gallery," Dawn lied. "My apologies."

"Ah, yes!" Raquel rose from her chair and joined everyone on the other side of the dining room. "Herb mentioned that you run a quaint little gallery in D.C." She laughed. "How sweet!"

Dawn eyed her stepmother.

Though Raquel was acting as if she was paying her a compliment, Dawn could tell from her tone that the comment was really a put-down. So it looked like everyone was pulling out the daggers tonight.

Quaint little gallery, my ass, Dawn thought indignantly. That "quaint little gallery" had pulled in almost two million in sales last year!

"It's actually a fairly large gallery, Raquel," Xavier said, clearing his throat. "And judging from the last time Herb and I were there, they do a lot of business."

Dawn turned toward Xavier with surprise. He was lecturing her to not take advantage of Herb only a few minutes ago. Now he was coming to her defense?

Make up your mind, honey. Either you hate me or you like me.

"Oh, I'm sure they do, Xavier!" Raquel cried, her bleached grin faltering slightly. "I'm sure they do! And no doubt, Dawn does a wonderful job!" She waved everyone toward the dinner table. "Well, now that everyone is here, I suppose we can begin dinner."

The family dinner was awkward at best. When Dawn wasn't trying to ignore her stepmother, who seemed hell-bent on making demeaning little comments, she was trying not to stare at the two lovebirds on the other side of the table.

Xavier and Constance held hands throughout the evening. Constance kept whispering in his ear and giggling. Occasionally, she kissed him on the cheek. At some point after they finished the soup course, Constance even took one of the dinner napkins and dabbed at the corner of Xavier's mouth.

Are you going to cut his food too? Dawn thought dryly.

To Xavier's credit, he tried to put a little distance between himself and Constance, but his fiancée wouldn't hear of it. That was her man and she was letting everyone at the table know it.

"So how is the Spencer situation settling out, Xavier?" Herb asked as one of the servants began clearing the table in preparation for dessert.

"Slowly, unfortunately. Byron and I are working on it, but I don't think it's something that'll be resolved overnight."

"At least Byron is working on it too!" Constance piped, patting Xavier's shoulder. "I'm sure he'll definitely help you fix it, pumpkin."

Pumpkin? Dawn didn't think she would ever get used to Constance's nickname for Xavier.

"Yeah, Byron is always incredibly helpful," Xavier said sarcastically.

"What do you mean?" Constance frowned. "What do you have against Byron?"

Xavier shook his head. "Nothing . . . nothing at all. I'm sure he'll . . . lend a hand when he can. There are a few issues at the community center that have to be resolved too that I haven't been able to pay attention to," he said, changing the subject. "Once this Spencer thing is settled, I can focus more on that community center stuff."

"Oh, please, not the community center *again!*" Constance exclaimed with a loud groan as she glanced around the table. "I am *so* tired of hearing about Xavier's street kids! I swear he talks about them *constantly.*"

"They aren't street kids." Xavier looked and sounded offended. "Some of them don't come from the best homes, but that doesn't mean they—"

"Be that as it may," Raquel said, speaking over him, "you donate so much time and effort to that center and those poor children, Xavier, and you aren't paid a dime for it! What little free time you do have could be better spent doing something more useful." She raised her wineglass to her lips. "It isn't *your* job to save the world!"

Raquel snapped her fingers and motioned for the maid behind her to place the crème brûlée on her plate.

"I've been volunteering there since I was in college," Xavier replied firmly. "I like working there and honestly, I think I'm needed there. They're already shorthanded as it is. I couldn't even consider quitting. Not now!"

"Well, in my humble opinion, I think it's laudable what you're doing, Xavier," Herb said, adjusting the napkin in his lap. "Helping those in need and giving those children something to aspire to is a good thing. Keep doing what you're doing, son."

Dawn noticed how Constance and Raquel exchanged a look, then rolled their eyes heavenward simultaneously.

"Thanks. I plan to, Herb, and if I can get a new coach and a new art teacher on board for the center, that would be even better."

"You need an art teacher?" Herb grinned. "Why, that would be a job perfect for you, Dawn!" He looked expectantly at her. "You know everything there is to know about art!"

Dawn, who had been trying diligently to stay out of the conversation and was breaking the crust of her brûlée with her spoon, stopped midmotion.

"Dearest," Raquel began, patting her husband's wrinkled hand, "I'm sure Dawn has absolutely no interest in volunteering at the community center."

"You don't know that," Herb insisted good-naturedly. "You didn't give her a chance to say yes or no."

Constance shifted uncomfortably in her chair and looped her arm through Xavier's. "I agree with Mom. Just because Dawn runs a gallery doesn't mean she wants to or *can* teach art, Daddy."

Dawn frowned, getting annoyed at being talked about at the table like she wasn't there.

"Perhaps," Herb conceded with a tip of the chin, "but maybe she—"

"That's all right, Herb." Xavier glanced at Dawn. "Really . . . we can find someone else. We've got a few feelers out there already. We aren't quite desperate yet."

Desperate? Well, it's not like I'm eager to work with you anyway, sweetheart, she thought indignantly.

"Will you all just give her a chance to respond?" Herb exclaimed. "You may have feelers out there, Xavier, but Dawn is—"

Then suddenly they all started talking at once.

"I know, but I don't think it's—"

"No one wants to impugn on—"

"Xavier, why can't you—"

"I'll do it!" Dawn blurted out, throwing up her hands. "I'll volunteer to be the art teacher."

Herb beamed while Constance, Raquel, and Xavier stared at her like she had just sprouted another head.

Dawn was somewhat surprised herself that she had said those words. She wasn't a bleeding heart by any means. Volunteering at a community center wasn't one of the activities at the top of her list. And after the little conversation she and Xavier had in the corridor, he wasn't one of her favorite people right now. But she was tired of everyone at the dinner table going around and around in circles, and irritated that everyone was making assumptions about what she would and wouldn't do even though they didn't know a damn thing about her.

"So where and when should I be there?" she asked before eating another scoop of her brûlée.

Chapter 8

Dawn opened the glass door to the industrial-looking concrete building, giving one last wary look over her shoulder at her Mercedes. She wondered if it would be okay in a sketchy neighborhood like this. She had no idea that the community center would be nestled in a city block filled almost exclusively with liquor stores and run-down buildings. She also wondered for the fifth time that morning what the hell she was doing up this early on a Saturday and why she had agreed to teach an art class to a group of pimple-faced teenagers. What drug had she been smoking when she agreed to do a favor for the likes of Xavier Hughes, the same man who acted like he had to protect Herb from her?

I must have been out of my damn mind, she thought ruefully, drinking some of her cappuccino from her oversized paper cup.

"Oh, suck it up," a voice in her head chastised. "Drink your coffee. Maybe you'll wake up a little and it'll brighten that surly mood of yours!"

She pushed her sunglasses to the crown of her head and walked across the rainbow-colored linoleum tiles, which had seen better days. A woman sat at the community center's reception desk and a few teenage boys lingered near the counter, laughing as they chugged bottles of Gatorade and dribbled a basketball between them.

There was a reason Dawn's mother had never trusted her to babysit any of her younger siblings. Dawn never would have drowned her sisters Stephanie or Lauren in the bathtub or left them alone on the side of the road, but she was not considered the "nurturer" of the Gibbons family—not by a long shot. Kids simply weren't her thing, and yet here she was with her chalks, pencils, and an oversized sketch pad tucked under her arm, prepared to teach Art 101 to a class full of kids.

I'm doing this for Herb, she told herself. Her father—not Xavier—had asked her a favor and she was granting it. *That's all.*

She sat her supplies and her coffee cup on the counter. "Morning."

"Good morning! How can I . . ." The receptionist paused to glare at the boys standing near her desk. "OK, Delonte and Eddy, if you guys are going to bounce that ball, do it in the gym!" She turned back to Dawn and gave an apologetic smile. "I'm sorry about that. How can I help you?"

"I'm supposed to teach an art class here today."

The Hispanic woman's smile faltered. "*Art class?* I'm not aware of any art class." She began to flip through a binder on her desk and scanned a column on one of the pages. "Are you sure it's today?"

Oh, good job, Xavier, Dawn thought. *They don't even know that I'm supposed to be here!*

"I think so. At least that's what I was told. Umm . . ." Dawn riffled through her purse in search of Xavier's business card where he had written the information on the back. "I think it was scheduled for ten-thirty. Xavier Hughes invited me to—"

"You lookin' for Professor X?" one of the teenage boys piped.

Dawn turned and stared over her shoulder to find a towering, rail-thin teen standing behind her. His mahogany-hued face was covered with acne and blackheads and he had a little peach fuzz over his lip that passed for a thin mustache. He wore a tank top, basketball shorts, and a baseball hat turned to the back. He twirled a basketball on his index finger and grinned.

"Huh?" she asked.

"You lookin' for Professor X?"

When she continued to stare at him blankly, he rolled his eyes. "Professor X . . . *Mr. Hughes?* That's who you lookin' for, right?"

First pumpkin, now *Professor X?* Dawn almost snorted with laughter. The kids at the center called Xavier by the same nickname as a superhero?

She turned away from the counter and faced the teenager. "Uh, yes, I'm . . . I'm looking for, umm, Professor X."

The boy jabbed his thumb over his shoulder. "He's down at the basketball court. I can show you where he's at."

Dawn turned back to the receptionist, who nodded. "Go right ahead. Delonte and Eddy can take you there. Just sign in and take a badge with you."

A few minutes later, Dawn trailed behind her two teenage escorts down a long hallway bordered by orange-and-gray-colored lockers and decorated with posters and construction-paper artwork.

"I'm Delonte," the one with the peach fuzz said.

"I'm Dawn."

"You the new art teacher?" He turned around, walking backward as he spoke to her. "I see you got all that stuff." He gestured to her supplies, then began to spin the basketball on his finger again.

"I guess you can say that. I'm the art teacher at least for today."

He smiled. "Then I'ma be sure to show up to art class from now on." He then gave her a wink and turned back around.

Dawn shook her head in exasperation. Teenage boys were a lot bolder than she remembered. She wondered if he realized she was old enough to have a son his age.

Delonte shoved one of the two heavy steel doors open and the trio stepped into the community center's indoor basketball court. The heavy thud of the bouncing basketballs, the squeak of sneakers over parquet floors, and the shouts and laughter echoed off the ceilings and cement walls, making Dawn instantly want to slap her hands over her ears to block out the sound.

It looked like she had walked in during the middle of a boisterous basketball game. A few boys and girls stood near the bleachers, either cheering on the players or barking taunts from the sidelines. Half of the twelve players were wearing T-shirts. The others were barechested. The boys raced up and down the court, passing the ball and attempting slam dunks.

Dawn smirked. *You'd think they were playing in the NBA finals, with this type of enthusiasm.*

"We can tell Professor X that you're here," Delonte volunteered. "He's playing right now, though."

"No, that's OK." She pointed toward a row of nearby bleachers. "I'll wait over here for him until he's finished."

Delonte and Eddy nodded before strolling off. Dawn walked toward the bleachers, climbed a few steps, then sat down with her sketch pad on her lap. She finished the rest of her cappuccino and watched the game.

It took a while for her to spot Xavier. She barely recognized him now that he wasn't wearing a business suit and tie. His shirt must have been among the pile of clothes on the other side of the gym because all he had on now was a pair of black drawstring basketball shorts and black sneakers. Standing there among the other players, he looked almost as young as they did.

He doesn't look bad, either, she admitted, admiring his physique as he dribbled the ball and shouted to his teammates.

Not bad at all.

He was lanky, but he also had sinewy cords of muscle along his arms and legs and an enticing set of washboard abs that glistened with sweat. A triangle of light, curly hair ran down his chest to his stomach, growing slightly denser at the waistband of his shorts. He had the swimmer-like build that Dawn had always admired, that she had always lusted after.

Xavier landed a jump shot and his teammates went wild.

I wonder if he's as good in bed as he is on the court, she thought as she watched him being given a series of high fives and fist bumps.

"OK, where the hell did that come from?" a voice in her head asked.

Not sure.

She thought that she had resolved that Xavier wasn't her type, that he left a nasty taste in her mouth whenever she was around him. And she knew lusting after her future brother-in-law was wrong in so many ways. But as she watched the basketball game draw to a close, Dawn's shameless thoughts didn't disappear. She imagined for a few fleeting minutes what it would be like to roll around naked with Xavier Hughes.

The boys dispersed and Xavier walked across the court to grab his T-shirt, a towel to wipe his face, and a bottle of water. He looked up and finally spotted her sitting on one of the bleachers. When he did, her heart fluttered a little.

Shit, she thought. *That was worse than sex fantasies! This nonsense has to stop!*

She didn't know what had gotten into her today.

"Hey!" he called out. "So you made it!"

"I told you I would, didn't I?" She pointed to the stack of supplies sitting on the bench beside her. "And I came prepared, but it looks like *you* forgot what time I was supposed to teach your class. You told me to be here by ten thirty." She pulled up the sleeve of her top and glanced down at her watch. "It's now ten forty-five."

Xavier climbed the bleachers, his long legs allowing him to take the stairs two at a time. He plopped down on the bench beside her. Unfortunately for her, he still didn't have his shirt on. Now the physique she admired from a distance was only inches away from her.

Damn, he even smells sexy.

"Stop that!" the voice in her head chastised. "He's your *sister's* fiancé!"

The world might think the Gibbons girls were wanton women, but in reality they operated by their own strict code of ethics. One of those rules meant that they never, *ever* competed for men. They certainly would never steal another sister's man! Constance hadn't grown up with Dawn, but she was still her sister by blood, and the same rules applied in this situation, in Dawn's mind.

To demonstrate her sincerity, she scooted to her right, putting even more distance between her and temptation.

She pretended not to notice his sweat-slicked body and willed her disobedient hormones to get the hell under control.

Xavier wiped the perspiration from his face then tossed his towel around his neck, unaware of the inner battle she was waging.

"I didn't forget the time," he explained. "I told you that it was at ten-thirty, but the class isn't really scheduled until eleven-thirty."

"Why would you tell me the class started an hour earlier?"

"Well, I figured if I gave you a fake time to show up, you'd definitely make it to the class when I needed you to be there."

"*Excuse me?* You thought you needed to trick me into being on time today?"

"In my defense, you *did* show up late to Herb's get-together last week."

"By fifteen minutes!" she shouted with mock outrage, making him laugh. "And you were late too!"

"I had a good reason, though."

"Oh, and I didn't?"

He shrugged and gave a knowing smile before drinking from his water bottle.

"Are you always going to be this easy to work with?" she asked sarcastically. "You're just hell-bent on being a pain in the ass, aren't you?"

He looked legitimately surprised by those words. "How am I a pain in the ass?"

"Well, let's start with you trying to trick me into being on time . . . also, you warning me not to take advantage of my father. You've been more than just a little off-putting, shall we say."

His smile disappeared. "I'm sorry about that. I just

had to be sure that both you and Herb were going into this with the same good intentions."

"And do you feel sure about it now?"

His gazed at her, assessing her silently for several seconds. "Yeah, I think I am."

Their eyes met and an odd sensation passed over her. The cacophony of sound in the gym around them seemed to fade. Dawn could feel a flush of heat in her cheeks. He licked his lips and her fantasies shifted from what it would be like to roll around naked with him to what it would be like to lean forward and kiss him right there in the gym.

Dawn looked away, breaking their mutual gaze. "So," she said, "how'd you end up working with kids at a community center anyway? You don't seem like the type to me."

He furrowed his brows and took another sip. "And what type would that be, exactly?"

"Oh, I don't know. I guess . . ." She shrugged. "Not you. You're pretty conservative. Straitlaced. You know what I mean. I would imagine this is more a gig for a dreadlocked brothah who does spoken word at Poetry Jam Fridays or walks around with a dog-eared copy of *The Autobiography of Malcolm X* in his back pocket."

Xavier lowered his bottle and grinned. "Well, as you can see, I don't have dreads. I don't think I could successfully write a haiku, let alone recite poetry onstage but"—he stood from the bleachers and she followed suit—"I do have a copy of *The Autobiography of Malcolm X*. It's not dog-eared, but I've read it a couple of times."

They slowly walked down the bleacher steps, back to the basketball court.

"I guess the real reason I like coming here is because I like being around kids," he explained. "They've got a good energy. It's a helluva lot better than what you find in the corporate world every day, that's for damn sure. I started volunteering here about nine years ago for a sociology project during my junior year in college. I've been coming back ever since."

Dawn paused as she climbed down the final step. She stared at him in shock. "Wait, you were a junior in college *nine* years ago? Exactly how old are you, Xavier?"

"Twenty-nine," he answered, casually taking another drink from his bottle. "I hit the big three-oh next month, though."

Twenty-nine? Dawn gaped. He was eight years younger than her! No wonder he had looked so young on the basketball court. She was lusting after an infant! But it made sense. He and Constance had practically grown up together. They had to be around the same age.

Damn, Dawn thought. Well, that was certainly the bucket of cold water she needed. He was off-limits not only because he was engaged to her sister, but because she didn't date younger men. A cougar-in-training she was not.

"So how old are you?" he countered.

"Too damn old for you to ask me that question."

"Fair enough." He started walking again and she followed him. "Look, I'm going to take a quick shower and change clothes. I'll definitely be back in enough time to show you where we're holding the art class, though."

"OK, I guess I'll wander around for a bit to kill some time." She looked around the gym. "I'll go exploring and meet you back here in thirty minutes, if that works."

He looked her up and down. "You know, I can show

you where the women's locker room is too if you need to change clothes."

Change clothes? Dawn looked down at herself. She was wearing a plum-colored, fitted V-neck cashmere sweater, dark-wash skinny jeans, and high-heeled black calfskin boots. Compared to what she usually wore, her current ensemble was pretty boring. It had been an inner battle not to throw on more accessories or a more eye-catching top.

"What's wrong with my clothes?" she asked.

"*That's* what you wear to paint?"

"We're sketching, not painting!" She dropped her hand to her hip. "Besides, don't tell me you're going to be anal about this too! If I had to clear my wardrobe with you before I came here, you should have told me, Professor X!"

He shook his head and raised his hand in defense. "Hey, wear what you want. It doesn't make a difference to me." He turned around and headed toward another set of steel double doors. "But if the guys in the class are more focused on you than on their sketches and no one gets any art done, then we know who to blame, don't we?"

"All right, quiet down! Quiet!" Xavier closed his eyes and sighed as the noise continued.

Dawn leaned against the steel desk behind her and fought back a smile. It looked like Xavier was having no luck calming down the room of thirty or so kids ranging in age from eleven to sixteen. They continued to laugh and shout at one another. One was dancing in the corner. Another was loudly reciting a popular hip-hop tune. Two were shooting spitballs across the room through bendy straws, using their sketch pads and easels as protective shields.

Finally, Xavier raised his fingers to his lips and let out an ear-piercing whistle that made everyone stop in their tracks. Dawn flinched at the harsh sound, but it worked. The clamor finally died down and all the kids looked toward the front of the room.

"Thank you." He then pointed to Dawn. "All right, I want you all to say hi to Miss Gibbons."

She waved to everyone. "Hello."

"Hi!"

"Hey!"

"What's poppin', cutie?" one boy yelled, making a few in the class erupt into a chorus of laughter.

Xavier gave the stare-of-death to the wannabe Casanova before he continued.

"Miss Gibbons was nice enough to fill in for Mr. Monroe. She'll be teaching today's class. So I'm going to hand things over to her for now. Tell them a little bit about yourself."

All eyes in the room suddenly focused on her.

Dawn was accustomed to hobnobbing at gallery openings and shaking hands at benefits, but she had never experienced the same level of nervousness that she felt now with more than two dozen teenagers staring at her.

She stepped forward. "Well, my name's Dawn Gibbons. I'm not a teacher, but I'm an artist and the director for Templeton Gallery in Northwest, so I think I know enough to get us through today's lesson." She laughed anxiously and looked around the room. "I heard your last lesson was sketching still life. I thought it might be a fun exercise to move on to portraiture."

"What's that?" one of the students shouted.

"It means sketching a person," she explained. "I want you guys to pair up and sketch each other."

"Do we have to get naked like in the movies?" another one yelled.

Dawn laughed again. "No, you don't have to get naked."

She spent the next fifteen minutes at the chalkboard, talking the students through a beginner's guide of how to draw a portrait. She started with the basic shape of an oval and eventually progressed to a recognizable face, answering questions as the students shouted them at her.

Meanwhile, Xavier sat quietly in the corner of the room in one of the student desks, watching her with his arms crossed over his chest. She tried to ignore him, but the whole time she could feel his eyes on her. He made her nervous all over again.

Dawn had been around fine men before. She had no idea why she was reacting so strongly to this one.

Forbidden fruit maybe, she speculated.

"All right," she said, wiping chalk from her hands and turning away from the board. "Everyone grab a partner and start sketching. I'll walk around the room to see how you guys are doing."

Dawn had expected the kids not to take the lesson very seriously, but she was pleasantly surprised to discover she had been wrong. The room was mostly silent after the students paired off and began sketching. She walked through the hushed maze of teenagers and easels, observing each kid and nodding with approval. When it looked like they were all diligently working on their assignment, she decided to stop hovering. Dawn walked back to the front of the room and sat down on a chair beside the teacher's desk.

"You aren't going to draw anyone?" Xavier asked, strolling toward her.

She looked up in surprise. She had managed for a few blissful moments to forget he was in the room, but now she was fully aware of him again—his height, his body heat, and the smell of his cologne.

"I hadn't planned on it."

"So I don't get a portrait?"

She lifted an eyebrow. "Why, Mr. Hughes, are you asking me to sketch you?"

"Sure, why not?" He grabbed one of the extra pads and pencils on her desk. "I'll sketch you too. We'll do each other."

Dawn had a saucy reply to that double entendre waiting to spring from her lips, but she bit it back.

Sister's fiancé, she reminded herself for the umpteenth time that day. *He's also not even thirty yet.*

"OK," she said, flipping open her pad. "Why not?"

He pulled up a chair in front of her and they both sketched for several minutes, not saying anything.

"You're good at this, you know," he blurted out, looking up from his sketch pad.

"I should hope so. I wouldn't be much of an artist if I wasn't," she mumbled, trying to get the correct arch of his brow.

"I meant *teaching*. I meant you're good at teaching, Dawn. I've never seen the kids this focused during art class."

She sketched the bridge of his nose. "Maybe my outfit was more of an inspiration than a distraction."

"Seriously, would you consider coming back here to teach again? Maybe volunteering? We could use the help."

"Would you consider holding still?" Dawn reached for him. "You asked me to sketch you, so stop moving!"

The instant she held his chin, she knew it was a mistake. An electric charge shot up her arm when she touched him. It made her catch her breath.

This time Dawn saw something lingering in those pale gray irises that she hadn't seen before. This time his gaze wasn't completely innocent.

"It's just your imagination," the voice in her head admonished. "Get a grip!"

Dawn dropped her hand from his chin. "Almost . . . almost finished," she whispered shakily, returning her attention to her sketch.

He returned to his sketch too.

"So how did you get into this?" he asked out of the blue a few minutes later. "What made you wanna become an artist?"

She relaxed a little. If there was anything she loved talking about, it was art. "I was doodling even when I was little. I would draw pictures of my mother, my grandmother, and my sisters. I took a few art classes in high school and won some awards for my watercolors and oil paintings. That's when I figured out what I wanted to do with my life. I wanted to be in the art world—in any shape or form. It didn't matter."

"But you have to have a preference. Which would you rather be, gallery director or artist?"

She chuckled as she drew his lower lip, retracing the line. "Artist, by a long shot. But being a gallery director pays the bills."

"You could get a rich guy to pay your bills for you," he suggested.

Her gaze shot up from her drawing pad. She narrowed her eyes.

"If you did, all your problems would be solved," he continued.

"Maybe . . . but I don't need a rich man to take care of me."

"You mean you don't need a rich man to take care of you *anymore*."

"No," she said tightly, not shocked that he had found out about that part of her past. Most people did eventually. She guessed that explained why he was suspicious about her. But it irritated her that he was bringing it up now. "Not anymore."

"So why the change?"

She sucked her teeth and lowered her pad and pencil. "Look, I don't know if this is really an appropriate conversation to have in front of a class of kids," she whispered.

He tilted his head and nodded. "Fair enough."

She returned to her sketching.

"So why'd you stop having rich men pay your bills?" he asked, making her sigh in exasperation and lower her pad yet again. She thought they were done talking about this.

"What changed?" he persisted.

"I'm pleading the Fifth on that one."

"We're not in court, Dawn."

"So stop with your line of questioning."

"I'm only making casual conversation."

"This is pretty damn heavy for 'casual conversation,' " she snapped.

"Are you always this evasive?"

"Are you always so *persistent?*"

He gave a charming smile that made her a smidge less pissed off. "I prefer to think of it more as curious than persistent."

"I bet you do."

"So come on! Tell me. What changed for you? What made you rule out rich guys?"

She relented. "Nothing, Xavier. I just want to focus on my work. It's hard to do both . . . serving two masters and all that."

"So no more time for rich men, then?"

"No more time for men *period*."

This time *his* eyes darted up from his drawing pad. He stared at her for several seconds. "I see," he murmured quietly.

The class ended half an hour later. Dawn was shocked when a few of the students came to the front of the class and said how much they enjoyed today's lesson. A few even gave her a hug.

Maybe pimple-faced teenagers aren't so bad, she thought with mild amusement as she packed her things. But she couldn't say the same for Xavier Hughes. All day long he had made her feel uneasy. His questions toward the end of class were the icing on the cake of awkwardness between them.

Dawn walked through the community center's doors and pulled her keys from her purse. She was only a few feet from her car when she heard the pounding footsteps of someone running up behind her. She turned and found Xavier striding toward her.

"Dawn! Wait up!"

"What?" she asked, frowning up at him.

"I wanted to . . . to catch you," he said between huffs of breath. "You never answered my question from earlier. I'm serious about that offer. I'd love for you to volunteer and teach here. We offer art classes about twice a month. Would you be interested?"

Me? A teacher?

The kids had made the experience at least partially fun today, but she couldn't imagine doing this all the time, let alone seeing Xavier twice a month. She didn't know if she could stand that torture.

"Xavier, I'm not—"

"Yes, you are," he insisted. "If you're going to say that you're not a teacher, I beg to differ. I saw it today."

She shook her head. "But I don't know if I can put the time into—"

"It's only two hours a weekend, two to three times a month, if you count the occasional field trip. I understand being busy. I'm general counsel for a Fortune 500 company. I'm busy too. And I get that you want to focus on your work, that you don't have time for men. You're an independent woman. Point made. But this . . . this doesn't take a lot of effort or time on your part, and as long as these kids are here, they aren't on the streets getting into trouble."

Damn, he's laying it on thick. Now he was making her feel like her refusal was the same as neglecting needy kids.

She pursed her lips.

"Try it for a month. See if you like it."

She contemplated his offer for a bit. "Fine," she finally said, wanting to kick herself even as she uttered the word.

He grinned. "You mean it? You'll do it?"

"*Yes!* I said I would!" She unlocked her car door and shooed him away. "Now leave me alone. This independent woman has about twenty errands she has to do today, and it's already almost two."

He nodded, still smiling. "Sure, don't let me stop you." He immediately stepped forward and opened the car door for her. "Sorry. You may be an independent woman, but I'm still an old-fashioned guy."

"Uh, th-thanks." She climbed inside, pretending not to feel the fluttering in her stomach as she brushed his arm. He shut the car door behind her.

"Drive carefully," he said through the glass. "And thank you, Dawn."

She nodded and pulled off.

The butterflies wouldn't be ignored. They were fluttering like crazy now, trying to beat their way out of her stomach.

Chapter 9

"Come on!" Cynthia yelled before blaring her car horn again. "We're going to be late!" she shouted out the lowered tinted car window.

She watched as her sister Dawn ran down the sidewalk toward her double-parked Lexus SUV.

"Ow, damn it!" Dawn shouted as the heel of her calfskin boot got caught in a crack in the cement.

Dawn's purse dangled from her forearm, dragging near the ground. She was still shoving her other arm into her wool coat as Cynthia beeped her horn again. Dawn swung open the passenger-side door and climbed inside.

"I'm coming! I'm coming! Jesus!" Dawn yelled as she landed on the leather seat and slammed the door closed behind her. "If I knew you were going to be like this, I would have driven to the cake-tasting appointment myself!"

"Uh-huh." Cynthia rolled her eyes, flipped on her turn signal, and pulled into traffic. She glanced at the speedometer and wondered how far she could go over the speed limit without getting a ticket. "That would mean you'd actually have to get involved in Mama's wedding planning and figure out where the hell the bakery is."

"Wow!" Dawn buckled her seat belt and eyed her sister. "So it's like that, huh, Miss Gibbons?"

"*Yes,* it's like that!"

"Cindy, what the hell crawled up your ass and died? What's with the attitude?"

Oh, where to start, Cynthia thought flippantly as she drove.

How about the fact that somehow all the planning for their mother's wedding had fallen squarely into her lap? Cynthia had suggested that their mother get a little more involved (hell, Cynthia had even found the cake baker and set up the appointment for today herself) or maybe even hire a wedding planner for the shindig, but Yolanda had shot down that idea. She said she sensed that something was going on with Reggie and he seemed to be getting more and more distant and ambivalent about their nuptials. Her mother worried that he was starting to get cold feet. Yolanda thought it would be better to concentrate her efforts on making sure her husband-to-be was taken care of and happy rather than deal with coordinating with a wedding planner to iron out the details.

"I'm sure whatever you organize will be wonderful, sweetheart," Yolanda had said over the phone.

Cynthia had been tempted to remind her mother that she had a full-time job and it wasn't *her* wedding, but out of respect, she bit her tongue.

Another reason for Cynthia's burgeoning bad mood: She was having little to no luck on the romantic front lately. Her own finances were starting to get a bit shaky now that her daughter, Clarissa, had started college and seemed to require an endless stream of money for books, architecture class supplies, sorority pledge events, and so on. Cynthia needed a man of means like *yesterday*, but the only candidates she had so far either had way too little cash or would require too much time and effort that she just didn't have right now.

But she couldn't reveal any of these worries to her sisters. No, all of them were too wrapped up in their own lives: Lauren with her restaurant and new family, Stephanie with her new man and her pregnancy, and now Dawn with her long-lost father.

No, none of them had time for *little ol' Cindy!*

"I told you that we needed to be at the bakery by four, and for some reason you can't understand why I have an attitude," Cynthia snapped at Dawn. "Mama is waiting on us, and you know how she hates to wait."

"Well, sorry!" Dawn flipped down the car visor mirror and began to reapply her lipstick. "But one of the things I had to do today ran longer than I thought it would. It threw off my entire schedule. I didn't want to be late, but it was out of my control."

"What thing?" Cynthia asked, glancing at her sister.

Dawn didn't respond but instead continued to stare at her reflection. She fluffed her bob, combing her hair into place with her fingers.

"What *thing*, Dawn?" Cynthia boomed.

"I was teaching an art class to teenagers! Damn!" Dawn muttered, flipping up the visor. "Cindy, you really need to chill the hell out."

"Teaching an art class?" Cynthia did a double take, almost missing the stop sign in front of her. She slammed on the brakes, barely missing an old woman who was hobbling through the crosswalk with her cane and a Yorkshire terrier. "Did you get a DUI and not tell anyone? Did the judge sentence you to community service or something?"

"No, I didn't get a DUI!" Dawn shouted as they pulled off. "I just agreed to teach at a community center in the city, that's all. Xavier said the center was in a bind and needed a replacement teacher, so I—"

"Wait. Who's Xavier?"

"I've told you about him before. I met him the same night that my father came to the gallery. Remember? He's general counsel at my father's company, seems to be the volunteer coordinator at the community center, and"—Dawn put the cap on her lipstick and dropped both back into her purse—"he's engaged to my sister, Constance, though I'm amazed those two are together. He's so serious and earnest and she's so . . . so ditzy. She's *really* self-involved and definitely not his intellectual equal."

"Oh, really?" Cynthia cocked an eyebrow. "Sounds like this Xavier guy has made quite the impression on you."

Dawn frowned. "What do you mean?"

"You don't think Constance is worthy of him, for one."

"I didn't quite put it *that* way, Cindy. Don't exaggerate!"

"Secondly, you agreed to teach art to a bunch of kids at a community center to help him out when I know damn well there is no way in hell you would normally do something like that."

"I was trying to be nice! He works for Herb. He's my future brother-in-law. I thought . . . I thought I'd do him a favor, you know? No big deal."

"Yeah, no big deal, which is why you're getting all flustered." Cynthia smirked.

"I'm not flustered! I'm simply trying to explain why . . ." Dawn loudly huffed. "Look, he's not even my type. He's boring, uptight, and way too young for me!"

"What's too young?"

"Twenty-nine."

"Nice! Twenty-nine, huh? Being that young isn't necessarily a bad thing, girl. It could mean he has *a lot* of stamina."

"Shut up, Cindy," Dawn snapped.

"Now who has an attitude? Sounds like somebody definitely has a thing for Mr. Sexy Young Lawyer."

"I do *not!*"

Cynthia giggled, knowing that when her sister denied anything this vehemently, it was definitely true.

"Oh, please! You don't fool me! You're attracted to the man. Don't lie!" She glanced at Dawn, who now looked sheepish. "Boring and uptight, huh? I know the truth! He's young, probably smart, and I'm guessing cute. Plus, he's a lawyer at a big tech company, so he has to be pulling in the low six figures—*minimum!* Sounds like a good candidate. So are you thinking of stealing him from under ditzy Constance's pretty little nose? Planning to work the ol' Gibbons charm on him?"

"I can't believe you would even ask me that. You know the rules! I would never steal my sister's man!"

"*Your sister's man?* By 'sister' you mean Constance?" Cynthia shook her head, sending her long hair whipping around her shoulders. "Oh, no, honey! The rules do not—I repeat—*do not* apply to her! She is not a Gibbons girl."

"But she *is* my sister! She's not my most favorite person in the world, but we have the same father, so as far as I'm concerned, the rules *do* apply to her. I have no interest in stealing her fiancé."

Cynthia squinted, trying to comprehend what she was hearing. "What in the hell are they putting in the Kool-Aid over there? What are they feeding you at Windhill Downs?"

"Huh? What are you talking about now?"

"You're acting like they're your family!" Cynthia

shouted. "You said you were just doing this to connect with your father, and now you're talking about how you consider Constance to be your sister! What's going on here?"

"Cindy, they *are* my family! I didn't grow up with them like I grew up with you guys, but they're still my relatives. I'm not going to treat them like total strangers just because their last name isn't Gibbons. Not when some of them are making a legitimate effort to reach out to me."

Cynthia pulled into a parking space in front of the bakery's glass front. Their mother's Mercedes was already parked in the space next to them.

"I knew it," Cynthia said, slamming her fist on the steering wheel. *"I knew it!"*

"You knew what?"

Cynthia unbuckled her seat belt and turned to glare at her sister.

She had suspected this would happen. All her other sisters had fallen into this trap at some point, but she had hoped that Dawn wouldn't be dumb enough to do it too.

"I knew that you would get all sucked up in this romantic idea of being around your father and having a new family. But what does Mama always say? *We're* important, Dawn! Not those people. You obviously are going through a crisis of allegiance!"

"A crisis of allegiance?" Dawn threw up her hands. "Would you listen to yourself? You sound like we're at war!"

"We *are* at war! We always have been! It's been the Gibbons family against the world. *Us* against *them!* But Lauren and Stephanie lost sight of that when they let their *vaginas* do the thinking for them! And now you look like you're about to fall in the same damn trap, except you're falling in love with another family instead of a man!"

Dawn closed her eyes and rubbed her temples. "I'm really trying to understand the crazy-ass line of reasoning you're following, Cindy, but I can't. There is absolutely nothing wrong with me trying to connect with my father and his family."

"Oh, there isn't? Then why haven't you told Mama about it yet? Huh?"

Dawn opened her eyes. "Well, because . . . because I . . . I mean, she's been so preoccupied with the wedding and . . . and I haven't had the chance to."

"Is that so?" Cynthia asked as she threw open her car door. "Well, why don't we tell Mama *right now?*"

Dawn's large eyes widened, almost popping out of her head. "What? Cindy, don't!"

Cynthia slammed the car door shut and strutted toward the bakery with her high heels clicking over asphalt.

"Damn it, Cindy!" Dawn shouted frantically as she unbuckled her seat belt and climbed out of the car. "You better not tell on me!"

"Watch me!"

Cynthia glanced over her shoulder to see Dawn running toward her. She raced to grab the door handle just as Dawn grabbed a fistful of Cynthia's gray-colored wool coat and pulled. Cynthia tugged back. The two women grunted as they tussled.

It was like they were reenacting one of their childhood fights, except this time they weren't racing to get the last Rocky Road ice cream in the freezer or fighting over who would get to wear the pink sweater to school that day.

When Dawn grabbed another part of the coat, Cynthia simply shrugged out of the sleeves, leaving the entire garment balled up in Dawn's arms. Cynthia bolted inside and raced down the short corridor.

"Damn it, Cindy! Don't do it!" Dawn shouted after her.

"Why? You said there's nothing to hide!" she called before stepping into the bakery.

The space was well lit and filled with the fragrant smell of vanilla and sugar. Several displays of fanciful fondant cakes sat on glass pedestals around the room. One looked like an imperial egg embellished with fake jewels and gold. Another looked like a medieval castle with a moat and towers with spires.

Their mother, Yolanda, sat at a table near the counter with the baker, smiling as she idly flipped through cake portfolios.

"Dawn has something to tell you!" Cynthia announced breathlessly, making Yolanda and the baker look up at her in confusion.

Dawn immediately skidded through the open doorway with Cynthia's coat still balled up in her arms.

"Tell her!" Cynthia ordered.

"Tell me what?" Yolanda asked as she turned in her chair to face both of her daughters. "Girls, what is this about?"

Dawn cut her eyes at her eldest sister. "This isn't the time or the place," she said through clenched teeth. "And you know it!"

Yolanda slowly rose to her feet. "The time or the place for what?"

"Nothing, Mama," Dawn said quickly, making Cynthia shake her head in bemusement.

"You are *such* a coward," Cynthia said.

"And you are such a bitch!"

"All right now! Both of you, stop it!" Yolanda caught herself, pursed her lips, and glanced at the baker, who seemed utterly astounded by what she was witnessing. Yolanda pasted on a polite smile. "I am so sorry. Would you please excuse us for a few minutes?"

The baker slowly nodded, closing the cover of one of the albums she had been showing Yolanda. "Sure, uh . . . Take your time."

Yolanda's smile disappeared as she strode toward her daughters. She snapped her fingers and glared at them.

"In the hall," she said tightly. They both followed her, though Dawn paused to give a menacing stare at her sister. She looked at Cynthia as if she could strangle her that very second. When they stepped into the corridor, Yolanda turned to them with her arms crossed over her chest. Her beautiful face was tight with rage.

"How dare . . . how *dare* you embarrass me like that! Acting as if you're bratty twelve-year-olds! I won't have it!"

Dawn's and Cynthia's gazes drifted to the floor.

"Now, you two better tell me what's going on and you better tell me quick," Yolanda ordered, shifting her gaze between both of her daughters. "So who's going first?"

Dawn and Cynthia stood silently for several seconds before Dawn sucked her teeth.

"Fine," she muttered, before stepping forward. "Look, Mama, I was going to tell you—eventually—but I just thought it would be better to . . . well . . . I've been seeing my father."

Yolanda's frown deepened. "What?"

"My father! You know . . . Herbert Allen. He showed up at my gallery one day a couple of weeks ago."

Yolanda's mouth fell open in shock.

"I don't know how he tracked me down. I guess a guy like him has his ways. He's not doing well, Mama. He's . . . he's really sick with terminal cancer, and he wanted a chance to get to know me, so . . . so I agreed to have lunch with him one day. Then he invited me to go to his family's pre-Christmas dinner party and—"

"Wait," Yolanda said, holding up her hand. "You ate dinner with *his family?*"

"I know, right?" Cynthia exclaimed, making Dawn glower at her again.

"It was just dinner, Mama," Dawn demurred. "Besides, he's my father. He reached out to me. I have the right to know the man!"

Yolanda raised her eyebrows. "You mean the same man that it took a team of lawyers just to get him to admit that he was your father? The same man who's spent thirty and some odd years pretending that you didn't exist? Are we referring to *that* man?"

"Herb knows what he did was wrong and he apologized."

"Oh, he apologized! Well, I guess that makes it all better, then, doesn't it?" Yolanda said sarcastically.

"Mama, he—"

"No!" Yolanda waved her hand, silencing Dawn. "I have no desire to hear any more about Herbert Allen," she said with a sneer, "especially when I have a wedding cake to choose and not much time to do it. If you're so eager to get to know your darling daddy, Dawn, I can't stop you." She walked back toward the bakery's entrance. She stepped over the threshold, then paused and turned back around to face them. "But just remember who gave birth to you and loved you since the moment she set eyes on you, who raised and nurtured you, and who would never *ever* deny you. I'm glad Herbert's had his grand awakening now that he's so near death's door, but if it were me, I would have told him he was a day late and a dime short."

Yolanda then turned back around and walked into the bakery.

"Now where were we, Glenda?" they heard her say in a syrupy-sweet voice, giving no hint to the sense of betrayal Cynthia knew her mother felt.

Cynthia gazed at her sister, whose eyes were downcast.

"She's right, you know," Cynthia said. "You don't owe him—any of them—anything."

Dawn looked up at her. She tossed Cynthia's coat at Cynthia's chest before turning on her heels.

"Where are you going?" Cynthia shouted as she followed her.

"To get a cab . . . or take the bus! I don't care. But there is no way in hell I'm doing that cake tasting with Mama or riding back with you. I could just kill you right now, Cindy!"

"*Why?*" Cynthia asked as Dawn opened the glass door and stomped outside. "Because the truth finally came out? We don't keep secrets like that from each other, Dawn. We never did! But now the only thing you, Laurie, and Steph do is keep secrets!"

Her sister didn't answer her, but instead continued down the sidewalk to who knew where.

"Dawn!" Cynthia shouted after her. "Dawn!" She stamped her foot in frustration and dropped a hand to her hip. She blew out a deep breath that caused her side bangs to flutter.

Well, this sucks, she thought. *So much for a fun day at the bakery!*

She turned and opened the glass door to go back inside, but she paused when she noticed the car parked on the other side of her mother's Mercedes.

The tan Grand Marquis looked familiar, as did the woman sitting behind the wheel. This time she wasn't wearing a fur hat or scribbling on a notepad. She was wearing a velvet tracksuit jacket and stuffing her face with a powdered jelly doughnut. When her eyes locked with Cynthia's, they went wide.

Was Reginald's ex stalking her mother now?

Oh, hell no!

Cynthia had little patience for crazy today, not with the fight she just had with her sister. She walked toward the car, putting her coat back on.

"Do I have to call the cops?" she shouted.

The woman lowered the car window. "Why would you call the police?" She raised her nose into the air. "I ain't done anything wrong. I have every right to sit here!"

"Uh-huh," Cynthia murmured blandly. "You're following us."

"You don't know for sure I'm following you!"

"Yes, I do! You're following us and that's considered stalking. Look, you've got sixty seconds and counting to pull off before I go inside and tell my mother to dial 9-1-1. You can either leave here in that car or in the back of a sheriff's office patrol car. It's your pick!"

The woman squinted. The grip on her powdered doughnut tightened, making red jelly ooze over her plump knuckles. She shook her head. "I ain't afraid of you."

Cynthia smiled icily. "Then you don't know who the hell I am, because if you did, you'd be afraid."

"Beatrice Little fights for what's hers," the woman continued. "Reggie is *my* man and no fast-tailed *heffa* is going to take him away from me!"

Cynthia tilted her head. "Well, considering that she's in there picking out the wedding cake that Reggie is buying for *their* wedding and you're out here alone eating a jelly doughnut, I think Reggie's already made the decision of who he wants to be with. Don't you?"

"You go to hell!" the woman screeched, tossing her doughnut out the window at Cynthia and almost hitting her with it. It landed at Cynthia's feet with a splat. "Your mama can go to hell too!"

"Sixty seconds," Cynthia repeated, tenuously holding back her own fury.

She watched again as the woman who she now knew was named Beatrice pulled off in a huff. When Beatrice's taillights disappeared around the corner, Cynthia shook her head, having the bad feeling that she would definitely see Beatrice again.

Chapter 10

"Can you pass the pasta, Connie?"

Constance looked up from the messages she had been scanning on her phone screen. "Huh?"

"Mom asked you to pass her the pasta primavera," Xavier said.

"Oh, umm, sure," she said with a little giggle, reaching for the ceramic bowl near her wineglass. She handed the bowl to Leslie Ann, Xavier's mother, before returning her attention to her phone, tapping at the screen with her manicured nails.

Leslie Ann placed some pasta on her plate and glanced at Constance again. "Connie, are you sure you don't want any more food?" She eyed the pile of salad and the half slice of chicken breast on Constance's plate, which Constance had yet to touch. "I made plenty!" She gestured to the smorgasbord of a family-style dinner that now sat at the center of the table: pasta primavera, roast chicken, slices of roast beef, ciabatta bread, and garden salad. "You don't want to at least *try* the pasta? It's tasty. I swear!"

Constance shook her head and wrinkled her nose. "I don't do carbs, Mrs. Hughes." She patted her hips. "I've got to maintain my figure, especially for the wedding!"

"Of—of course," Leslie Ann said. She pursed her lips and gazed across the table at her son.

Xavier locked eyes with his mother, whose eyes were an identical light shade of gray to his own. He looked away after a few seconds, pretending to be engrossed with Lenny instead. His mother's sheepdog was nudging his knee with his nose and head and whimpering plaintively, begging Xavier for food. Squiggy, Leslie Ann's other sheepdog, had tried to beg Constance, but she wasn't having any of it. She had shoved him away multiple times before he finally wandered off, dejected.

At that moment, Xavier would rather look at the dogs than his mother. He knew what Leslie Ann was thinking. He could see the silent judgment in her eyes. She didn't approve of his fiancée, Constance. Frankly, she never had.

Since his father and Herb had been such close friends when his father was alive, Xavier had assumed that his mother would be happy when he and Constance got together. She had loved and adored Xavier's father, Malcolm, and had always admired Herb. But instead of being pleased when Xavier and Constance became engaged, it seemed to annoy her. Even after all these years, his mother still couldn't see the Constance that he knew: the innocent, charming, beautiful girl who could light up a room. Instead, she thought Constance was shallow, selfish, and "an all-around nitwit."

He took a piece of chicken from his plate and handed it to Lenny, who ate it quickly and started to lick the remaining juice from his hand.

"Xavier Christopher Hughes!" his mother exclaimed.

"What?" he asked with mock innocence, making the graying strawberry-blonde shake her head with amusement and laugh.

"How many times do I have to tell you, *do not* feed the dogs from the table?" she admonished, though her smile showed that she wasn't really that mad. She pointed at him. "I won't be able to finish a decent meal if they beg every time I sit down to eat because *you* have no willpower and can't tell them no!"

Shamefaced, Xavier patted Lenny's flank, then shoved the dog away. "Go on, boy. Mom doesn't like having you at the table."

Lenny whimpered again but followed Xavier's command and walked away, plopping down next to Squiggy on the Afghan rug in the adjacent living room.

"So how are things with you guys?" his mother asked, raising a wineglass to her lips. "How's the wedding planning going?"

Constance lowered her phone to the table and grinned, happy to talk about their impending nuptials. "Oh, it's going well, Mrs. Hughes! Mommy and I are finalizing the details! We've been zipping from appointment to appointment!" She gave a side glance to Xavier and playfully nudged his shoulder. "Unfortunately, *someone*—who will remain nameless—hasn't been as involved as I would like."

"But I've apologized and explained that I've been busy, baby," Xavier said softly.

"Busy doing everything else, you mean," Constance said as she jabbed a finger into his rib cage. "But *I* manage to make time to plan our wedding. I've made it a priority!"

"Xavier works full-time, Constance," his mother said before slicing into her chicken breast. "He's a lawyer for a major software consultant company. He also volunteers. It's understandable that his schedule is busy."

Constance shifted uncomfortably in her chair. "Yeah, but . . . I have a job too."

"You mean the job that you go to twice a week?" Leslie Ann asked with mock innocence before she bit into her chicken.

Xavier gritted his teeth. *Mom, don't start,* he thought.

"Actually, I work three times a week now," Constance said proudly.

His mother finished chewing her chicken. "*Three whole times?* You don't say. Must be tiring!"

"Don't listen to her, baby. Mom's from a small town in the Midwest. She thinks if someone isn't working sixty hours a week killing themselves at their job, they're being lazy."

"Not lazy, Xavier," his mother corrected him. "But I grew up in farm country, where everyone was expected to earn their keep."

"I don't think I could grow up on a farm." Constance wrinkled her nose again as she played with her salad. "It's way too dirty and farm animals are just gross." She shuddered.

Leslie Ann opened her mouth, perhaps to give another sarcastic retort, but Xavier stopped her before she could.

"So did I tell you that Dawn is going to take over the art teacher position at the community center?" he suddenly interjected. "It took some convincing, but I'm glad she agreed. She's better with the kids than I expected."

"Really?" His mother's face softened. "You know, I'm looking forward to meeting your sister, Connie. She sounds like a very interesting woman."

"*Half sister,*" Constance whispered sullenly, still picking at her salad.

"She's an art gallery director in the city. And Herb says she went to Georgetown," his mother continued, not hearing Constance's comment. "She sounds so . . . so sophisticated. I bet she's really smart too."

"She is," Xavier concurred as he drank his beer. He turned to find Constance glaring at him. "Well, she *is,* baby."

"You should invite her to your birthday celebration, hon!" his mother suggested. "You know, the little get-together you're having. I could meet her there."

He nodded. "That doesn't sound like a bad idea."

"I can't wait to meet her there!" Constance exclaimed in a high voice with a roll of her eyes an hour and a half later. They were walking down the brick walkway toward Xavier's car. His mother had already bid them good night and shut the front door to her Georgian-style home behind them. He could still hear the dogs barking inside.

"She can't wait to meet *Dawn,* but she hates me!" Constance lamented.

Xavier wrapped an arm around Constance's shoulders and squeezed. "She doesn't hate you."

"Fine, then. She just doesn't *like* me," she mumbled with a pout, pushing her hair out of her eyes. "It's true! Don't deny it, pumpkin!"

Xavier unlocked the passenger-side door to his Audi and held it open as she climbed inside. "Mom is just . . . she's just . . . set in her ways," he explained. "I told you, it's how she grew up."

"On a farm, I know! But you can't tell me she doesn't like me because I didn't grow up milking cows and shoveling hay!"

No, that wasn't the reason, but he could never reveal the truth to Constance without hurting her feelings.

"Dawn didn't grow up on a farm and your mom seems all eager to meet her!" Constance crossed her arms over her chest and glowered out the windshield. "Maybe she . . . maybe she'd rather you'd be marrying Dawn than me."

Xavier frowned, wondering where that statement came from. "Why would my mother want me to marry Dawn?"

"I don't know," Constance said with a shrug. "She's so smart and *sophisticated*. Even you said so!"

Yes, he thought Dawn was very intelligent and sophisticated—even stunning when the light caught her at the right angle. But he wasn't naïve. He knew enough about Dawn's background to remind himself not to be too enamored by those qualities. Women like her—who excelled at seducing and using men—had to have all those traits to be good at what they did. You could be a polite acquaintance or even friends with someone like Dawn, but a man with any brain would be smart to always be on his guard around her lest he fall for her charms and end up heartbroken and just plain broke.

No, I much prefer women like my Constance, he told himself, who were more honest and less calculating. He didn't have to be on guard with her.

Xavier leaned down, dropping to one knee on the cold cement of his mother's driveway. He ran his finger along Constance's cheek, then jaw. He cupped her chin. "Look at me, baby."

She stubbornly continued to stare forward.

"Connie, look at me."

She took a deep breath and slowly turned to face

him. He leaned toward her and kissed her, savoring the taste of her and the plumpness of her lips. When they parted a minute later, she was smiling.

"That's what I like to see, that beautiful smile." He tapped her button nose. "I hate to see you upset."

"But how can I not be upset? Your mom—"

"What Mom wants doesn't matter, all right?" He rubbed her cheek again. "*I'm* the one who asked you to marry me. *I'm* the one who's in love with you."

"You really love me, pumpkin?" she whispered.

"Of course I do! Hell, I'd marry you tomorrow if I could." He paused, knowing he was about to wade into an argument they had had on many occasions. "I've even offered to marry you sooner, if you remember. We can keep the ceremony small, with just family, and hold the big reception later in May, like you wanted. With your dad being so sick, we—"

"Xavier, you know we have plans. Things are already booked. My dress alterations couldn't be finished that soon! We can't just move up the date! I've been fantasizing about the perfect wedding almost my entire life and I can't—"

"I know that. Point taken! But I'm just talking about the ceremony, baby. We don't know how much time your dad has—"

"Shh," she whispered, holding a finger to her lips. "Let's not talk about that right now, OK?" She kissed him again. "I don't want to fight, pumpkin. I just want to hear you say you love me. That's all I need."

But when would they talk about it? *How many times can we put this off?* he thought.

But like with many disagreements with Constance, he surrendered. He just wanted to make her happy.

"I love you, Connie." He rose to his feet. "So don't worry about anything but planning our wedding, OK?"

She nodded.

With that, he shut her car door, hoping that put an end to her insecurity about their relationship and about Dawn Gibbons.

Chapter 11

"Size eight, please?" Dawn said tiredly as she walked toward the counter.

The redhead in the brown golf shirt nodded before turning her back to Dawn in search of size eight ice skates. Dawn stood by patiently as the woman scanned the rows upon rows of skates stacked on the shelves behind the counter.

Decades ago, Dawn had owned a pair of skates—some pretty cute ones, in fact. They were white with Day-Glo pink laces and petite pompoms on the front. Back then, she and Cynthia (who she still wasn't talking to, by the way) would regularly go to the ice-skating rink outside of Chesterton, though admittedly they went there less to skate than to hang out with friends and flirt with boys. But Dawn hadn't set foot in any rink in *years,* which was why she still didn't understand why Xavier insisted she co-chaperone this little field trip with him.

"You realize that I haven't skated since Bobby Brown was skinny and everyone had beepers instead of iPhones, right?" she had asked Xavier a week ago when he told her that he was taking several kids from the community center to the local rink and wanted her to go with them.

Xavier had laughed. "You can't help but keep reminding me how old you are, can you? It's become like a reflex."

She had shrugged in response. "I'm simply saying that it's been a while."

"Point taken. But you don't have to skate. I need you there to help make sure no one breaks a leg and no one disappears."

"But there *has* to be someone better for this than me!" she had insisted. "I swear, Xavier, I think you have me confused with Mary Poppins or something. I agreed to teach the art class, but a day at the ice rink with twenty or so teenagers sounds like my perfect idea of hell on earth! Get one of the other volunteers to do it!"

"It won't be *that* bad," he had argued. "Look, I'd go ask someone else, but all the other volunteers are either busy or even older than *you* and will probably bust a hip out there on the ice. It'll only take a couple of hours at most. You might actually enjoy yourself, you know."

She highly doubted that.

Dawn didn't know why she had said yes. *Temporary insanity, perhaps?* Either way, after a few more minutes of Xavier's pleading, Dawn had agreed to co-chaperone, which was how she now found herself tugging on a pair of worn skates while more than two dozen rowdy teenagers ran past her on the rubber-matted floor, all pushing to get on the ice.

"So are you going out there?" Xavier asked.

Dawn had finished tying her laces. She turned to find him standing over her shoulder, smiling down at her.

Of course he looked slim, trim, and handsome as usual. He was wearing dark jeans and a gray fitted sweater that was a few shades darker than his eyes. His curly hair was casually ruffled. The black skates he was wearing were his own.

"Not if I can help it," Dawn muttered dryly, watching the children as they zipped and stumbled around the rink. "I'm here to sit on the sidelines, remember? I'll hop in there if someone needs me. Besides, I'm not that good a skater anyway."

"I can skate with you, if you'd like," he volunteered. "You know, guide you around the rink until you get the hang of it again."

She shook her head and tugged her wool jacket tighter around her, adjusting the jacket belt. "That's OK. I'm fine here."

"Come on! I won't even charge you for the lesson."

Dawn glanced at him again. He had extended his hand to her in invitation.

She was half tempted to take him up on the offer, but a voice in her head said that was a bad idea. Though Dawn could grudgingly admit that Cynthia had hit the nail on the head when she figured out that Dawn had a thing for "Mr. Sexy Young Lawyer," that didn't mean Dawn was going to act on it. She didn't care what Cynthia said! She would never take her sister's man! Unfortunately, having him hold her as he tried to teach her how to ice-skate was a bit much for her nerves and hormones to bear. It would probably make her question her resolve.

"Go ahead without me," she said casually, waving him away. "Like I said, I'm fine right here."

"*I'll* skate with you, Mr. Hughes!" a voice piped.

Xavier and Dawn turned.

Dawn instantly recognized the young woman standing next to Xavier who had volunteered to skate with him.

She was one of the girls in Dawn's art class: a thirteen-year-old named Nikki who had the body of a woman ten years older, wore a heavy layer of eye shadow and lip gloss, and had most of the boys in Dawn's art class salivating over her.

Dawn suspected that Nikki had a bit of a crush on Xavier. The light-skinned, teenaged temptress was certainly looking rather dewy-eyed at the moment. She was smiling adoringly at Xavier like angel wings had sprouted from his back and a halo dangled over his head.

He grinned at Nikki. "Thanks for the offer, Nick. I'm okay with skating alone. I was just offering to skate with Miss Gibbons because she said she doesn't know how to. She's out of practice."

"She doesn't know how to skate?" Nikki exclaimed, wrinkling her nose in disgust. She then eyed Dawn derisively. "Everybody knows how to skate! I mean, even *I* learned how to skate when I was like . . . five years old!"

"Well then, neither of you should have any problems out there," Dawn said while rising from her bench. "Meanwhile, I'll watch. Have fun!"

Xavier looked as if he was going to say something more, but Dawn waved and walked off, wobbling slightly on her skates.

Dawn wasn't sure if it was her imagination, but Nikki had been throwing her a tremendous amount of shade. It was kind of amusing in a way. Dawn had gotten the snake eye before from grown women, but this was the first time she had gotten it from a thirteen-year-old.

Don't worry about me, Nikki, Dawn thought as she made her way to a relatively quiet section on the perimeter of the rink. *I'm not even in the running with Xavier. That one is already taken, honey.*

Dawn finally found an inconspicuous spot and sat down again. She gazed at the scene in front of her, watching the children whip around in circles or stumble on the ice. After about fifteen minutes, she was lost in boredom.

I should have brought a book with me, she thought. *This is going to be a long damn day.*

She glanced beside her and saw another girl sitting on one of the benches. The girl was staring listlessly at the other children on the rink with her knobby shoulders hunched. She picked at the hem of her pink wool sweater, pulling at the loose string. Dawn definitely recognized this girl. Her name was Tanisha and she was one of the more talented artists in Dawn's class. She also seemed rather quiet and withdrawn. While most of the kids would huddle together, laughing and talking before and after class, Tanisha seemed to prefer being on her own.

In some ways, how withdrawn she was reminded Dawn a lot of her niece, Clarissa. Though Clarissa had since broken out of her shell since entering college, she had been a very soft-spoken girl for many years.

"You're not going to skate?" Dawn called to Tanisha.

The petite, dark-skinned girl seemed to snap out of her daydream. She turned and squinted at Dawn through her thick glasses. She shook her head. "Nah, I don't . . . I don't really like skating," she mumbled.

Dawn got up from her bench and took shaky steps toward Tanisha. She sat down beside her and grinned. "Me neither," she confided. "But you're here. There's a rink. Might as well take advantage of it! I'm sure Mr. Hughes would want you to."

Tanisha shook her head again. "That's OK."

The two fell into awkward silence. Dawn's first impulse was to get up and return to her bench. It was obvious Tanisha wanted to be alone. But another part of her insisted it wasn't right that Tanisha was sitting all by herself in an ice-skating rink while the other children enjoyed themselves. It was rather sad, actually.

"Well, I'll go out there . . . if you'll go out there," Dawn heard herself saying.

Tanisha stared up at her in surprise.

"I mean, we could even go out there together," Dawn continued, trying to sound casual. "We can go around the rink once. Call it a day. At least, we could say we did it, and," she leaned toward Tanisha, whispering conspiratorially, "it'll get Mr. Hughes off our backs. He's really into 'participation.' "

She gave a droll roll of her eyes that made Tanisha giggle.

"So what do you say?" Dawn asked. "One go-round, then we head back here?"

Tanisha hesitated, seeming to contemplate Dawn's offer. She bit her lower lip as she thought. Finally, to Dawn's shock, Tanisha nodded.

"OK, we can go around once," Tanisha said.

A minute later the two stepped hand-in-hand onto the ice. As Dawn stumbled forward slightly, she laughed at herself. *Lord, I'm worse than I thought!*

"Man," Tanisha said, tugging Dawn's hand to keep her from falling, "you aren't very good at this, are you, Miss Gibbons?"

Dawn was laughing too hard to be offended. "No, not really."

"I can show you how to do it . . . if you want. You're trying to walk on your blades and that won't work. You've gotta push off." Tanisha let go of Dawn's hand and glided forward to demonstrate. "See?"

Dawn smiled. "I didn't catch that. Do it again."

Tanisha glided another few feet. "Got it now?"

The two made it a third of the way around the rink before Dawn stopped.

"I'm only slowing you down," Dawn said, waving her off. "Go ahead without me."

"You sure?" Tanisha seemed to really be into it now. She was even doing occasional figure eights. "I don't mind if you aren't that good, Miss Gibbons."

Dawn chuckled. "No, go ahead. Have fun!"

"Well, O . . . OK," Tanisha said. She gave one last glance at Dawn. Dawn waved at her. Tanisha waved back before skating off, confidently sailing across the ice with her braids flying behind her. Tanisha slowed down slightly when another girl yelled to her and asked if Tanisha could show her how to do a figure eight. Tanisha obliged her.

Dawn beamed with pride as she watched Tanisha. She wasn't usually sentimental, but she felt a warmness swell inside her chest knowing that she had helped the young girl overcome her timidity.

Maybe Xavier was right. She wasn't such a bad teacher after all!

"Good job, Gibbons!" she heard Xavier shout.

Dawn turned and gazed across the rink. He grinned at her and gave her the thumbs-up.

"Thanks!" she shouted back, cupping her hands around her mouth like a megaphone. "But I didn't really do any—*Ack!*"

Dawn's words were cut short when she was shoved forward. She almost landed face first on the ice, and only managed to break her fall by landing on her knees and forearms instead. Crashing that hard still hurt like hell.

She looked up in bewilderment to see what Mack truck had hit her. Instead, she saw Nikki sail by, mocking her with an innocent smile.

"Sorry, Miss Gibbons," sang the busty teenager ever so sweetly while skating backward. "I guess I slipped. My mistake."

Mistake? That wasn't a goddamn mistake!

Dawn gritted her teeth as she watched the young woman skate away. Nikki's hips swayed as her fiendish giggles filled the air.

"You little bitch!" Dawn wanted to shout. But she bit back those words. She didn't want any of the other children to hear her.

So much for that warm, fuzzy feeling, she thought. Now, instead, Dawn was blazing with anger.

She pushed herself to all fours and tried to rise to her feet, but wasn't having much success.

"You all right?" Xavier asked, coming to a smooth stop beside her.

Dawn nodded and blew her hair out of her eyes. "Yeah, I'm fine. Just had a little . . . accident. Remind me never to underestimate thirteen-year-olds."

"Huh?"

"Nothing. Forget it. Help me up, please?"

She held a hand to him, but instead of taking it, he hooked his arms under her armpits and pulled her to her feet in one swift motion. She yelped in surprise again as she seemed to levitate in the air for a few seconds. When he gingerly set her back down, she winced and breathed in sharply.

"What's wrong?" he asked, frowning with concern.

"My goddamn ankle!" Dawn looked down at her feet. "The left one. I guess I twisted it when I fell." She put weight on it, and the dull throbbing in the joint turned to a spiky pain. "Shit! Ow, that hurts!"

Xavier wrapped an arm around her waist and tugged her toward him. "Lean against me. I'll take you back so we can have a look at it. Hopefully, it's only a light sprain."

Dawn's face flushed with heat. She wasn't sure what was more overwhelming: the pain in her ankle or the liquid fire that surged over her body now that Xavier was holding her so close. She politely pulled away from him.

"No . . . no, I'm fine. I can make it," Dawn insisted, trying to mask her grimace. "You keep skating. Worry about the kids. I'm a big girl. I can take care of myself."

She started to limp off, but he caught her by the arm.

"Look, either you let me help you off the ice," he said softly, "or I embarrass the hell out of you by picking you up and carrying you off."

Dawn smirked. "Sure you would."

She turned back around but he didn't let go of her arm.

"Don't think I will?" he challenged. "Try me."

She stared at him in disbelief. He wasn't smiling. He actually looked serious. "You . . . you wouldn't dare!"

"I told you I would, and I meant it. We both know you wouldn't be here if it wasn't for me. *I'm* the one who begged you to come to the rink in the first place. So if you're injured, it's *my* fault. Let me take a look at your ankle. It probably isn't that bad, but I'd rather see for myself."

Damn it, she thought. Why was he making such a big deal about this? She could probably make it off the ice herself. She didn't need his help.

"We walk together or I carry you," he said, sounding firm. "Those are your options."

Dawn sucked her teeth and crossed her arms over her chest. "Fine," she mumbled.

Seconds later, he had his arm wrapped around her waist and her arm was loosely draped around his shoulder as he guided her from the ice to one of the small openings that led to the seating area. Dawn saw that he was steering her toward the condiment stand. She could smell the popcorn and corn dogs even from here.

Though having him this close made her uncomfortable, Dawn took some pleasure in seeing the look on Nikki's face as the teenager watched her and Xavier together. The young woman looked mad enough that lasers would shoot out of her eyes.

Your fault, Dawn thought.

Let that be a lesson to Nikki on the proper way to take out a rival when competing for a man.

Xavier guided Dawn to yet another scuffed bench and urged her to sit down. "Let me see your ankle."

"So you're a lawyer *and* you have an M.D., Dr. Hughes?" Dawn asked as she slowly untied her shoelaces. "You're going to give me your diagnosis?"

"All the sarcasm in the world isn't going to keep me from looking at that ankle." He sat down beside her. "I used to play sports in high school and college. I've sprained my ankle enough times to know what it looks like. I don't *need* an M.D."

She removed her left skate and extended her foot toward him. He took off his gloves and—to her astonishment—quickly removed the sock she was wearing too and tossed it aside. He raised her leg and placed her foot on his knee. He shoved up the damp pants leg of her boot-cut jeans and exposed her calf. He began to gently touch her foot, ankle, and the lower half of her leg, examining them all.

If Dawn thought her ankle was throbbing, it was nothing compared to the throbbing that was starting to bud between her legs as his warm hands skimmed over her bare flesh. She had always been a sucker for foot massages. Damn, this was starting to get distracting!

He furrowed his dark brows as he worked, completely oblivious to the lustful thoughts that were floating through her head. "Your ankle *is* a little swollen. Does it hurt when I do this?" He increased the pressure of his touch, making Dawn wince again.

"Yes . . . unfortunately."

"OK, I know what to do." He stood up and delicately placed her foot on the bench. "I'll be back in a sec."

Now where is he going? She watched in exasperation as he walked toward the concession stand. Yeah, she could use a hot dog, but she didn't know how that was supposed to help her ankle.

He returned a few minutes later with a plastic bag filled with ice and a cup of hot chocolate. He handed both to her.

"The ice is to keep down the swelling," he said, smiling, "and the hot chocolate is my apology for getting you out here."

She laughed and shook her head, taking both the cup and bag from him. "You don't have to apologize, but thanks."

She began to ice her ankle and sip the hot chocolate. It wasn't one of her favorite gourmet lattes, but it was good enough.

"I'm having a party in a couple of weeks at my place," he suddenly blurted out.

She lowered her cup from her lips and raised her eyebrows in surprise.

"It's a small dinner party . . . in honor of my birthday. Constance will be there, of course, and so will Herb and Raquel. I wondered if . . ." He paused. "I wondered if maybe you'd like to come too."

Dawn stared at him, dumbfounded. *An invitation to his birthday party?* This definitely wasn't something she expected. Her stunned silence must have unnerved him because his grin quickly disappeared.

"I mean, you don't have to feel obligated to come," he suddenly rushed out. "I just wanted to—"

"No, I'd like to. I'd *love* to. Just . . . just tell me what time and give me the address."

The two gazed at one another and fell into silence again. She broke their mutual gaze and glanced back at the rink. "So I guess you're going back out there now that you've done your med work?"

"Yeah, I should," he said, though he still lingered.

"I'm OK, really, Xavier. You don't have to stay. I've got my ice. I've got my hot chocolate." She held up the paper cup. "My ankle is already starting to feel a little better. Go ahead. I'm fine."

"I saw what you did with Tanisha," he said quietly. "That was really nice of you."

Dawn shrugged and drank again. "No big deal. I wanted her to enjoy herself. She seems like a nice kid. She shouldn't be huddled in a corner all day."

"But you didn't have to and you did it anyway." He shook his head. "Every time I think I've figured you out . . ." His voice drifted off.

"Why are you trying to figure me out?" She frowned. "This isn't about me trying to take advantage of my father again, is it? Look, I told you that—"

"No . . . no, it's just . . ." He paused. "You're a complex woman, Dawn Gibbons."

Dawn was caught off guard again by his words. "I never claimed not to be."

He nodded and gave her one last lingering look before walking off.

Dawn watched him as he made his way back to the ice. *I'm not the only complex one, Xavier,* she thought.

Chapter 12

"You have someone waiting for you," Ramona said as Xavier walked through the office doorway.

His greeting instantly died on his lips and he stopped midstride. He had just come into the office for the day, and as far as he knew, he had no meetings scheduled first thing that morning.

"I do?"

His secretary slowly nodded, giving him a look that spoke volumes, and pointed over his shoulder to the far-off corner. When he turned and saw who was sitting there, he almost gaped in shock.

"Good morning, Mr. Hughes," said the balding white man in the dour-looking black suit. He wore wire-framed glasses that he absently pushed up the bridge of his nose. Beside him sat an attractive black woman in a red dress.

Xavier knew instantly who this woman and her companion were—the infamous Monique Spencer and her lawyer, Marvin Finklestein.

The last meeting Xavier had with them had ended disastrously with Spencer storming out of the conference room and Finklestein apologizing before grabbing his briefcase and running after her. Xavier had made it clear to them both that a two-million-dollar settlement for her sexual harassment claim was out of the question. He also stated that Allen Enterprises wanted some proof beyond mere verbal allegations that Spencer had actually experienced sexual harassment while she was employed at the company. They would need that before they even would consider giving her a dime.

Xavier watched as Spencer and Finklestein stood. The bulge at the woman's waist was noticeable. Though her sexual harassment charge was still questionable, it looked like at least her pregnancy claim wasn't fictitious.

"To what do I owe this surprise?" Xavier said, extending his hand.

Finklestein instantly shook it, while Spencer kept her hands clasped in front of her and her lips pursed.

"I've had a chance to talk to my client, Mr. Hughes, and we are willing to present the proof that you asked for," Finklestein said, holding up a manila envelope.

Xavier's eyes widened. His workday was certainly starting off with a bang.

"All right." He turned toward Ramona. "Ramona, would you hold all my calls and let Pierce know I may be a little late for that ten a.m. meeting we have scheduled?"

Ramona nodded and began to dial Pierce's extension.

"Miss Spencer, Mr. Finklestein, please step into my office," he said, gesturing toward the other open door.

Finklestein walked first, striding confidently through the doorway. Spencer seemed to hesitate. She took a few steps, then stopped and gazed up at Xavier.

"I didn't want to do this," she whispered fiercely through clenched teeth. "He left me with no choice."

She walked into his office.

"So," Xavier said minutes later as he sat in the chair behind his desk, "you said you had something to show me."

Finklestein, who sat on the opposite side of the desk with his client, nodded.

Xavier had already been through the pleasantries of offering them something to drink and one of the office scones. He had even stepped out and quietly asked Ramona to call Byron to see if he also wanted to sit in on this meeting, since Byron seemed to be so eager to offer his assistance in the matter. Not surprisingly, Byron's secretary said he wasn't in yet. He rarely made it into the office before nine thirty.

"Yes, we do have something to show you," Finklestein said, opening the manila envelope. "My client has copies of emails dated *during* her employment that show proof of systematic sexual harassment."

He pulled out several sheets of paper that were covered in highlighted text and started to hand them across the desk to Xavier, but Spencer stopped her lawyer midmotion by grabbing his wrist.

"Wait," she said. "Before we do this, I want to know first what will happen to him once this comes out."

Finklestein sighed. "Monique, that's not what we agreed to," he said softly. "Remember we talked about this, and I explained—"

"I know what you explained, but I wanna know first!" she boomed, then suddenly turned her gaze to Xavier. Her long, dark hair whipped around her shoulders. "What's going to happen? Is he going to get fired?"

"I can't disclose information like that. That would be left to the discretion of Human Resources and his superiors."

"Come on!" she snapped. "Don't give me that! We're

playing ball with you guys, aren't we? I'm not backing out. I only want to know the truth! Is he going to be fired?"

Xavier took a deep breath. He didn't have to reveal anything to her, but if he wanted this arbitration to finally move forward, he might have to cave on this one.

"I can't say for sure," he began cautiously, "but if your allegations are true, his termination would be a strong possibility. Yes."

She released her lawyer's wrist and let her eyes drift to her lap. "Thank you for at least telling me," she murmured.

Finklestein finally handed Xavier the sheets of paper. Xavier began to read them and when he did, his stomach plummeted. The language in the emails was pretty salacious—definitely not PG-13. But what astounded him wasn't the kinky, naughty banter between Spencer and her "harasser," but the other name in the heading of the emails. When Xavier saw whom she was accusing, his head snapped up and he glared across the desk at Finklestein and Spencer.

"*Byron Lattisaw?*" he asked, almost choking on the name. "Byron Lattisaw? *That's* the manager who you're alleging sexually harassed you?"

"Yes, it is." Finklestein nodded, speaking for his client and smiling triumphantly. "And you can see plainly that Mr. Lattisaw was the aggressor here."

Xavier dropped the sheets of paper on his desk, now dumbstruck.

Well, this explained why Byron had been so eager to help out with the arbitration and why he had been equally eager for the company to settle with Spencer. Byron knew that eventually the identity of the man who had started this whole debacle would come out. He had been trying to protect his own ass this whole time!

"So Byron is also the father of your baby?" Xavier asked quietly.

Finklestein loudly cleared his throat. "That question isn't relevant to—"

"Yes, he is," Spencer blurted out, making her lawyer grumble beside her. "And I still love him. I still love him!" She sniffed and looked at Xavier, teary-eyed. "I didn't want to do this. Please tell Byron that I didn't want to do this to him, but I didn't know what else to do!"

"Monique," Finklestein said, looking like he wanted to clap his hand over his client's mouth, "I urge you not to—"

"He promised me that he'd take care of me," she lamented, ignoring her lawyer's warnings. "He said that he would leave his wife. He said he wanted to marry me. Then when I told him I was pregnant, he acted like he didn't even know me!"

Xavier opened his desk drawer and pulled out a pack of tissues he kept on hand. He slid them across his mahogany desktop toward her and she quickly grabbed a handful. She dabbed at the corner of her eyes, smudging her mascara, and blew her nose.

"I don't have a job, Mr. Hughes. I don't have any money! How could Byron do this to me? *How could he?*" She burst into uncontrollable sobs.

Xavier didn't know how to tell her that promises from a man like Byron should never be taken seriously. Byron would never marry a woman like Monique Spencer. His wife Kelly came with her own trust fund and had been handpicked by Byron's parents. Byron only saw Spencer as a fling—a fling that went cockeyed when she became pregnant. Rather than impact his own wallet and ruin his reputation, Byron had let this poor woman go forward with suing the entire company in order to secure money to take care of her child. Byron was a selfish asshole, a man with no honor. Xavier didn't know how to tell Spencer any of this without crushing her further, but he knew what he had to do next.

He turned to Finklestein. "Thank you for sharing this information. I'll convey it to the proper people."

"It can't be," Herbert Allen murmured, shaking his head. "Xavier, are you sure?"

Xavier laid the email copies on the desk in front of his mentor and nodded. "It's all there, Herb. The stuff that Byron wrote to her is pretty graphic, definitely not work appropriate."

Herb reached for the papers and began to scan them. "Good Lord! The boy is *married*. What the hell was he thinking?"

"Byron was being Byron. You've heard the rumors about him just like I have. I had only assumed he wouldn't pull this same crap here at the company. I guess I assumed wrong."

"Please tell me the relationship was at least consensual. Not that it makes much difference, but . . . He didn't badger her, did he? For my own peace of mind, I hope she didn't feel pressured to enter a sexual relationship with him."

Xavier lowered himself into the wingback chair facing Herb's desk.

Being the CEO of the company, Herb had by far the biggest office in the entire building, but it didn't feel hollow. Herb kept the space warm and much like an at-home library with leather and mahogany furniture, towering bookshelves, and lamps with an antique bronze finish. In fact, the office's atmosphere was so warm that Xavier always felt like he was visiting an old friend here—not his boss, which was why he had no problem being perfectly candid at that moment.

"Byron was pretty aggressive initially, but yes, I believe based on what I've read and how Spencer feels about him that it *definitely* was consensual. She fell in love with him. She's been trying to protect him this whole time."

"That poor girl," Herb whispered as he stared at one of the sheets of paper. He finally raised his eyes to look at Xavier again. "Well, this is quite the situation. Byron knows the rules. We'll give him a chance to explain himself, but more than likely he'll have to be let go."

Xavier nodded in agreement. "More than likely."

Herb lowered his head and closed his eyes. "Oh, the fallout from this is going to be horrendous. Raquel and Byron's mother have been friends for *years*. Hell, Byron went to school with Constance!"

"I know, but Byron did it to himself. When he was hired here, he signed an agreement forbidding sexual harassment just like we all did and—"

"I know. I know," Herb said, waving his hand to silence him. He opened his eyes. "Well, I guess I better call him in to speak to him personally. I at least owe his parents that, I think." He sighed and slumped back in his chair. "There go my plans for the day."

"Hey, I'm with you. I had to cancel a meeting with Pierce because of this. I've rescheduled with the guy twice already. I bet he's starting to think I'm avoiding him."

"And I wanted to stop by Dawn's gallery around lunchtime to give her a check," Herb lamented, looking crestfallen.

At the mention of Dawn's name, Xavier instantly perked up. He hadn't seen her since the field trip to the ice-skating rink several days ago. He had been thinking about her off and on since then.

"A check?"

"Yes, I told her that I was interested in purchasing a

few of the paintings she had at her gallery," Herb continued, "and I wanted—"

"I can take her the check for you!" Xavier instantly volunteered. "I had planned to head into D.C. later this week, but I could do it today. It wouldn't be . . . It wouldn't be a problem."

Herb smiled. "Xavier, you're many things—my lawyer, my future son-in-law, and my confidant—but the one thing you are *not* is my errand boy." He chuckled. "I'm not going to ask you to take this to Dawn. I could have one of the messengers in the building do it if I needed to. Besides, it doesn't need to be done right away."

"But it's no big deal," Xavier insisted as he rose from his chair. "I can take it to her. Besides, I-I wanted to check on her. She twisted her ankle at the ice skating rink. I talked her into going, into being a chaperone. I'd like . . ." He cleared his throat. "I'd like to make sure she's recovering OK."

Herb squinted and stared at Xavier for several seconds. He then slowly reached for one of his desk drawers and pulled out an envelope. "Well . . . if you insist." He held the envelope toward the younger man.

Xavier grabbed it, but he noticed that Herb hadn't released the other end of the envelope. He gazed at his mentor, perplexed.

"You two are getting along rather well, aren't you?" Herb asked.

"What do you mean?"

"I mean you and Dawn seem to be hitting it off. In fact, I think you're getting along better with Dawn than Dawn and Constance are getting along with each other. Those two haven't connected at all."

"Well, they're two women who just found out a

month or so ago that they're sisters, Herb. It has to be awkward. And there is the age difference between them."

Herb finally released the envelope. "There's an age difference between you and Dawn *too,* Xavier, and it doesn't seem to have made much of a difference."

"I . . . I suppose not," he said, clearing his throat again. "Good point." Was it his imagination or was the temperature rising in the room? He tucked the envelope into his suit breast pocket. "I'll let you get back to your work. In the meantime, I'll take care of this check for you." He turned and began walking toward the office door.

"Oh, Xavier!" Herb called after him.

Xavier stopped and turned around. "Yes?"

"I appreciate you being so welcoming to Dawn. I want her to feel like she's part of the family, and I'm glad you're making an effort to do that, but . . . you don't have to try *too* hard. All right? We wouldn't want to make Connie jealous."

Herb was still smiling, but Xavier could see something in Herb's eyes that made him uncomfortable. Was it caution, maybe? But why was Herb warning him off? Xavier was still keeping a safe distance from Dawn. He hadn't crossed any lines. He had no interest in her.

"Of course not, Herb."

He opened the office door, stepped out of the office, and shut the door behind him.

Chapter 13

Dawn grumbled to herself as she riffled through the pile of papers and envelopes on her desk. Her sprained ankle was elevated on the chair beside her.

She had planned a leisurely morning of enjoying a freshly baked croissant and her French-pressed coffee, then maybe checking her e-mail. But that whole plan was shot to hell the instant she walked through the gallery's revolving glass doors.

Her heaven-sent assistant Kevin was regretfully on vacation in Napa Valley with his longtime boyfriend. That meant Dawn now had to fend for herself, and her to-do list was growing longer by the hour. Not only did she have to review the draft of the press release for an upcoming exhibit, but she also had to redo all the invitations. Last week, Dawn had handed off the task to her new intern, who promised he had the invitations covered.

"No problem, Miss Gibbons," her new intern had assured her with a wink.

But this morning she was stunned to realize the intern did *not* have it covered. He had used an out-of-date invite list and accidentally deleted the new one, so now

Dawn was frantically trying to gather names and addresses to create mailing labels.

If you want something done right, you have to do it yourself, she thought with frustration.

She also had an interview scheduled with a style magazine reporter for later that morning and several phone messages from florists and caterers to return. This was in addition to the less-than-glamorous office work she had to take care of as part of her day-to-day responsibilities as gallery director.

"I'll be lucky if I get out of here before midnight," she mumbled, picking up another envelope and ripping it open.

"Good morning, darling!"

Dawn flinched at the sound of the booming voice. Oh, this was the last thing she needed!

She slowly raised her eyes from the mountainous pile on her desk and saw gallery owner Percy Templeton sailing through her office doorway. He grinned down at her.

He was wearing another one of his ridiculous outfits today: stone-washed skinny jeans that sagged on his thin hips, a studded leather belt, red combat boots, and a black shirt that was open at the collar. He was also wearing another one of his many expensive leather jackets.

She wondered if he realized wearing clothes that were meant for a man almost thirty years younger than himself actually made him look a lot older.

Probably not . . . but it's not my place to tell him.

"Good morning, Percy," she answered flatly, barely masking her annoyance.

He eagerly rubbed his hands together. "All right, darling, put away that rubbish! I've come to rescue you! I'm taking you out to brunch."

With one careless brush of the hand, he swept her

pile of papers aside, wiping out two hours of work, making her jump back in shock.

Dawn clenched her jaw and silently counted to ten. She forced a smile. "Percy, I can't go out to brunch with you. I have a lot of work to do today, and most of it is time sensitive. Why don't we—"

"No! I won't hear it!"

Percy walked around her desk and grabbed her arm. He roughly tugged her to her feet, making her sputter and wince at the sudden weight put on her ankle.

What the hell has gotten into him? Has he lost his damn mind?

Percy looped an arm around her waist and dragged her toward him. "Now grab your coat! I'm not taking no for an answer."

Dawn tried to pry Percy's arms from around her waist, but it was a challenge. He might have been skinny, but he certainly wasn't weak. His grip was oppressively strong.

"Percy," she said, holding on tenuously to what little patience she had left, "I already told you that I can't go with you. What part of what I said did you not understand?"

"Darling, I am offering to treat you to a wonderful meal at one of the best restaurants in town. I can't tell if you're playing hard to get or—"

"I'm *not* playing hard to get, but I am getting annoyed!" She shoved at his chest. "Now stop kidding around and let me go!"

He leaned toward her and she took a step back and bumped into something hard and metallic. She tried to shift but realized she was pinned against her own desk. He pressed his thighs and chest against hers. She leaned back and winced again, feeling the pain flare up in her sprained ankle.

Dawn looked up, prepared to tell Percy that enough was enough and it was high time that he got the hell out of her office. But when she saw the look in his eyes and the expression on his face, those words died in her throat. Something in his gaze had hardened, and for the first time, she was frightened of him.

She glanced nervously at her office door. The new intern wasn't scheduled to show up until noon, and the only other staffer who had been in the gallery with her that morning had left an hour ago to run an errand. She and Percy were completely alone.

"Dawn, this little dance we've done for the last year or so has gotten rather tiring. Hasn't it?" Percy asked.

"What . . . what dance?"

"Well, I repeatedly ask you out to dinner or for drinks, and you turn me down, making some absolutely asinine excuse, insulting my intelligence. Frankly, darling, I find it quite rude. When I hired you to work for my gallery, I did it not only because you were talented, but you had a"—he looked down at her breasts—"another quality that I greatly admired. I hired you with the assumption that—"

"You'd get a piece of ass?" she asked tersely.

He chuckled. "If you wish to put it so crudely . . . yes, I did. *Why not?*"

"Well, pity for you, Percy, because you were mistaken," she said, glaring up at him. "Signing my paycheck doesn't mean you automatically get me too! I'm not a prostitute!"

She gave him another hard shove, but he didn't budge. Instead, he laughed again.

"*Really?* I've heard differently."

Dawn stilled.

"I've indulged you for far too long. Now stop playing games!"

He dipped his head lower, bringing his mouth dangerously close to hers. To avoid his lips, Dawn had to turn her head. She grimaced as he pushed her farther back against the desk. The glass top cut into the backs of her thighs as he forced one of his knees between her legs.

"Why don't we do this, darling?" He lowered his mouth to her neck. "Why don't we close the door, push aside all those little papers of yours, and—"

Someone loudly cleared their throat, making both Dawn and Percy jump.

Xavier stood in the office doorway with his knuckle raised as if he had intended to knock on her door. His wool coat was draped casually over his forearm and an envelope was in his hand. He was wearing one of his staid suits today. This one was charcoal with pinstripes. His handsome face was set in a scowl.

Percy's hold around her waist instantly loosened. Now free, Dawn fled to the other side of the room.

"I guess I came at a bad time," Xavier said.

"No! *No!*" Dawn pushed down the front of her pencil skirt, which had ridden up during her tussle with Percy. She walked across the room, grabbed Xavier's hand, and tugged him inside her office. "No, you came at a-a *great* time, a perfect time!"

And she meant that. If Xavier hadn't shown up at that moment, she didn't know what Percy might have done.

Now that he had been caught red-handed trying to force himself onto an employee, Percy's face had paled considerably. He licked his lips. "I didn't know . . . y-you had an appointment, darling."

"Well, now you do," she said angrily. "So you can leave, *darling!*"

He glanced at Dawn, then Xavier, and nodded before adjusting his leather jacket and making a quick exit from her office. She strode across the room and slammed the door shut behind him. When she turned back around, prepared to thank Xavier again for his wonderful timing, she found him glowering at her.

"Who the hell was that?" he asked.

She closed her eyes and took a deep breath. "That's just Percy. He's the gallery owner . . . that self-entitled asshole! I should have known that he would—"

"And you let him grab you like that?" Xavier shouted before throwing his coat onto one of her office chairs.

Let him? Dawn opened her eyes, not liking Xavier's question or his tone.

"Umm, I don't know if you noticed, but I was trying my best to push him away! I didn't want him grabbing me! I was working, and Percy barged in here and—"

"Oh, bullshit!" he snarled, making her flinch. "I saw you and I saw him, and frankly, you didn't look like you were putting up much of a fight!"

"Then maybe you need to go to an optometrist and get some damn glasses, because that was exactly what I was doing!"

He shook his head. "So much for being done with rich guys, huh?"

"What?"

"Is this Percy guy the next in line?" Xavier challenged.

"Excuse me?"

Where is all this coming from? This was a complete

about-face from the guy at the skating rink last week-end. Where was the guy who had charmed her, iced her sore ankle, and brought her hot chocolate?

"So much for that shit about focusing on your work and being an independent woman!" Xavier continued. "So much for not needing rich guys to pay your bills anymore! You're a pragmatic woman, Dawn. This way is much easier, isn't it? You can paint all you want with a guy like that around to foot the bill!"

She balled her fists at her sides.

Who the hell was he to question her? The last she checked, she was single, and Xavier was engaged to the cookie-cutter cutout of perfection known as Constance Allen. Even if Dawn was having sex with Percy, it was none of Xavier's concern.

"Not getting any at home?" Dawn taunted, crossing her arms over her chest.

She could tell she hit a nerve with that one. His gray eyes went glacial.

"You've been asking me a lot of questions. Is that why you're so worried about *my* sex life? Is Connie not giving it to you on the regular?"

"I don't have to listen to this shit!"

"Neither do I! So you get the hell out of my office!" She pointed at the door. "How dare you question me about using sex to climb my way up the ladder when you're sexing up the boss's daughter? You can get off your moral high horse, honey!"

"So you admit that's what you've been doing?"

"I'm not admitting a damn thing! I'm just pointing out that you have little room to talk when it comes to blurring the lines between personal and professional! Xavier, you have no lines!"

"Constance and I are in love! We're engaged! The re-lationship that she and I have is *nothing* compared to the tawdry shit going on between you and that British asshole! So don't even try it!"

So Constance Allen was the princess who could do no wrong, while Dawn was the ho who obviously only had gotten where she was today because she slept her way there.

Typical. So goddamn typical!

She should be used to it by now. Women like her—the women in her family were always judged this way. She and her sisters had commiserated about it endlessly over the years. But the sting of other people's judgment never subsided. The sting she felt now was particularly painful.

"Let's get this straight!" Dawn said, pointing at him. "For the last time, he pushed himself onto me! It wasn't the other way around!" She sucked her teeth in frustration. "Besides, why the hell am I even defending myself to you? Why do you care? How is what I do or *who* I do any concern of yours? Huh?"

Xavier fell silent. He adjusted his necktie and ran a hand over the crown of his head, looking uncomfortable at suddenly being put on the spot by her question.

"I . . ." He swallowed. "I've known Herb for a very long time. I'm his lawyer, and you're his daughter. He pays me a considerable amount of money to make his business my business. His interests are my concern, and by extension *you're* my concern. I'm sure Herb wouldn't want you to make a mistake like this. He'd be . . . disappointed."

"Well, isn't that sweet," she murmured sarcastically as she walked toward her office door. She opened it. "But you don't have to be concerned about me. I'm an adult. I'm thirty-seven years old! Hell, I'm *older* than you are and—"

"You're not that much older than me! Stop acting like I'm a fucking toddler!"

"And I'm completely capable of taking care of myself," she continued, ignoring him. "I've been doing a fair enough job of it for a couple of decades now. I think I can stand a few more decades without your helpful guidance, Mr. Hughes." She gestured toward the empty hallway. "So thank you, but again, you can get the hell out of my office."

She watched a tic form along his jaw. He was angry, but she didn't care. She had been sexually harassed by Percy, then yelled at and insulted by Xavier. She was mighty pissed herself!

Dawn watched as Xavier tossed an envelope he held onto her desk, which was now in complete disarray thanks to Percy. Papers, envelopes, and opened catalogs were strewn everywhere.

"A check from your dad for artwork," Xavier said. He grabbed his coat from the office chair beside him.

He walked toward the doorway and she averted her eyes, stubbornly refusing to meet his gaze. When he reached her, he paused.

"I'm . . . I'm sorry if I . . . overreacted," he said softly. "I guess I just . . . misunderstood what I saw."

She nodded, though she still didn't look at him, and she wasn't sure if she believed his apology either. She believed that his knee-jerk reaction to seeing her with Percy was probably the most honest one: He still thought she was an opportunist, and worse, he also thought she was a whore. Obviously, in the back of his mind, he had been thinking that about her all along, despite the progress she had thought they had made in becoming friends. That realization hurt.

"Dawn?"

"What?" she snapped.

She felt him place a hand underneath her chin, surprising her. He gently tilted it upward. She could have pulled away from him, but she didn't. All her anger dissolved with one touch. When their eyes met, it felt as if all the air had been sucked out of the room.

Xavier leaned down and drew close to her mouth. Percy had done the same minutes earlier, totally revolting her. But with Xavier she didn't shy away. Her lips parted. She exhaled slowly. She welcomed his proximity and his touch and, for a fleeting moment, hoped that he would lean down and kiss her and end the agony she had been in for weeks.

"I don't give a damn what you say," Xavier whispered. "Like it or not, you *are* my concern now and I *will* watch out for you. And if I find him—or anyone else, for that matter—touching you like that again, I'll . . ."

His words drifted off. He dropped his hand and abruptly turned away from her, not giving her the chance to respond before he strode down the hallway and out the gallery's door.

Dawn took an unsteady breath, watching him as he retreated. With shaky legs, she walked back to her desk and sat down, taking another calming breath, but it didn't work. Her stomach was still in knots. Her heart still thudded wildly in her chest. And the agony of delayed gratification returned.

Delayed? a voice in her head mocked. *Girl, he's never going to kiss you!*

Because he was with Constance and men like Xavier didn't cheat.

Chapter 14

"Laurie, would you pass me the pepper?" Cynthia asked.

Lauren leaned toward her left, picked up the crystal pepper shaker, and handed it to her sister.

A few minutes later, Dawn also turned to Lauren. "Laurie, can you hand me the coffee pot, please?"

Lauren hesitated. The sterling silver coffeepot sat only inches in front of Cynthia, but Dawn seemed to be making a point of ignoring their eldest sister. In fact, she wouldn't even glance Cynthia's way.

Cynthia supposed that Dawn was still angry at her for making Dawn confess to their mother about connecting with Herbert Allen and his family. That would be the only thing that could explain Dawn still giving her the cold shoulder.

"Umm, OK," Lauren said as she reached over Cynthia and grabbed the pot. She handed it to Dawn.

"Thanks," Dawn murmured.

The table fell into painful silence again.

This was undoubtedly a rough start to Saturday brunch at Mama's, a weekly tradition in the Gibbons family. Cynthia had been looking forward to having brunch with her sisters, knowing it would be the first in a long time that would include just the women in the family. Crisanto was away on a business trip. Keith was doing some investigative work for one of his cases. No husbands or boyfriends would be intruding into their happy little female circle—or so Cynthia thought. She hadn't known that Dawn would arrive at the brunch with a stick shoved up her ass, ruining all the happiness.

Fine with me, bitch, Cynthia thought flippantly as she continued to eat her eggs Benedict and glower at Dawn, who sat on the other side of Lauren at the table. *Two can play at that game.*

Cynthia made a big production of loudly clearing her throat. "Steph, can you hand me a croissant?"

Stephanie, who now took eating as seriously as she once took a Louboutin shoe sale, stopped midbite of bacon and cheese biscuits. "Why me? The basket is right in front of Dawn," she said between munches.

"I didn't ask Dawn to pass the croissants. I asked *you,*" Cynthia answered tersely through clenched teeth.

"Well, excuse me!" Stephanie exclaimed, reaching for the basket.

Dawn sipped from her glass of orange juice and shook her head. She laughed coldly. "I swear, some people so petty."

"*I'm* petty?" Cynthia shouted with outrage. "What about—"

"Enough!" their mother declared, tossing her napkin onto the linen tablecloth, making her silverware clatter. Her voice echoed in the sunroom. "Enough of this nonsense!"

Everyone fell silent again.

"Cindy, Dawn, whatever problem you two have with each other, you better end it *right now!*" Yolanda ordered.

"I don't have a problem," Cynthia said, casually fluffing her sun-kissed curls. "Dawn's the one acting like someone ran over her dog."

"Of course you don't have a problem!" Dawn spat. "You're always the one to light the match, start the bonfire, and then act like you can't smell any smoke!"

"That's it," their mother said as she pushed her rattan chair away from the table. "Thanks to you girls, I've lost my appetite. If you are going to continue to act as if you're ten-year-olds, I'm not going to sit around and watch. I've got too many other things to do today!"

Just then, Crisanto Jr.'s wails filled the sunroom. He lay in his baby-blue bassinet, not too far from the table where the women sat. Lauren furrowed her brows with worry as she reached for her son.

"What's the matter, Pooh Bear?" Lauren cooed.

"No," Yolanda said, walking around the table toward the bassinet.

Lauren stopped.

"No, you finish your breakfast, Laurie. And talk to your sisters. Maybe you can snap some sense into them. Meanwhile, I'll take care of the baby. Come with Grandma, honey." She reached into the bassinet and scooped her weeping grandson into her arms. She adjusted his blanket and gently bounced him up and down. She eyed Cynthia and Dawn. "I need a break anyway."

Their mother strode across the room and up the short flight of steps from the sunroom.

When the sound of Little Cris's cries and their mother's high heels disappeared, Lauren gazed at her sisters. "What the hell was that about?"

"Whatever it was, Mama's pissed," Stephanie whispered between chews.

"She's pissed," Dawn explained, "because Cindy doesn't know how to keep her big fat mouth shut."

"No," Cynthia clarified loudly, "Mama is pissed because she found out that Dawn has been sneaking behind her back, secretly having family dinners with her father—the *same* man who deserted Dawn decades ago!"

"Wait . . . how the hell did Mama find out about that?" Lauren asked.

Dawn crossed her arms over her chest and glared at Cynthia. "Cindy told her."

Stephanie dropped her biscuit back to her plate and breathed in sharply. "You *didn't!*"

Cynthia pursed her lips, feeling under siege. Why was everyone turning on her like she had done something wrong when clearly Dawn was the one at fault?

"Of course I told her!" Cynthia said defensively. "Mama had a right to know!"

"No, she didn't! I'm not some little girl looking for my daddy! I'm a grown woman who chose to reconnect with my father. I don't need my mother's permission to do that," Dawn argued.

"Well then you should have had the balls to stand up and say it instead of sneaking around!" Cynthia yelled back.

"OK! OK, guys, stop shouting," Lauren urged, holding up her hands.

"This wasn't just about me reconnecting with Herb or 'sneaking around'!" Dawn continued, ignoring Lauren's request for them to quiet down. "You were angry because I consider him family now. You see this shit as some weird competition!"

"It's not just him!" Cynthia bellowed, slapping her hand on the table, making her water glass tip over and water slosh all over the chenille tablecloth.

Stephanie grimaced as she slid back from the table to keep from getting soaked. "Damn, watch it!"

"You had the audacity to call that chick Constance your sister, like she's one of us!" Cynthia yelled.

"No, I had the audacity to refuse to seduce her fiancé *because* she's my sister!" Dawn insisted. "And she *is* my sister, Cindy. We have the same father. That's just a statement of fact!"

"Wait," Lauren said, holding up her hands again. "Wait! What's this about seducing someone's fiancé?"

Dawn's eyes widened with alarm. "Forget I said that."

"No, tell them!" Cynthia said. Her wicked smile broadened. "Tell them about your sexy young lawyer."

Cynthia watched as Dawn gritted her teeth. "He isn't *my* sexy lawyer. Like I said, he's Constance's fiancé and nothing is going on between us. *Nothing!*"

"So why does Cindy think you want to seduce him?" Lauren asked.

"Because she's a shit stirrer!" Dawn proclaimed. "Look, can we please change the subject? I don't want to talk about Xavier. To even suggest that he and I have something going on is just . . . just ridiculous. Trust me!"

"Why is it so ridiculous?" Stephanie asked, rubbing her pregnant belly.

"Because he would never hook up with me." Dawn took a deep breath and closed her eyes. "He's not like that. It's not in his makeup."

Cynthia was taken aback by that revelation and even more shocked at the longing she heard lingering in her sister's voice.

"Besides, this has nothing to do with him. The issue at hand is Cindy's big mouth!" She opened her eyes and glared at Cynthia again. "You couldn't keep a secret to save your life!"

"Oh, yes, I can!"

"She does have a point, Cindy," Stephanie ventured before sliding back to the table and returning to her plate.

"Yes, I can!" she said adamantly. "I can keep a damn secret! I've kept plenty of secrets over the years, I'll have you know!"

"Name one!" Dawn challenged.

"Well, Mama has a stalker, for one." Cynthia triumphantly raised her pert nose into the air. "None of you knew about that!"

The entire table fell silent again as her sisters stared at her, aghast.

"*A stalker!*" they shouted in unison.

"Mama has someone stalking her? *Who?*" Stephanie asked, clutching her chest in alarm.

"Why the hell am I just hearing about this?" Lauren cried. "Cindy, of all the secrets to keep—girl, this isn't one of them! Why did Mama tell you and didn't say anything to the rest of us?"

Cynthia rolled her eyes. "Because she doesn't know about the stalker either."

They all stared at her, confused. She gave a furtive glance at the sunroom entrance to make sure their mother wasn't standing there, then told her sisters the story of her past run-ins with Beatrice.

"Well, I'll be damned," Dawn mumbled as she slumped back in her chair after Cynthia finished telling her story. "She sounds like a nutball."

"That bullfrog is cheating on my mama!" Stephanie exclaimed, looking outraged. She slowly shook her head. "Damn, times must be hard when a guy like that has women fighting over him."

"I wouldn't call it a real fight. So far all she's done is

talk a good game. All she does is follow Mama around," Cynthia said. "She hasn't actually *done* anything."

"So far," Lauren clarified. "You say 'so far,' but what if that changes, Cindy? What if Mama could seriously be in danger? Why haven't you told her?"

Cynthia shrugged. "She's been so focused on the wedding, I just didn't want to upset her."

"Yet you had absolutely no problem telling her about what I was doing," Dawn said petulantly.

"All right, ladies," Lauren huffed. "Please let's not start that again. Let's focus on Mama and this stalker lady."

"Don't worry. I'm keeping tabs on it," Cynthia assured. "Like everything else around here, I've got it covered."

"You better," Dawn warned, sipping from her glass of orange juice again. "We don't want Mama to end up with a knife in her back or with dead rabbits boiling in her kitchen pot."

Stephanie stopped slicing into her sausage link, looked up from her plate, and frowned. "But Mama doesn't have any rabbits."

At that, her sisters all turned, stared at her, and burst into laughter.

Chapter 15

Dawn sat down in the wingback chair, feeling like a big ball of nerves. She gripped the chair's padded armrests so tightly that her royal purple nails dug into the upholstery. She had to remind herself to let go lest she make nail-sized crescent indentations in the leather—which wasn't quite the "impression" she wanted to leave behind. So she let go of the armrests and clasped her hands together in her lap instead.

"Are you sure I can't get you anything to drink?" Madison McGuire asked as she lowered herself to the sofa facing Dawn.

The two women sat in Madison's lavishly decorated living room, which had bay windows that overlooked a small arbor and Maddie's vegetable garden, both of which were covered in icicles and a fine layer of snow. Dawn could hear Maddie's son, Nicholas, playing video games in the next room. Maddie's lobbyist husband, Rick McGuire, was in their French country kitchen, having a hushed conversation on his cell phone. Meanwhile, the two women gazed at one another in uncomfortable silence.

"No, I'm . . . I'm fine," Dawn finally answered.

Maddie fluffed one of the gold dupioni silk sofa pillows behind her before slumping back. "Well, I must admit, I was surprised to hear from you. I hadn't spoken to you since the exhibit in December. So what brings you here today?"

Dawn hesitated, not sure how to answer that question. Should she come straight out and say why she had come here to Maddie's Capitol Hill townhome on a Friday afternoon, or try a more tactful approach? What exactly was the proper etiquette for begging someone for a job?

Maddie gazed at her, assessing her shrewdly. "I'm guessing this is more than a social call."

Dawn nodded. "You're right."

"So don't beat around the bush!" Maddie beckoned her with her hand. "Tell me why you're here."

Why she was here, in short, was because Percy's last sexual harassment attempt had been the final straw. Though Dawn loved Templeton Gallery and the staff, she knew she couldn't work there anymore. What if Xavier hadn't made his unexpected appearance last week? What if she hadn't been able to fight off Percy? Even now, she shuddered at how badly things could have gone wrong that day.

Feeling as if she was left with no alternative, Dawn had turned in her resignation and packed her office. Unfortunately, she had given little thought to what quitting her job as Templeton Gallery director would mean for her professionally and financially. She had been so filled with anger and indignation that she'd given little thought to *anything* that day. Thankfully, she had remembered Maddie's offer in December to take over the helm of Sawyer Gallery. She just prayed that Maddie's offer was still good and she hadn't given the gallery director position to anyone else.

If she has, I am so *screwed,* Dawn thought.

"Well, I was wondering if you were still interested in having me at Sawyer Gallery," Dawn finally said, making Maddie look taken aback.

"*Really?* You're considering leaving Templeton? But I thought you loved working there."

"I do, but it's not the best situation for me anymore," Dawn answered candidly.

"I see." Maddie reached for a cup of espresso that sat on the coffee table between them. "Does Percy know you're leaving?"

"Yes, he knows. I've already given him my resignation."

"I see. And how did Percy take the news?"

Dawn thought back to how Percy had responded when she told him she was quitting. He had thundered on the phone for a good fifteen minutes before declaring that she would "never work in this town again."

"You'll be lucky to be working behind a counter taking orders for Happy Meals when I'm done with you!" he had bellowed before slamming down the phone.

"He didn't take it well," Dawn now answered dryly.

Maddie chuckled. "I didn't think he would. Percy has"—she paused to take a sip of her espresso—"a bit of an ego. He doesn't seem like he would take rejection well."

At the sound of Maddie's laughter, Dawn's tenseness eased a little. "Saying that Percy has 'a bit of an ego' is like saying Antarctica is a little bit cold."

"That is definitely true. *Definitely!*" Maddie laughed again before quickly becoming somber. "He's also bad at keeping things professional."

"That he is."

Maddie lowered her espresso cup back to the table. She gazed at Dawn again. "Forgive me for asking this, Dawn, but I'm sorry, I have to."

Dawn steeled herself. She knew what question Maddie was about to ask.

"You said things were fine for you at the gallery, and now you've had a sudden change of heart. Knowing what I know about Percy and the . . . the rumors that I've heard, I—"

"He and I weren't sleeping together," Dawn said bluntly, cutting her off. "He wanted to. He wasn't subtle about letting me know that he wanted to, but I don't mix business with pleasure—no matter what reputation I may have."

Maddie lowered her eyes sheepishly. "I'm sorry for bringing it up."

"No, it's all right." Dawn tried her best to hide her bitterness. "This is a very image-conscious job and I'm sure you're aware of my image. But contrary to popular belief of some in our social circle, I took my job very seriously. I wouldn't jeopardize it by canoodling with the boss. Unfortunately, Percy didn't appreciate that. That's why I had to leave."

"That's good to know. Because I respect your work and your talent, Dawn. It would be a shame to have a reason not to hire you, because I'd love to have you as my gallery director."

Dawn broke into a grin. "Really?"

"*Of course!* Percy was an idiot to drive you away! But his loss will be my gain. You're hired!"

Maddie stood first and Dawn breathed a sigh of relief as she also stood from her chair. Now that the conversation was over, the tension in Dawn's body released instantly like a deflating balloon.

"I'm so happy that we'll be working together," Maddie said.

"I am too!"

You have no idea how much, she thought as she and Maddie shook hands.

Minutes later, Dawn walked down the brick steps of Maddie's home, feeling as if a massive weight had been lifted off her shoulders. As she walked toward her car, she heard the tinkling sound of her cell phone. She pulled it out of her leather purse and glanced at the number on her screen, expecting it to be one of her sisters. When she saw who it was, she smiled with surprise.

"Hey, Herb!" she said after pressing the "answer" button.

"Hi, sweetheart! How are you?"

"Good . . . great, actually!"

"Great? You sound like you're in a good mood."

"I am!" She pressed the remote button to open her car door. "I just got a new job. I'm really excited."

"A new job?" He paused. "May I ask what was wrong with the old one?"

I was working for a lecherous asshole and I should have quit it a year ago, she wanted to say, but answered instead, "Nothing. This is just a better situation for me."

"Well, I-I wish I knew you were looking. I don't have too many contacts in the art world, but I could have made a few phone calls and—"

"Thanks but no thanks, Herb. That's not how I roll," she said as she juggled her phone and her purse and climbed behind her steering wheel. She shut the car door behind her. "Besides, I didn't need any help. I can find a job on my own."

"Yes, you can. I know you can. I just . . . I just would like to help you whenever *I* can. It would make me feel good to help you."

"You're sweet, but again, it isn't necessary."

And it wasn't just the fact that she was too proud to accept Herb's help that would have made her turn down his offer to find her a job. She would hate to hear what Xavier would say if he found out that Herb had pulled strings to get her a position at another gallery. Xavier already seemed to think the worst of her.

The sanctimonious jerk, she thought angrily.

She didn't want him to think yet again that she was out to use Herb.

"Well, then," her father said, "the least I can do is help you celebrate! What are you doing this afternoon?"

She had just put her key into the ignition. She paused. "This afternoon? You mean *today?*"

"Yes, *today!*" He laughed. "I can meet you at five-thirty if that works for you. I can meet you in Georgetown at your favorite tea shop," he said. "The raspberry scones will be my treat."

"How can I resist? I'll see you then."

Dawn walked into Big Ben's tea shop, still smiling. She spotted her father instantly at a small bistro table on the other side of the room. It was the same table where they had sat at on their first "date." He was also overdressed again—this time in a tan suit jacket and charcoal slacks. She could even see that he was wearing gold cuff links. Behind him was a table of Georgetown University students in Abercrombie and Fitch T-shirts and sweaters and wrinkled jeans, leaning over their laptops as they drank from coffee mugs. He looked like he could have been one of their professors.

"Well, well," she said as she strode across the shop toward him. "Who is this handsome man sitting all alone?"

Herb grinned, grabbed his bamboo cane, and slowly rose to his feet. "Why, I was only waiting for a lovely lady to join me." He leaned forward and kissed on her on the cheek, making her giggle. He patted the back of the chair beside him. "Now have a seat and tell me about this new job of yours."

For the next half hour Dawn told him about Madison and the new gallery. She glossed over the more embarrassing details regarding her last days as gallery director at Templeton, choosing to avoid the discussion about the groping incident. Her father seemed genuinely happy for her.

"But enough about me," she finally said, after taking a sip of white tea. "What have you been up to?"

"Not much," her father confessed. "Allen Enterprises is thankfully a ship that pretty much steers itself, with little or no intervention from me. Most of my days now are filled with listening to Constance and Raquel go on and on about wedding preparations." He rolled his eyes and laughed. "I must confess that I don't find conversations about stationery and ribbons quite that fascinating. Thankfully, they've recently started to talk about Xavier's birthday, which is tomorrow. But you know that already. He told me you're coming to his party."

At the mention of Xavier's name, Dawn's smile faded. "Actually, I don't think I'll be able to make it," she replied before finishing her scone.

Herb frowned. "*Really?* Why not?"

"Something came up," she lied, brushing away the crumbs from the napkin on her lap. She waved her hand dismissively. "Besides, I doubt I'll be missed. I bet he only invited me because I'm a relative now. Just wish him a happy birthday for me. You guys have fun."

"Xavier will certainly miss you if you don't come to his party, sweetheart. He didn't just invite you because he only sees you as family now. He's very fond of you."

Dawn cocked an eyebrow as she raised her teacup to her lips. "Frankly, sometimes it's hard to tell, Herb."

"But he does!" Herb chuckled before sampling his cookie. "In fact, he's so fond of you that I was starting to wonder if ol' Xavier was a little smitten with you."

Dawn had to stop herself from spitting out her tea. Her heart seemed to skid to a halt. She stared at her father in disbelief. "You've got to be joking!"

"I said I was only starting to wonder," he quickly corrected himself. "But then I remembered that he's been crazy about Constance since he was a teenager."

Exactly, Dawn thought, though she was a little crest-fallen.

Herb leaned forward. "He *does* like you, though, Dawn, even if it isn't in a romantic way."

She lowered her teacup back to the table. "Guys like him don't like women like me, Herb."

He squinted. "Women like you?"

"Yes, women like me. You know what I mean."

When he continued to look at her with an expression that conveyed confusion, she blurted out, "Gold diggers."

Her father looked offended by that word. He opened his mouth as if to disagree with her, but she stopped him before he could.

"I know the truth. Like I said, guys like him—serious to the point of anal-retentive, self-righteous, almost austere in how they live their lives—they see us as trouble. They're wary of us." She shrugged. "It's a small-minded world. I'm used to being judged that way."

Herb gazed at her in silence for several seconds. "And you don't think you're being small-minded by judging Xavier?"

"What do you mean?"

His face became stern. " 'Guys like him,' as you say—anal-retentive, self-righteous, austere—it seems that you've painted Xavier into a little box too. You're also stereotyping him."

"I wasn't stereotyping him! I was just . . . just . . ." She sighed helplessly. "Look, I'm sorry if what I said offended you."

And she was sorry, not for how she felt, but for saying her thoughts aloud. She had allowed her frustration with Xavier to make her way too candid. She should have known better than to bad-mouth him in front of Herb. He was Xavier's friend and mentor, after all.

"You didn't offend me. I just don't think your judgment of Xavier is very fair. Do you know why he comes off as so anal-retentive and self-righteous?"

"Bad programming at the robot factory?" When he didn't laugh at her flippant remark, she shook her head. "Sorry. Bad joke," she said softly, feeling contrite.

"He didn't choose to be this way, Dawn. He used to be a lot more carefree when he was younger." A smirk crept to Herb's lips. "Why, I remember the stories his father, Malcolm, would tell me about the hijinks Xavier got into. Malcolm worked for me back then, but he was more than just an employee. We were also very close friends. We spoke a lot and the stories Malcolm would tell about Xavier would shock even *you*." He chuckled. "But then his father died when he was seventeen. Xavier was alone with Malcolm when it happened. They were on a fishing trip together. They were driving back and his father had a heart attack. They pulled over to the side of the road and Xavier tried to resuscitate him, to bring him back, but he couldn't. That's a hard thing for a boy to experience. After that . . ." Herb paused. "After that, he became very somber. He became a very serious young man."

Dawn suddenly went from feeling contrite to feeling like a big pile of dog poop.

"I'm sorry," she mumbled. "I didn't know."

"Of course you didn't. He doesn't usually talk about his father, or that part of his past. I believe it might be painful for him. But now do you see why he is the way he is?"

She lowered her gaze, feeling rightly chastised. "I suppose."

"So maybe you can rethink whatever else you have going on tomorrow? Maybe you can attend his party?"

"Maybe," she answered, though she knew at this point that she'd feel like dirt if she didn't go.

Chapter 16

Xavier tossed his hand towel onto the granite counter-top and strode out of the kitchen at the sound of his ringing doorbell. When he reached his front door, stared through the peephole, and saw who was standing in the hallway, he paused.

It was Dawn, clutching a bottle of wine, holding a gift bag, and staring off into space as she waited.

Holy shit, he thought. *She came!*

After what he had said to her at her gallery when he caught her with that British asshole, after the shameful way he had treated her, she had still come to his birthday party.

Xavier had been so embarrassed at how he had behaved. He still had no reasonable explanation for why he had blown up at her, but the instant he had stumbled upon her locked in that bastard's arms, he had seen red. He kept insisting to himself that it wasn't jealousy. No, he was just concerned for her. He didn't want her to slip back into her old ways. That was all.

But he couldn't ignore the fact that he had behaved terribly and he had wondered if she would ever speak to him again, let alone show up tonight. To say he was shocked to see her standing in his hallway was putting it mildly.

He unlocked the door and swung it open.

"Happy birthday! I've come bearing gifts," she said as she handed him the bottle of wine.

"Uh, thanks." He glanced at the chardonnay, then back at her in bewilderment. "You didn't have to, though."

"What do you mean I didn't have to? I wouldn't show up to a birthday party empty-handed!"

He nodded and continued to stare at her.

"So . . ." She gazed over his shoulder. "Can I come inside?"

"Oh! Oh, yeah. Sure. I'm sorry. I should have . . ." His words drifted off as he stepped aside and gestured for her to enter.

"You will note," Dawn said, pointing down at her wristwatch as she stepped over the threshold, "that I am here at seven-thirty *exactly!* I didn't want to be late to your party. We all know how judgmental you can be," she chided with a smirk.

Xavier winced at her jab. "Dawn, I'm sorry about what happened at the gallery. I know I—"

"I was just joking, Xavier! No need to apologize again."

He shook his head. "But it was wrong the way I reacted. You were put in an awkward situation. I should have seen that. He's your boss and—"

"Not anymore," she said, making him pause.

"Huh?"

"Not anymore. I quit. I'm tired of his groping and his bullshit. I work for another gallery now. So see, it's done. All is forgotten . . . really."

She patted his shoulder soothingly and he instantly

relaxed. She then tugged off her leather gloves and stepped around him into his condo.

As she passed, he caught a tantalizing whiff of her perfume—an exotic, zesty fragrance that he couldn't quite place but that made his mouth water. He was tempted to lean forward to smell her again, but resisted the urge.

"You're not attracted to her. Remember?" a voice in his head reminded him.

He glanced down and saw that she had a blue gift bag in her hand. "Is that for me too?" he asked as he reached for it.

She winked and pulled the bag out of his grasp. "Yes, it's for you. But I want to give it to you after dinner—not before." She turned in a circle and gazed around his condo.

He knew from being at her workplace that they had a similar aesthetic. His home was just as clean and modern as her office, though with a more masculine touch. Her eyes shifted from his charcoal-colored simple sectional to his steel-framed leather chairs to the glass-topped coffee and end tables. He could see her admiring the few tasteful paintings and Masai warrior masks on his walls.

"Nice place. Very nice." Dawn paused as she looked around his living room. "It's also very empty. Where is everybody, by the way?"

"You're the first guest besides my mom, and she's helping me in the kitchen," he said, alluding to the clatter of pots and pans they could both hear coming through the closed kitchen door. He set the wine bottle on his coffee table and reached out to Dawn. "Let me take your coat."

"Thanks." She undid her belt and unbuttoned her tweed cloak. "Your first guest, huh? Oh, I *definitely* get extra points for this one, Mr. Hughes!"

She shrugged out of her cloak and handed it to him. When he saw what she was wearing, he swallowed audibly.

She had chosen for tonight's birthday dinner to wear a form-fitting, off-white cashmere sweater and a tight, camel-colored leather pencil skirt that showed off her taut, sleek frame. The fabric whispered as she walked across his living room. She bent down to examine one of the picture frames on his end table and he got a full view of the swell of her breasts over the top of the V-neck sweater. He clenched his jaw and hastily looked away, busying himself with hanging her cloak in his coat closet.

"Is this you?" she exclaimed as she stood up and pointed at one of the photos.

Xavier nodded and shut the closet door. "Yeah, that's me with my dad."

"*Your dad?* He's very handsome." She gazed at the picture. "Herb told me you guys were close."

"We were," Xavier answered softly.

He had idolized and adored his father. It had been very painful to lose him.

"And you weren't so bad-looking yourself," she added playfully. "Look at you! Look at those braces!"

"Don't remind me," he said with a chuckle.

"He was adorable back then, even *with* those chunky braces, though he hated wearing them! Let me tell you," his mother said as she stepped out of the kitchen and began to untie the apron from around her waist. She smiled as she walked toward Dawn with her hand extended. "Hi, I'm Leslie Ann, Xavier's mom."

Dawn shook her hand. "It's a pleasure to meet you, Leslie Ann. I'm Dawn. I'm Herb's—"

"*Daughter!*" his mother finished for her. "Yes, I know! I've heard so much about you." She looked Dawn up and down, still smiling. "And may I say you're even more striking in person than I've heard."

Dawn blinked, seemingly caught off guard by his mother's compliment. She opened her mouth, then closed it, at a loss for words.

"Mom, please stop. You're embarrassing Dawn."

His mother turned to him and waved her hand. "No, I'm not! What's there to be embarrassed about? I'm just stating the truth." She looked at Dawn again. "You *are* striking. . . . very beautiful."

"Uh . . . well, th-thank you." Dawn glanced at the apron his mother held in her other hand. "You know, if you could use some help in the kitchen, I'm more than happy to help out." She shrugged. "I'm not the best cook in the world. That's more my sister Lauren's department. She's the chef. But I'm good at taking instructions."

His mother laughed. "Most of the cooking is done already, but Xavier and I were just about to set the dinner table, if you'd like to do that."

"*Set the dinner table?* Well, that sounds like a safe one! You can't burn a glass or a fork, right?" Dawn asked, making his mother laugh again. "Show me the way and I'll get started."

His mother and Dawn walked back toward the kitchen, chatting animatedly with each other.

Xavier watched them until they disappeared behind the kitchen door. The two women were a study in contrasts: Leslie Ann Hughes, the cute, petite strawberry-blonde wearing the simple shift dress and sweater, and Dawn, the towering dark-skinned beauty in the form-fitting clothes. But despite their differences, the two seemed to be hitting it off well.

Xavier suddenly remembered what Constance had said almost a month ago, that his mother would much rather he married Dawn than her. He knew that wasn't the case, but he had to admit his mother had never responded to Constance the way she was responding to Dawn tonight.

What was it about Dawn that could make her win over so many people around him: Herb, the kids at the community center, and now his mother? Dawn's charm no longer seemed to be the machinations of a woman who excelled at seducing men, who knew what she was doing. Instead, she seemed to do it naturally, making it harder for Xavier to keep up his guard, making it harder to fight his attraction.

"So you're finally admitting that you're attracted to her?" the voice in his head mocked.

Yes, he answered grudgingly.

He couldn't keep ignoring it. When he was in a room with her, he thought he felt an electrical charge radiating between them. It made his skin tingle and caused less-than-proper reactions in other parts of his body. Though he had been firmly in denial, his subconscious had obviously been more than happy to indulge. Last night, he had even had an erotic dream about Dawn and this morning, he had awoke hard with arousal, groggy eyed, and unsettled.

I'm a good man, Xavier reminded himself as he lingered in the living room, pretending to straighten up the space a bit more in anticipation of the rest of his dinner guests. *I respect my fiancée and our relationship. They're just dreams ... fantasies. I'm only human. It's not like I would ever cheat on Constance.*

But the mere fact that he had to keep reminding himself of this made him uneasy.

It didn't bode well. It didn't bode well at all.

"Do you remember the song, hon?"

Xavier sighed as everyone at the dinner table began to laugh. "Yes, Mom, I remember the song."

"You can't sing a few bars for us?" his mother pleaded.

"No, I can't."

"*Why?*" she whined. "It was so adorable! You used to sing it every night to me and your dad before you went to bed."

"Because I'm thirty years old now, not three," he answered succinctly.

"Thirty years old as of two hours ago." She sipped from her wineglass and grinned. "Oh, come on! I'll pay you!"

"There ain't enough money in the world," he said, making almost everyone break out into uproarious laughter.

The dinner had gone well with easy conversation among his guests. Xavier had felt a little tension when Herb, Constance, and Raquel arrived and the two women saw that Dawn was there. He wasn't sure why. He thought Constance knew that Dawn also had been invited. She was family now, after all. But after about an hour, the tension seemed to dissolve and everyone settled into the meal.

His mother had helped him cook her usual smorgasbord of food and even had brought along a few extra casseroles. "Just in case we run out," she had said. By the time they sliced his chocolate ganache birthday cake, half of the casserole dishes hadn't even been touched and everyone looked stuffed.

Xavier now surveyed the half-eaten bounty in front of them, then looked across the table. Through the glow of the fading tapered candles between them, he locked eyes with Dawn, who was slowly shaking her head at him. He smiled. She smiled back. He started to feel the electric charge between them again, but it was abruptly cut off when Constance dropped her head to his shoulder, landing with a thump that caught him by surprise.

"I bet you had a cute singing voice, pumpkin," Constance said, gazing up at him lovingly.

He wrapped an arm around her, pulling her close. "Probably not as cute as you would think." He glanced around the table again. "But let's change the subject. I'll talk about anything but my childhood rendition of 'Twinkle, Twinkle, Little Star.' I mean it, absolutely *anything*: the basketball season, the tax code, work . . ."

"Speaking of work, I'd like to say thank you for resolving that Spencer issue," Herb said, holding up his wineglass in praise. "I know it was ugly and it wasn't easy. But I'm glad it's finally been resolved . . . for the most part."

Raquel leaned back in her chair and frowned. "How could you possibly say it was resolved, darling? The Lattisaws' lives will be ripped apart! I heard Byron's wife is considering a divorce. I spoke with his mother, Jackie, just the other day and she is *so* embarrassed . . . totally horrified. She doesn't know how she could possibly show her face at the country club now that everyone knows you fired Byron for sexual harassment," she said accusingly.

Herb lowered his wineglass back to the table and pursed his lips. "Well, I'm sorry, dear, but to be frank, Byron brought this upon himself. I can't consider the social comings and goings at the country club when I'm making business decisions. What he did was inappropriate and definitely in violation of—"

"You've never liked Byron," Constance said bluntly, again catching Xavier by surprise. "Just admit it, Daddy."

"Sweetheart," Herb said softly, looking hurt. "This has nothing to do with whether I like or dislike Byron. As CEO of Allen Enterprises, it is my responsibility to maintain the welfare and credibility of my company. Byron was putting both at risk by carrying on an affair with an employee."

Constance raised her head from Xavier's shoulder and shook it. "You do favors for people *all* the time, Daddy! Byron and I have known each other since grade school. We've been friends for, like, forever! You could have done a favor for him. You could have looked the other way, but you didn't!"

Xavier squinted at his fiancée.

What was going on here? Why the hell was Constance coming to Byron's defense? Xavier stared at her, bewildered that she was picking a fight with her father. It was so out of character for Constance. Had something happened before they arrived at the dinner party that he didn't know about?

Xavier looked at his mom, who was starting to appear uncomfortable with the whole argument. Meanwhile, Dawn's brows were furrowed. Her lips had tightened. She opened her mouth like she was about to come to her father's defense, but Xavier cut her off and defended Herb instead. He didn't want the two sisters to argue.

"Come on, baby. Cut your dad some slack," he urged softly, squeezing her shoulder. "It's not like he was out to get Byron. And he's right. Byron *did* do this to himself. If his marriage and his family's reputation are ruined, then it's Byron's fault, not your dad's."

Constance shoved away from him. "You don't like Byron either. You didn't want Daddy to hire him in the first place! Be honest!"

"Well," Dawn said, finally joining the conversation, "considering that neither Herb nor Xavier liked him very much, as you claim, sounds like this Byron guy had it coming, Constance. They're pretty good judges of character. I would trust their opinions."

"Oh, what the hell would you know?" Constance snapped, making everyone stare at her in shock. "You just met all of us two months ago! Now, suddenly, you're an authority on *our* family?"

Leslie Ann loudly cleared her throat and rose from the table. She clapped her hands. "It looks like everyone is finished now," she said anxiously. "Xavier, we should probably start cleaning up, shouldn't we?"

"Yeah," he murmured, his eyes shifting uneasily between Constance and Dawn as he reached for one of the dirty plates.

He had to give Dawn credit. She was staying tight-lipped, even though she looked furious, even though he knew from experience that she didn't shy away from a fight. He wondered if she was holding back because her father was here.

"Raquel and I should probably be leaving," Herb said quietly. "We have to get back home, and frankly, I'm . . . I'm feeling a bit under the weather today."

Dawn tossed her napkin aside and pushed her chair back from the table. Her face was marred with concern. She touched her father's shoulder. "Are you OK? Maybe you should—"

"I'm fine, sweetheart." He patted her hand. "I'll get some sleep and I'm sure I'll be right as rain in the morning."

Herb and Raquel departed soon after. Constance had

already made plans to spend the night with Xavier, so he wasn't surprised she didn't leave with her parents, but in some ways, he wished she had. If she was in a bad mood, he wasn't in the right mind-set to deal with any bullshit tonight.

Dawn lingered behind to help with the cleaning after the meal while Constance sat at the table, silently drinking chardonnay and looking sullen. A distinct chill now radiated between the two women. If they had any chance of building a relationship before, he was pretty sure that it was now ruined.

He carried the remaining dirty plates into the kitchen and began to load the dishwasher.

"Need any help?" he heard a few minutes later.

Xavier looked up from the dishwasher racks to find Constance standing in the entryway smiling at him.

"You want to help me?" he asked, surprised.

She stepped into his kitchen. "Don't look so surprised." She reached for one of the hand towels on his granite kitchen island. "I wanted to make a peace offering for that little blowout we had earlier."

He turned to face her. "Yeah, what was that all about? I wasn't sure how the argument even started."

She released a long breath and shrugged. "I have no idea, pumpkin. I guess I was just . . . upset. Mommy said that Daddy vetoed one of the things I wanted for the wedding. He said the cost was just 'too outlandish.' Daddy never tells me no, but since Dawn came into the picture, now he says he doesn't want to just spoil me anymore. He gave me some speech last week about being more self-sufficient! 'Learn from Dawn's example!' " She rolled her eyes. "I guess I was pissed at him and it came out during dinner. Then Dawn had to make it worse and butt in her big fat nose and I . . ." She shook her head angrily and tucked a lock of hair behind her ear. "Look, I don't want to talk about it anymore. I came in here to make up with you, pumpkin. To say I'm . . . I'm sorry for how I behaved."

"I appreciate that, baby. But you don't have to do manual labor for us to make up."

"I know. It's just . . . It's not like I'm needed out there. Your mom and Dawn are busy with their own little conversation. It looks like they're becoming *fast* friends." She seemed perturbed at the idea, but didn't make any further comment. "Besides, I know how to clean!"

"I know you do, baby. It's just . . ."

You've never offered to clean before, he wanted to say, but didn't.

Constance had grown up with servants who catered to her every need. She didn't think to offer to clean up after herself or anyone else. He didn't hold it against her. She was just a product of her upbringing.

The one time he had seen Constance pick up anything dirty, it was while she volunteered at a soup kitchen event that Allen Enterprises had sponsored. She had done her best to keep on a smile for the photographers as she removed used paper plates and plastic forks from the tables, as she scrubbed down the scuffed linoleum surfaces, but the instant the cameras disappeared, Xavier had seen Constance's perky façade disappear. She looked tired and bewildered.

"Don't worry about it," he said now, waving her away. "I've got it covered."

"Oh, it's no big deal! Let me help you." Constance eagerly walked toward the sink and peered down at the pile of dirty dishes. She paused, making him chuckle.

"Any second thoughts?" he asked, loading another plate into the dishwasher.

"No!" she answered stubbornly. "I'm supposed to be more self-sufficient now. Right?"

She grimaced, reached into the sink, and retrieved a dirty wineglass. She began to place it on one of the dishwasher racks.

Xavier shook his head and removed the glass, setting it on the counter. "No, sweetheart, that's Mom's crystal. All those glasses have to be washed by hand."

At that, she frowned. "I didn't know washing dishes was so complicated."

For the next ten minutes, she made a halfhearted attempt to help him—mostly holding the dirty dishes with two fingers and quickly rinsing them off before handing them to Xavier. But finally, she let out a dispirited sigh.

"I don't think I'm cut out for cleaning, pumpkin," she said, wiping her hands on one of the towels. "This is just *gross* and the water is making my hands all prune-y," she muttered, staring down at her fingers.

"That's OK, baby. I appreciate you trying to help at all." He leaned down and gave her a quick peck on the cheek before returning his attention to his work.

"But you know," she said, placing her hands on her hips, "you look pretty sexy cleaning and working in the kitchen like this."

He did a double take. *"I do?"*

"Definitely." She wrapped her arms around his waist. "Seeing you like this even makes me a little horny," she whispered seductively with an impish grin.

Horny? He frowned down at her in disbelief. But then she suddenly turned him around, stood on her toes, wrapped her arms around his neck, and kissed him. She tugged his bottom lip between her teeth and raked her fingers through his hair.

Xavier didn't know how to respond. Constance rarely initiated things sexually, so for her to take the reins now was pretty astonishing, to say the least. But it didn't take him long to fall under her spell. He kissed her back just as fervently. When he started to get into it, she abruptly pulled her mouth away. She then began to unbutton her top, making his eyes widen. He stopped her hands midmotion and looked toward the kitchen entrance. He could still hear Dawn and his mother laughing and talking in the dining room. They sounded like they could walk into the kitchen at any moment.

"Baby, are you sure you don't wanna wait until they leave?" he whispered. "Believe me, I'm ready to go if you are, but—"

"We'll just be quiet about it."

He opened his mouth to say more, but she silenced him by raising a finger and placing it on his lips. "I'm horny *now*, pumpkin. I don't wanna wait until they leave!"

Constance went back to unbuttoning her blouse, revealing the pink lace bra underneath. She took one of his hands, placed it on her breast, and kissed him again.

The logical part of him thought this was a bad idea. Who the hell had sex with his girlfriend with his mother and his future sister-in-law on the other side of a wall, less than ten feet away? But the logical part was losing out to the hunger that was building inside him. Admittedly, he and Constance didn't have sex quite as often as he would like, so when she presented him with an offer like this, it was hard for him to say no. Maybe that was the *real* reason why he was having fantasies about Dawn. Sex with his fiancée might be the balm that he needed to push Dawn out of his mind.

When Constance pressed her torso against his and began to unbuckle his belt, he didn't argue with her. When she lowered his zipper and plunged her hand past the elastic waistband of his boxer briefs, all he could do was close his eyes and let her do whatever she wanted. He groaned against her lips when she started to stroke him, and he tugged down the lace cups of her bra and toyed with her nipples. They kissed again and he began to raise the hem of her skirt, easing her back onto the counter.

"Xavier," Dawn said as she walked into the kitchen, holding a casserole dish, "your mom said you need to soak this in soapy water as soon—"

At the sound of Dawn's voice, Xavier tugged Constance's hands out of his pants. He turned toward the entryway to find Dawn staring at them.

"Hmm, looks like we've been caught red-handed," Constance said, closing her top. She grinned.

"I'm . . . I'm so . . . so sorry," Dawn stuttered, looking embarrassed. "I wasn't . . . I mean, I didn't . . . I was only bringing this in. Your mom asked me to—"

"No! No, that's OK, really," Xavier said, hastily raising his pants zipper. "We were just—"

"Pumpkin, Dawn *knows* what we were doing." Constance giggled and wrapped an arm possessively around Xavier's waist. She licked her lips and laid her head on his shoulder. "Sorry, Dawn. Xavier and I got a little carried away. You know how it is though, right?"

"Yeah," Dawn replied, smiling tightly at Constance. "I know how it is."

Her dark eyes then shifted to Xavier, and he instantly felt guilty. He didn't know why. Constance was his fiancée. He had every right to kiss her and to do a lot more than that if he wanted to, but still, the last person he had wanted to stumble upon them at that moment was Dawn.

Dawn stepped forward and placed the eggplant-crusted casserole dish on the granite island. She then quickly backed away. "Well, like I said . . . your mom asked me to bring this to you. I was about to head out and—"

"Leaving already?" Constance asked.

"Yeah, I should be . . . you know . . . getting home." Dawn cleared her throat. "Enjoy your birthday, Xavier."

"Oh, believe me, *he will!*" Constance gloated, then laughed. "Won't you, pumpkin?"

Xavier could be wrong, but at those words, he thought he saw Dawn flinch.

"Good night," he called to her.

"Thanks for coming!" Constance sang.

Dawn nodded. "No problem. Have a-a good night."

He watched her turn and walk out of his kitchen.

Chapter 17

Dawn poured herself another glass of sauvignon blanc, grabbed her cell phone, and began to scroll through the contacts list on the glass screen.

She had arrived home from Xavier's dinner party half an hour ago, and thanks to the hot-and-heavy love scene she had witnessed in the kitchen between Xavier and Constance, Dawn was now hell bent on getting drunk and getting laid—*in that order!* She was tired of obsessing about that man. Dawn Gibbons was not a woman who mooned over someone who neither wanted nor desired her. Plus, it wasn't like she could have him anyway. He was Constance's man, and that Malibu Barbie bitch had made that abundantly clear tonight. It was about time Dawn realized that fact and moved on, and what better way to do that than with a booty call?

"You're hurt, but are you sure you don't want to call one of your sisters and lament to her instead?" a small, rational voice in her head suggested. "You'll feel much better in the morning about it than having sex with some random guy!"

To hell with that, Dawn thought with a snort as she continued to scroll through the list and took a gulp from her glass. The time for talking was over! She wanted a man to make her moan and make her scream and push whatever lingering thoughts she had of Xavier Hughes out of her head with an earth-shattering orgasm. Her only challenge now was finding the right candidate.

While Dawn and her sisters had been taught by their mother to look for certain qualities in men—wealth, power, and a willingness to skip signing a prenuptial agreement—Dawn knew some men had other laudable qualities that weren't on her mother's list. In this area, Dawn didn't break the family rules exactly, but merely bent them a little. Over the years, she had secretly hooked up with a half dozen guys who didn't have a lot of money or prestige, but were definitely skilled in the bedroom. She would never commit to them, only call on them from time to time, whenever she had an itch. Unfortunately, those times were further and further apart now that she had become so preoccupied with her career, but still she liked to keep a few around for emergency situations like these.

"*Mark?* No," she said as she scanned her phone screen, searching for the names with the gold star beside them. "*Jean Claude?*" She tilted her head and drank more wine. "Eh, maybe. But I'll see who else is in here. *Miguel?* Oh, yes! Yes! Yes! *Yes!*"

She had met Miguel two years ago at a fund-raising gala at the Capital Hilton. He wasn't one of the rich men who had placed insanely high bids on the items up for auction that night. He was instead one of the bartenders who handed out watered-down drinks and collected tips in a snifter. He had kept looking at her with sexy caramel eyes and had given her a seductive smile every time she'd go to the bar to refill her glass. When the night wound down, he asked her if she'd be willing to go with him to a salsa club after the gala. Her first instinct had been to say no. She was exhausted from a night of schmoozing, and he was a hotel bartender, for God's sake! But there was something in those eyes and in that smile that held a lot of promise. The next morning, Dawn was happy she had agreed to go out with Miguel. It turned out he was just as good in bed as he was on the dance floor—and that man could salsa damn well!

They had hooked up a few times since then, but she hadn't spoken to him in more than a year.

"Time to check in," Dawn murmured as she pressed the button to dial his number. She finished the last of her wine and listened to the phone ring, already brainstorming what lingerie she would wear when he arrived at her apartment later that night.

"Hello?" a woman answered.

Dawn paused. That certainly wasn't the voice she expected to hear on the other end of the line. She lowered her wineglass to her night table. "Hi, uh . . . I'm sorry. I was trying to call Miguel Sanchez."

"Who is this?" the woman asked. "How did you get this number?"

Dawn went stark still.

"How the hell did you get my husband's cell number?" the woman continued, raising her voice. "Damn it, the number is blocked but you don't fool me! Are you that bitch from the leasing office? I told you not to call my husband anymore unless you want me to come down there and kick your ass!"

Her husband? Oh, hell, Dawn thought, rolling her eyes heavenward. So she guessed quite a great deal had happened in Miguel's life in the past year. Luckily,

Dawn had run into her fair share of angry girlfriends and wives, and she knew how to do some fancy footwork to get out of this one.

"I'm sorry, ma'am. I'm not sure what you're referring to," she said, taking on a bureaucratic tone. "I was trying to get in touch with Mr. Sanchez to let him know about the new low interest rate he can receive on his Visa card. He's one of our valued customers, but I'll try calling back at another time that's more convenient for him."

"Oh," the woman said. "Well, I . . . I didn't know it was a sales call. You should have said that at first."

"No problem. Thank you very much for your time, ma'am. Enjoy your evening!" Dawn chirped.

After she hung up, she flopped back onto her pale blue satin comforter and blew out a breath that sent the bangs of her bob flying.

Well, that was a big fat disappointment! *So much for a hot night with Miguel,* she thought.

"Good! Now maybe you'll give up this stupid idea, throw on some pajamas, climb into bed, eat a carton of Ben & Jerry's, and call it a day," the voice in her head chastised.

Dawn ignored it and instead went back to scrolling through her phone list, looking for more contenders.

She paused when she reached the name *Hosea.* She slowly sat up from the bed.

Hosea . . . Now there was a chocolate honey-dip she wouldn't mind seeing again. He had been her personal trainer for a while. One day last year, an intense evening workout at the gym doing push-ups and crunches led to an equally intense workout in his bedroom that also required her to get on all fours. She was sore for days after that, and for all the right reasons. She wondered if Hosea was willing to do an encore performance.

Dawn pressed the button to dial his number while crossing her fingers that no angry wife or girlfriend answered the phone this time.

"What's up? Hosea speaking," he answered casually in his rumbling, deep baritone, instantly making her toes curl.

"Hey, Hosea, it's Dawn. Remember me?"

He chuckled on the other end. "Of course, I remember you, girl! You had the best abs I've seen in quite a long time."

"*Really?* That's all you remember is my abs?" she purred with a laugh.

"Oh, I remember a lot more than that! Don't even get me started! So what have you been up to, sexy?"

"Oh, a little of this and a little of that." She walked across her bedroom to one of her dressers. "I was sitting all alone in my bedroom wondering what *you* were up to, specifically what were you up to tonight."

"Nothing so far." He paused on the other end. "Why? Did you have something in mind?"

"Well . . ." She tugged open one of her dresser drawers and pulled out a black and purple bustier. "I was thinking you could drive over here. I'd open a chilled bottle of wine, set the lights and the music on low, and wear the sexiest lingerie I could find. Then we'd go from there. Who knows? Maybe you'll even get to see my abs again."

"Give me your address, sexy," he said instantly. "I'll be right over."

At the sound of her doorbell ringing, Dawn tightened the belt of her silk robe and finished yet another glass of wine. She was starting to get that light buzz that let her know she was only one or two glasses away from being drunk, which was right where she wanted to be. She had just enough alcohol in her veins to make her bolder and to perk up her libido.

"And to make a world-class ass of yourself," the annoyed voice in her head iterated yet again.

Oh, hush! I've had enough of you. I'm going to get some booty tonight and no one *is going to stop me!*

She sat down her glass on her dresser, gave one last glance at her reflection in her bedroom mirror—opening the top of her robe a bit to reveal the lace cups of her bustier—and dashed to her apartment's front door. She took a moment to gather herself, unlocked the door, and swung it open. She grinned.

In the hallway stood Hosea—all two hundred pounds of hard muscle and chocolate delight. His dreads had grown longer since the last time she had seen him, and he had shaved off all his facial hair. But besides that, he was as handsome as she remembered and he still emanated the same sexiness and virility that made women do double takes when he passed them at the gym.

His eyes slowly trailed over Dawn from head to toe, lingering on her breasts and the exposed thigh that peeked through the slit in her robe. She could tell from the expression on his face that he liked what he saw.

"Hey!" She leaned seductively against the door frame. "Thanks for coming."

"Hey, sexy," he drawled then stepped forward. He wrapped his arms around her, eased her back into her apartment, and shut the door behind him. He tugged at the knot in her belt, catching her off guard. Hosea pushed her robe open and lowered his mouth to hers. The next thing she knew, he was shoving his tongue down her throat and groping for the bustier clasps at her back. She could barely get her bearings before his other hand was toying with her thong, trying to tug it down her hips.

Whoooooa! Slow down there, honey!

Yes, this was a booty call, but that didn't mean that they were going to skip all foreplay and any pretense that this was about more than just sex. Hell, he could at least have a drink first!

Dawn pulled away and yanked at his hands.

"I didn't know we were on a timer," she said hesitantly with a chuckle. "Why the rush?"

"Why the rush?" He stared down at her, looking exasperated. His jaw clenched. "Damn, girl, I thought you wanted to do this! Isn't that why you called me?"

"Of course it is," she said, bristling at his tone. "But we've got all night." She ran her hands along his coat lapels. "At least take your jacket off. Sit down. Have a glass of wine."

He looked like having a glass of wine was the last thing on his mind, but he sighed and nodded. "Whatever. Go ahead and pour me some."

And the evening pretty much went downhill from there. While Dawn tried to engage Hosea in a little conversation, he stared off in the distance and swilled back a few glasses. After a half hour, he didn't even bother to pretend anymore. He started groping at her again. When they made it to the bedroom, Hosea showed just as little patience and restraint. The man went straight for the bustier and the panties. Within seconds he had on a condom and her legs spread wide.

This certainly wasn't the lover that she remembered from a year ago. This guy could take a lesson or two in how to please a woman.

"You like this, huh?" he grunted as he pumped his hips and plunged inside her. "You want this? Is this what you want?"

Dawn didn't respond but instead stared at the bedroom ceiling, completely bored. She grimaced when he roughly pumped again.

"Take it, girl! Take it!" he ranted like some demented porn star.

She stifled a sigh.

Why had she called this man?

"Because you were under some misguided notion that this would help you forget about Xavier," the voice in her head answered. "I told you this was a bad idea!"

Finally, after about ten minutes—the longest ten minutes of her life—Hosea gave one last grunt and collapsed on top of her. He slowly raised his head. "Aww, man! Damn, that was good! I'm worn out, girl!"

Dawn didn't comment. Instead, she shoved him off her and rose from the bed.

"Wait, now! Don't leave yet," he said, wiping the sweat from his brow. He turned on his side and hooked a finger toward her. "I'm just getting started, sexy. Give a man a few minutes to recover and we'll go another round."

Dawn threw on her robe. This time when she put on the belt, she did a double knot so that there were no delusions that she was taking off her robe again. "No, that's OK." She walked around her bedroom and gathered his clothes. "I've got an early morning tomorrow. I really should get some sleep."

"*Early morning?*" He frowned, sitting up from the bed as she tossed his shirt and pants at him. "But tomorrow's Sunday."

"Yes, but sometimes I . . . I work weekends," she

said, which was true. Sometimes, she *did* work weekends, just not this weekend. But he didn't know that, and frankly, she would tell any lie to get this man out of her bedroom and her apartment.

"Uh-huh," he said, looking doubtful. He began to put on his boxers and slowly shook his head. "Females," he muttered.

Dawn cocked an eyebrow. *"Excuse me?"*

"Y'all just don't know what the hell you want!" He rose from the bed, pulled his T-shirt over his head, and stuck his arms through his sleeves. "First, you call me to come over here like you're hard up to get fucked in twenty minutes or less! Then you tell me you want to 'talk' first," he said with widened eyes. "Whatever the hell that means! *Now* you're giving me some bullshit story about working tomorrow, when you know damn well—"

"No, Hosea, I know *exactly* what I want!" she said, crossing her arms over her chest. "And it's not you shouting, 'You like this? You want this?' when it's pretty damn obvious that I don't!"

"What am I? *A mind reader?* How the hell was I supposed to know that you weren't into it?" he asked, dragging on his jeans.

"Hmm, I don't know!" she shouted sarcastically. "Maybe it was the fact that I looked like I was counting ceiling tiles, or that my vajayjay was as dry as the Sahara desert! Maybe one of those things would have given you a clue!"

He glared at her. "Man, to hell with this . . . and to hell with you, you moody-ass bitch! Don't call me again. In fact, forget my damn number!"

"Don't worry. It's already forgotten," she replied as he stormed out of her bedroom.

A few seconds later, he slammed the front door of her apartment closed behind him. After that, Dawn slumped onto her bed and dropped her head into her hands.

Whatever buzz she had before this little episode had completely disappeared. Dawn was both sober and re-morseful—not about what she had said to Hosea, but about calling him in the first place.

Her hope had been to forget about Xavier, but she didn't feel any better now than she had when she saw Xavier and Constance together in his kitchen earlier that night. Actually, she felt a lot worse. The heartbreak was both painful and raw.

"Damn it," she mumbled with a sniff. Tears welled in her eyes and spilled onto her cheeks. She impatiently wiped them away. She wished she could blame the alco-hol for her crying, but she knew that was a lie.

Why couldn't she get that man out of her damn head? Why did she hurt this bad? It didn't make any sense!

"You can't chose who you fall in love with," the voice in her head urged.

I'm not in love, damn it, she thought vehemently.

"Sure, you aren't," the voice ridiculed.

Dawn sighed. *Okay, maybe just a little.*

She finally understood what her sisters Lauren and Stephanie had meant when they said the same thing when they both fell in love. But while her sisters found their own happy endings, she knew she wouldn't with Xavier. That's why she desperately wished for these feel-ings to go away. They didn't serve any purpose other than to make her miserable.

It's time to be a grown-up about this.

She guessed her only alternative was to suck it up, to

keep pretending. Out of respect for her father, out of respect for the family rules, Dawn would continue to play the good future sister-in-law and not interfere with Xavier and Constance's relationship. She would continue to be "just friends," no matter how much it hurt.

With that she rose from her bed, walked into her living room, and locked her apartment front door. Minutes later, she turned off her bedroom lights and fell asleep.

Chapter 18

Xavier pushed up the front of his black wool hat. It had started to droop into his eyes, making it even harder to see the roadway in front of him.

The glare from last night's record snowfall was almost blinding in the morning sun. It was so bright that he wanted to open his glove compartment and try to dig out his favorite pair of Ray-Bans. But he worried that if he took his hands off the steering wheel—even for a second—he could easily fishtail out here. It wasn't noon yet and the snow was already transforming to a murky gray slush in some spots. He had hit patches of black ice twice along the way.

No, Xavier thought as he squinted at the street in front of him, *I'll tough it out.*

He only had a few more miles until he arrived at his mother's house anyway, even though he probably wouldn't get there until evening, with the thirty miles per hour he was clocking on the speedometer.

Most people were still indoors, waiting for the snow removal and salt trucks to finish their handiwork, but Xavier had braved highways and back roads in his ill-equipped Audi S4 because he knew his mother would probably be snowed in for the next few days, if not the whole week, unless he came and shoveled her walkway and driveway. Leslie Ann Hughes would stay holed up in her house with her two beloved Old English sheepdogs until the snow melted or until Xavier came to rescue her.

"It's no big deal, hon," his mother had assured him over the phone when he called to check on her earlier that morning. He could hear the dogs barking in the background. "I've got plenty of soup, toilet paper, and Dog Chow. The boys and I will be fine! Just *fine!*"

Yeah, like he was really going to leave her to fend for herself.

He had taken on the responsibility for caring for his mother since his father had died more than a decade ago. It was a responsibility Xavier took very seriously.

He finally pulled onto her street, feeling his tires slip a little as they fought to gain traction in the packed snow. He tentatively pressed on the gas and lurched forward again. When he drew near his mother's white Georgian colonial with its black shutters and Christmas lights still dangling around the windows, his eyebrows shot up an inch in surprise.

His mother's neighbor, Jake Mahoney, was in her driveway, pushing a snowblower. The plump man was in a blue parka, jeans, and furry snow boots. A St. Louis Blues cap was on his bald head. When Xavier pulled to a stop, Jake cut the engine to the snowblower, and waved his mitten-encased hand.

"Hey, Xavier!" Jake shouted as he carefully made his way down the almost-cleared driveway. "What the heck are you doing out here? Are you trying to hit a tree?"

Xavier shifted the car into park, turned off the engine, and opened his car door. "I came to shovel Mom's driveway and walkway," he said as he climbed out and shut the Audi's door behind him. "But it looks like you've taken care of it for me."

Jake smiled. At that moment, he looked like Santa Claus with his thick gray beard and rosy cheeks.

"Ayuh, got it all covered," Jake said. "I should be done with the whole thing in about an hour."

"Hi, hon!" Xavier's mother called.

Xavier looked up to find her standing in the doorway, pushing Lenny and Squiggy back inside, though the rambunctious pets tried their best to squeeze around and through her legs. They started to bay and bark excitedly the instant they saw Xavier.

"You go on and visit with your mom," Jake said, walking back toward his snowblower. "I'll finish this up."

"Thanks."

Xavier trudged through the snow, which was almost up to his knees. He finally reached his mother's front door. As he wiped and stomped his boots on her welcome mat, she stood on her toes and kissed his cold cheek.

"Told you that you didn't have to come!" she chided.

Xavier walked inside and shut the front door behind him, drowning out the buzzing sound of the snowblower. He gave attention to the "boys." They ran in circles, hopped on their hind legs, pressed their paws against Xavier's chest, and slobbered down his face. Xavier rubbed their heads and muzzles. He scratched their chins before thumping both on their sides and shooing them away.

"You could have told me that you already had your boyfriend out there with a snowblower. I could have saved the trip," Xavier said with a smirk as he lowered the zipper on his wool coat.

His mother looked offended. "Xavier Christopher Hughes, that man is *not* my boyfriend!"

He tugged off his hat, ran his hand through the matted curls on his now-sweaty head, and followed his mother down the hall. The dogs raced between them. "I'm only joking, Mom."

"And it wasn't funny!" She pursed her thin lips and adjusted her blue wool shawl around her shoulders. "I told him that he didn't have to do it. Jake took it upon himself to clear my driveway."

"Maybe he figured if he got rid of the snow, you'd finally go on a date with him," Xavier ventured, needling her again.

His mother obstinately tossed back her strawberry-blond head. "I'm afraid there isn't *that* much snow in the world." She turned on her heel and strode toward the kitchen, making Xavier shake his head in exasperation.

He glanced at the living room wall and frowned at the collage of framed pictures. Most were old photos of his father, either alone or posing with her and a teenage Xavier. It was her little shrine to Malcolm Hughes. She hadn't changed it since Malcolm's death. In fact, if you removed the photos from the wall, you'd probably see the dusty silhouette of each picture frame. They had been nailed to the wall for so damn long.

She had always been in awe of Malcolm, ever since the day they met on a flight from Chicago to London back in 1980. She had been the shy, small-town girl from Indiana who was going on her first trip to Europe. Malcolm was the smooth-talking, worldly lawyer who indulged her and talked to her the entire flight, answering all her questions about London. When the plane touched down at Heathrow and Malcolm asked Leslie

Ann what her evening plans were and if she would like to join him for dinner in the West End, she had been dumbstruck. She was enthralled by him, but she had never dated a black man before. She had hardly even spoken to one until that day. But he was so handsome, smart, and charming that she couldn't say no. She had been lost ever since. Even now, Xavier's dad still cast a magic spell over her from the grave. No other man seemed to compare to him. Poor Jake Mahoney didn't stand a chance.

Xavier and his mother had chosen to mourn his father's passing in very different ways. Though Xavier had chosen to push aside his emotions, locking away his mourning for his father under a staid façade, his mother wore her emotions on her sleeves. Everyone could tell that his dad still held a firm and prominent place in her heart.

It's not healthy, Xavier thought, turning away from the photographs. *Her keeping vigil like this isn't good for her.*

"You know, maybe you *should* consider going out with Jake, Mom," Xavier ventured. He could hear her rummaging around in the kitchen, opening and closing cabinet doors and digging through drawers. He tossed his coat and hat on the back of her flower-printed, dog-hair-covered sofa and tugged off his leather gloves, adding them to the pile of outerwear. "You might actually have fun. Remember that word? *Fun?* It'd be good for you to get out of the house for once. Lenny and Squiggy could handle it."

His mother poked her head around the kitchen door frame and gazed into the living room. "You want some hot cocoa?"

"Sure, and don't pretend like you didn't hear me. I

mean it, Mom. When Dad died, I'm sure he didn't expect you to stay a single widow forever. It's been thirteen years and you still haven't seriously dated anyone."

She emerged from the kitchen a few minutes later with two steaming coffee mugs in her hands and a stubborn expression on her face. She walked toward Xavier and handed him one of the mugs. "Thanks for the romance advice, but I'd focus more on *your* love life than my own."

Xavier sat on the sofa while she took one of the nearby armchairs. The dogs plopped on the rug between them.

Xavier stared at his mother, now baffled. He took a drink from his mug. "What's wrong with my love life?"

"Well, what's the story with Dawn Gibbons, for one?"

He shook his head, puzzled by the subject change. "Well, you spoke to her at the party, didn't you? She's Herb's daughter. She works at a gallery in D.C. as a—"

His mother shook her head. "I know *who* she is and what she does, sweetheart. I talked to her last week. She seems like a very charming, intelligent woman. What I mean is, what's the story with *you* and Dawn Gibbons?"

Xavier gaped. How the hell did his mother know about Dawn? He hadn't told anyone about his mixed feelings toward her. How had his mother found out?

"I have no idea what you mean," he said softly with a forced laugh, letting his gaze drift to his coffee mug, deciding to play stupid. He drank some of his cocoa.

Leslie Ann sighed heavily. "I mean are you *having sex* with her, Xavier?"

At that, he almost spat out his cocoa onto the living room floor, but instead swallowed the burning liquid in one gulp, scorching his throat. He coughed into his fist.

"Are you all right?" she asked.

He nodded then finally stopped coughing. "Of course I haven't had sex with her!" he said between gasps. "What the hell . . . Why would . . . Why would you ask me a crazy question like that?"

Her face softened. "I didn't think you had, but frankly, your behavior last week left me a bit confused. The whole night at dinner you had your arm wrapped around Constance but your eyes on Dawn. I noticed. It was hard not to. If you didn't stop staring at her like that, I thought you were gonna make your fiancée jealous."

Damn, was I that bad? Had Constance noticed too? That would definitely explain why she had been so clingy during dinner and had practically jumped him that night after the party.

"I thought it would be funny to rib you about it," his mother continued, "but then I noticed Dawn stealing glances at you too, so I knew s*omething* was going on. I've never known you to be a cheater, so I wanted to know what it was."

He clenched his jaw and put his mug on the oak coffee table. "Nothing's going on between us. You're mistaken, Mom."

"Not only are you not a cheater, but you're not a good liar either, so don't start now."

Xavier looked down at the Afghan rug beneath his feet and gnawed the inside of his cheek as he contemplated telling his mother the truth. But he didn't know how to say it. What would she think of him if he admitted he was attracted to his fiancée's sister? What would his mother think if he admitted that not only was he attracted to Dawn, but he also suspected he was starting to fall for her? He would be declaring that not only could he feel himself drawing closer and closer to doing something that would break Constance's heart, but he also wasn't the loyal and reliable man he had always believed himself to be. He would be declaring himself to be no better than that asshole Byron Lattisaw.

"I'm telling you the truth. Nothing's happened."

"But you've thought about it?"

He didn't answer her, but instead kept his eyes downcast.

"Hon, why are you marrying Constance?"

He gritted his teeth. "Mom, we've been through this before."

"That girl is shallow. She doesn't match you at all!"

He laughed ruefully, finally meeting his mother's eyes. "So what are you saying? Are you suggesting that I marry Dawn instead? Constance said that's what you probably wanted, but I told her she was wrong. Now I'm starting to wonder!"

Leslie Ann sat aside her mug on a nearby end table. "Not marry her. Of course not! But at least she seems to have more going on than Constance Allen! *She* matches you! Dawn is sophisticated, articulate. She's an artist and a gallery director—"

"You've also failed to mention that she's been divorced *twice*," he countered, playing devil's advocate. "And she's probably been through more boyfriends than any woman who—"

"So she's divorced! So are half of the people who've ever been married. So she has boyfriends! You told me that I should get out and date and have some fun! Now you're looking down on her for doing the same?"

"You know that's not what I meant. Dawn has got a lot of mileage behind her and—"

"*Mileage?* Well, aren't we being judgmental! Would you say the same if she were a man?"

"We wouldn't be having the conversation if she was a man, Mom!"

"At least she has a *real* job!" his mother continued, ignoring his sarcasm. "What does Constance do for a living?"

"Constance works part-time. You know that."

"*Works part-time?* You mean that little clothing boutique job she does three days a week when she feels like it?" She blew air through her pert, freckled nose. "Admit it! That girl does *nothing* except spend poor Herb's money! I swear she has cobwebs between her ears with how empty her head is."

"Look, I'm not going to sit here and listen to you talk trash about my fiancée. Constance *is* the right woman for me. She . . . she makes me happy. She fits me. We make sense!"

"She makes you so happy that you're making wolf eyes across the dinner table at her sister?" his mother asked incredulously.

Xavier clamped his mouth shut, pushing down his frustration. He rose to his feet. "Well, that was a nice visit," he muttered dryly, reaching for his coat. "I guess I'll head back to—"

His mother grabbed his wrist. He turned toward her.

"Hon, I'm not trying to make you angry. I'm not trying to hurt you. I don't want you to do something you'll regret later. I married your father because I loved him. Because I couldn't imagine being with anyone else in the world but him. I don't want you to get married because you feel it's the right thing to do, because you feel it's your obligation."

"You think I'm marrying her because I feel *obligated* to do it?"

His mother released his wrist. "I think you've been

incredibly grateful to Herb for all the things he's done for you since your dad died, for him being there for you. You tried to hide it from me, but I knew you took it just as hard as I did. Maybe . . . maybe even worse," she said softly. Tears pooled in her eyes. "I know you, Xavier. You believe in doing the right thing, the honorable thing, and you want to pay back Herb. What better way to pay him back than by marrying and taking care of his daughter?"

Xavier grimaced, feeling a punch to the gut at his mother's words. He wanted to deny it, to argue that what she was saying wasn't true. But he knew deep down that in many ways, it was. Yes, he thought Constance was beautiful and he was attracted to her. Most men would be. But was he *in love* with her? Was he in love with her the way his parents had been in love with each other? Xavier had always assumed that his desire to protect her *was* love. Constance was so innocent and naïve. She needed to be taken care of and shielded from the disappointments and realities of the world, as Herb had done for him thirteen years ago. But was that love?

Shit, Xavier thought as the realization swept over him.

Lenny rose to his feet and bumped Xavier's knee with his nose in sympathy, sensing Xavier's mood shift.

"Please think about it," his mother persisted. "Think about what *you* really want."

But what he really wanted wasn't what he could have. He was about to marry a woman even though he was falling in love with her sister, a sister who had said several times that she had no time for men or the distraction they presented. And Dawn was a complicated woman with a less-than-stellar past. She was nowhere as simple as Constance. A woman like Dawn could only lead to heartbreak and frustration. There was no way he was tearing his life apart and hurting most of the important people in his life for someone like her. He couldn't and *wouldn't* risk everything for what could be nothing more than a meaningless fling to her.

He knew what he had to do. He had to stick to his word. He would keep a respectful distance and expunge Dawn from his mind and his heart as much as possible.

Chapter 19

Dawn was removing the last of the easels and paint supplies from the classroom closet, preparing for the start of her art class when she heard Xavier's voice. It drifted in from the hallway and a faint smile came to her lips.

She hadn't seen him since his birthday dinner and that disastrous night with Hosea, and she hadn't had the chance to give Xavier his gift when she'd rushed out after catching him and Constance together. She had brought the gift today with the expectation of eventually running into him. The instant she heard his voice, she rushed across the classroom, grabbed the gift bag from her desk, and dashed into the hall.

"Hey! I'm glad I finally ran into you!" she shouted with a grin. "I wanted to . . ."

Her words faded when she realized he wasn't alone. She found him strolling with a dowdy-looking older white woman who was wearing an oversized green sweater, long skirt, and Crocs. Her long brown hair was held back by a yellow scrunchie. She stared at Dawn quizzically.

"Oh, I'm sorry! I-I didn't know you were with . . . I

mean, I didn't know that you were busy," Dawn said. "I can come back later."

Xavier shook his head and motioned her forward. "No need to apologize." He turned to the woman beside him. "Margaret, this is Dawn. Dawn, this is Margaret. Dawn is our current art teacher." He gestured to Margaret. "Dawn, Margaret's volunteering at the community center starting next month and I was showing her around, giving her a feel for the place."

Dawn extended her hand to her for a shake. "Pleased to meet you."

The woman nodded timidly before hesitating and shaking Dawn's hand. "Same here."

The three fell silent and Dawn looked expectantly at Xavier, then Margaret.

"So you're volunteering?" Dawn asked, trying her best to make conversation. "Well, that—that's great! Welcome aboard. I know we've been shorthanded. It's always nice to have more people. I know we've been looking for an assistant football coach too. I could be wrong, but I guess you aren't filling that position."

Margaret grinned for the first time. Her mousy face brightened. "No, actually, I studied folk art at Bryn Mawr and I work out of my studio in Arlington. I've always been interested in teaching. I thought this might be a wonderful opportunity to explore it here." She fidgeted with the strap of her leather satchel. "Xavier said the children can be a rowdy bunch, but I'm . . . I'm willing to try."

"Well, he's right. They're rowdy but tamable. Besides, I'm sure we could tag-team them. I'm more than willing to help out a fellow art teacher." She turned to Xavier. "So we'll have two teachers now, huh? I didn't know you guys were so invested in the art program. Are you adding more classes for the kids?"

Xavier loudly cleared his throat. "Uh, no, actually. Those, uh ... Those plans aren't in the works right now." He turned back to Margaret and pointed down the hall. "So would you like to see our gym? I don't know if you'll be using it often, but—"

"You're not adding any art classes?" Dawn asked, now confused. "What do you mean you aren't adding any? Are she and I sharing a class, then?"

Dawn noticed the friendly expression on Xavier's face begin to falter. "Uh, can't really say. We can ... we can work through the details later, though."

Dawn nodded, though her confusion was slowly turning to uneasiness. Why was Xavier being so evasive?

"Well, enjoy your tour," she said to Margaret, deciding to let the subject drop—for now. "Sorry for interrupting."

"No problem at all." Margaret nodded. "It was a pleasure to meet you, Dawn."

Dawn watched the two walk down the brightly lit hallway and disappear around the edge of the corridor. She glanced down at the gift bag in her hand, not quite sure what to do with it now.

Dawn managed to put thoughts of their conversation aside during her class, getting easily distracted by trying to simultaneously keep the attention of and keep the peace among the more than two dozen teenagers she taught that day. Between one paintbrush-flinging incident that almost caused a fight among a couple of boys and trying to explain the intricacies of shading to her students, she had little time to think about Xavier or his caginess.

"Okay, that's it for the day, guys!" she said at the end of class. She dropped her paintbrush into a water-filled can. The kids began to gather their backpacks and loudly stream out of her classroom. "Enjoy the rest of your weekend." She cupped her hands around her mouth so that she could be heard over the clamor. "And stay out of trouble!"

A few of the students muttered replies and good-byes before running out the door into the hall.

Dawn shook her head and turned her attention to cleaning up the room. Though she asked the children to clean their paintbrushes at the end of each class, only two-thirds of them actually did it. She started to walk toward the back of the room to gather dirty brushes and scrub them at one of the industrial sinks down the hall when she heard a soft knock at the door. She turned to find Xavier leaning against the door frame.

"You busy?" he asked.

"Not really. Just tidying up," she said casually, gathering discarded supplies. "How was the tour with Margaret?"

Xavier shrugged, walked across the room, and sat on the edge of her desk. The same tenseness radiated from him now as it had earlier. "It went OK, I guess. Margaret seems fine with working here."

"That's good." Dawn dropped the dirty paintbrushes into a can she held. She hesitated. "Look, sorry if I came off as rude, but if you had told me you were getting a second art teacher, I wouldn't have asked so many questions. I wasn't trying to scare her off. You caught me off guard, that's all."

"We're not getting a second art teacher, Dawn." He took a deep breath. "In fact, that's what I came back here to talk to you about."

Now she really was confused. She sat down the soup can and dropped her hands to her hips. "What do you mean? Then why was Margaret here?"

She could see his jaw clench. He evaded her gaze.

Suddenly, the answer to her question dawned on her, or more accurately, fell on her like a ton of bricks. She gaped at him in shock. "Wait, are you . . . are you *firing* me?"

Xavier glanced at the door leading to the hallway. A group of kids were lingering by the lockers, near the classroom's entrance, and talking animatedly. He rose from the desk and quietly shut the door. He turned back toward her.

"You *are* firing me, aren't you?" she asked with disbelief, feeling a stab to the chest.

"Dawn . . ." he began softly.

"No, don't . . . Don't *Dawn* me! Damn it! Just spit it out! Answer the question! Are you firing me?"

She hoped he would deny it. She hoped this was some gross misunderstanding and that he wouldn't do something like this, especially considering that she hadn't wanted to teach the art class to begin with but had only done it because he asked her to do it, considering how hard she had tried to be his friend. But she could tell from the expression on his face that such a hope was futile.

"I can't fire you," he finally said. "You're a volunteer. We just don't need you anymore." He took a step toward her. "Look, you were only supposed to be temporary . . . an emergency fix. Remember? Margaret is willing to take over as a long-term replacement and—"

"So this is how I find out about it? While you're giving my long-term replacement *a goddamn tour!* When the hell were you planning to tell me this?"

"I'm telling you now!" he bellowed, then closed his eyes. She could see he was trying to regain his calm.

"Look, don't act so offended. You told me yourself you don't like to teach, and you're a busy woman. You have your gallery work . . . your own life. I thought you'd be relieved that—"

"*Relieved?* Relieved? You practically *begged* me to teach this damn class and now you go behind my back and do this?"

He opened his eyes. The pale gray irises seemed to darken to a stormy shade of gray as he glared at her. "I didn't go behind your back," he said tightly.

"No, Xavier, that is *exactly* what you did!" Another thought popped into her head, making her stop in her tracks, making her even more furious. "Wait, are you firing me because of Constance? Is that what this is about? I bet she's not too jazzed about me working here with you! She certainly doesn't like me! She's made that abundantly clear!"

"Constance has nothing to do with this."

But Dawn knew he was lying—*again*. She could see the lie written all over his face. She wondered if Constance had done it the night of his birthday party, coaxed him into getting rid of her while giving him a piece of ass. Dawn should have known if Constance had issued him an ultimatum that he would put her on the chopping block. She didn't know why she had expected anything else from him.

"Great! That's just great!" She laughed coldly, shaking her head. "You're getting rid of me because you don't have the *balls* to stand up to your fiancée!"

"I told you that Constance has nothing to do with this!"

"Yeah, right," she snarled, feeling tears of anger and humiliation well in her eyes.

She had never been fired before—*never!* Even Percy hadn't given her the pink slip despite all their drama, and yet Xavier—the man she had fallen for—could be so callous to do this to her now.

She wiped at her eyes, strode across the room, and grabbed her wool coat and purse—her cleaning efforts now forgotten.

"Fuck Princess Constance and *fuck you*, Xavier! I'll stay on until Margaret can take over the class next month. I'll do it so the kids won't be left high and dry, but that's the only reason. You, on the other hand," she said, tossing her purse strap over her shoulder, "can kiss my ass, you ungrateful, pussy-whipped son of a bitch!"

She strode toward the classroom door, but stopped when she suddenly remembered something. Dawn turned on her heel and stomped back toward Xavier. She opened her desk drawer and pulled out the gift bag she had meant to give to him earlier.

"Oh, before I forget . . . Here's your damn birthday gift! You don't deserve it, but I've got no use for it."

"Dawn . . ." For the first time, he looked and sounded contrite, but she didn't want to hear it.

She tossed the gift bag at him, startling him. She had aimed for his head, but instead it landed against his chest and fell to the floor. She turned again to leave.

"Dawn, don't storm out like this! Don't put this shit on me like I did something wrong!"

She ignored him and reached for the door handle. She only stopped when he grabbed her. Dawn angrily whipped around and shoved him away—or at least she tried to. Despite her efforts, she was still locked firmly in his grasp.

"Don't act like I did something wrong!" he shouted again, clutching her shoulders, looking desperate. "I'm trying to do the right thing, God damn it! I'm trying to . . . to . . ."

"I get it! You're trying to be a good little boy and make your fiancée happy!" The tears she had been holding back were spilling onto her cheeks now. "Fine! You get your wish! I'm leaving! Just let go of me so I can get the hell out of here!"

But he didn't let go of her. Instead, he lowered his mouth to hers and knocked the bluster right out of her.

"What . . . what the hell are you doing?" she sputtered against his lips. They were the last words she uttered.

She wasn't prepared for the sensuous kiss or what it would do to her. All her anger and indignation were instantly forgotten. She even forgot about Constance.

His lips weren't full, but there was more than enough strength behind them to rival the fullest of lips. He worked against hers, taunting her, toying with her mouth until she gave in with a whimper. Her lips finally parted and she kissed him back. When she did, he seized the opportunity and licked inside her mouth, tasting her. Dawn tasted him too. Their tongues met. He released his hold long enough for her to drop her coat to the classroom floor, then her purse. She looped her arms around his neck. His hands went from her back to her ass and he tugged her closer.

They were panting now and tilting their heads so that the kiss could deepen. Dawn's heart was thudding wildly in her chest. A surge of heat crested over her body. She rubbed her pelvis enticingly against his and felt a bulge in his jeans urgently pressing back against her.

He shifted her back toward her desk and eased between her thighs so that he stood between her legs. He shifted his kisses from her mouth to her neck, nibbling at her skin along the way.

They had to stop this soon. She could feel herself getting hotter and wetter by the second. If one of them *didn't* end this kiss, he could have her right here on the tiled classroom floor if he wanted to.

Lucky for her, Xavier regained his senses first. He suddenly pulled away and took several ragged breaths.

"Shit," he murmured. He closed his eyes and clenched his teeth. He shoved his hand into his hair. "God damn it . . . God . . . *damn it!* I shouldn't have done that. I shouldn't have done that!"

"You shouldn't . . . but you did," she said softly. "Why did you?"

"Because I've wanted to kiss you since the moment I saw you standing in the hallway this morning." He licked his lips. "Hell, I wanted to do it since the first night I met you at your gallery back in December. But I've been fighting it this whole time." He slowly shook his head. "Shit, I've been fighting it without even realizing it."

She stared at him, dumbstruck. He suddenly glared at her.

"Do you get it now? Do you get why I can't do this again? I'm not a cheater!"

"Why are you acting like it's my fault?" she asked, pointing at her chest. "I haven't done anything to you! I wasn't trying to make you cheat! All I've done is—"

"You don't have to try! That's my point! You're *way* too tempting." He shook his head ruefully. "And if you keep working here, if I keep being around you, I know this shit is gonna happen again and I can't afford that. I can't let that happen!"

He was shoving her away, both emotionally and mentally. Part of her understood why he was doing it, but the knowledge still hurt. "So is that why you want me to leave? That's why you're replacing me?"

"I *have* to. I'm marrying Constance in less than three months. I don't need any complications."

"I'm a 'complication'?" She chuckled and crossed her arms over her chest. Her lips still tingled from his kiss, depressing her even more. "Well, I've been called many things, but that's a first."

"Yeah, go ahead and laugh," he spat. "This all may be fun and games to you, but this is my life! Constance is important to me. Herb and the respect he has for me is important to me! I'm not going to toss that aside because—"

"Xavier, you kissed me! It wasn't the other way around! I'm not playing games with you! I've tried my best to respect your relationship with Constance! I haven't . . ."

Enough, she thought. *Enough! I'm so tired of this shit.*

She threw up her hands in surrender. "Don't worry. I won't 'complicate' things for you any longer. I quit."

In more ways than one, she wanted to add, but didn't.

She leaned down and grabbed her coat and purse. She turned around, walked across the room, opened the classroom door, and let it slam shut behind her.

Chapter 20

Xavier was out of sorts as he sat at Herb's bedside. He felt odd in a business suit, looking so formal, while his mentor lay in a navy blue bathrobe and striped pajamas, being held up by several down pillows. A nurse stood at Herb's side, checking his IV bag before checking his vitals with a pressure cuff and thermometer, catering to him like he was an infant with a fever.

Lying there in bed, Herb seemed so vulnerable. It didn't seem right to see him this way.

"Can I get you anything, Mr. Allen?" his nurse asked in a too-loud voice in her heavy Caribbean accent.

"No. No, I'm fine. Thank you," Herb answered, looking uncomfortable at being hovered over.

He was a proud man. Knowing what he knew about Herb, Xavier figured it had to be demoralizing for Herb to be babied this way. But Herb had suffered a major health setback that would mean having to suffer being babied for a while.

Xavier had gotten a call yesterday that Herb had to be rushed to the hospital. Xavier had known for months that Herb's cancer treatments weren't going well and that the older man's body was growing weaker and weaker, but Xavier hadn't been prepared for the emotional punch he suffered when he heard that Herb had fallen seriously ill. It was similar to the punch he endured a few days ago when he had to shut the door on his feelings for Dawn.

He could still recall the yearning he felt when he watched her walk out the classroom door. That feeling would probably haunt him for the rest of his life. He had wanted to run after her. He had wanted to kiss her again, and it took Herculean strength to fight those impulses.

I made the right decision, he silently reminded himself as Herb's nurse shifted to the end of the bed to adjust the sheets. *I made Constance a promise. It was the honorable thing to do.*

"And if there's anything Xavier Hughes is, it's honorable," a voice in his head mocked, but he quickly shut it out.

Mock all you want, but I did what I had to do.

"Thank you so much for visiting me today, Xavier," Herb said, snapping Xavier out of his heavy thoughts. "I know things are busy for you at the office. You have better things to do than to check on an old man."

Xavier slowly shook her head. "You know damn well that isn't true, Herb. Things are never so busy that I couldn't come here to see how you're doing. I heard that you had a real scare yesterday."

Herb waved his hand dismissively. "I have scares *every* day. That's part of the fun of being terminally ill," he said with a smirk. "Compared to everything else, it wasn't quite that bad. My doctor merely overreacted to my last lab results."

"Humph," the nurse grunted as she fluffed his pillow, looking incredulous.

Herb narrowed his eyes at her. "That's quite enough pillow-adjusting, don't you think, Hortense?"

She stood back and grunted again in response.

"You know, you don't have to stay here," Herb said to her. "I am perfectly—"

"I'm supposed to stay with you at all times, Mr. Allen. Those were my orders," she insisted. "I'm fine *right* here. I'll just read my book."

She then pulled out a raunchy paperback romance and a pack of Oreos from her pocket, sat down in a chair on the other side of the bedroom, and flipped to one of the book's pages.

Herb let out a beleaguered sigh, making Xavier chuckle.

"She's right," Xavier whispered. "You need someone to watch over you until you feel a little better. I'm sure Constance and Raquel would agree."

"Feel a little better?" Herb glanced at the nurse again. "I'm afraid we both have to accept the truth, Xavier, that it's only going to go downhill from here."

Xavier felt his throat tighten at those words. His eyes got a little misty. But he quickly pulled himself back together. His congenial expression stayed locked in place.

"Either way, you need a nurse," he said.

"Which is why I agreed to let Raquel hire one. She wanted to make sure I was taken care of while she and Constance take their trip to St. Thomas. I said, 'So be it. If that's what you want, darling.' "

Xavier did a double take, wondering if he had heard Herb correctly. "What do you mean while they take their trip to St. Thomas? They're canceling it, of course."

Herb shook his head. "No, they aren't."

"But . . . but how could they still go? I mean . . . with you being so sick. They can't go to the Caribbean now!"

"I doubt having them here will make much of a difference. I'm not going to miraculously get better. And

Constance has had her heart set on this trip forever. You know that. She and her mother have been planning this for months. I told them that unfortunately, the cancer is really starting to take its toll now and I would no longer be able to go with them, but they shouldn't let me hold them back. Have a good time."

Xavier frowned. "But you're on your sickbed, Herb. You're . . . you're . . ."

His voice faded as he let Herb's words sink into him. Constance and her mother planned to take a trip to St. Thomas while Herb was hooked up to an IV bag and lying in bed? The idea sounded so absurd and so selfish that there was no way it could possibly be true. Or was it? He had to talk to his fiancée about this.

"Where is Constance?" Xavier asked.

Xavier found his fiancée ten minutes later in one of the workout rooms. She was running on one of the treadmills with earplugs in her ears and her ponytail flopping wildly behind her. Her back glistened with sweat, and her rear end and breasts bounced with each stride. The digital screen in front of her showed a moun-tain trail. She seemed to be making her way up a steep hill at the moment.

"Constance?" Xavier called as he walked into the brightly lit room, tripping over pink hand weights that littered the floor. He mumbled under his breath as he made his way toward her. "Constance!"

She glanced over her shoulder, saw him, and smiled. She held up her finger, motioning for him to wait as she quickly pressed a few buttons on the treadmill screen. The tread belt gradually lowered and decelerated to a slower pace. She went from a jog to a power walk.

"Hi, pumpkin!" she said, taking out one of her

earplugs. She wiped her damp forehead with a white hand towel that hung off the treadmill's guardrail. "What are you doing here?"

"I came to see what's going on with your dad."

"*Oh?*" She turned back toward the screen. "That was nice of you. He had a little scare yesterday, but he says it's no big deal."

"Your dad *always* says it's no big deal. But obviously it *is* a big deal if he's on bed rest!"

"But he's only on bed rest until, you know . . . he regains his strength. No big deal!"

Xavier closed his eyes and took a calming breath. How could Constance not see how serious this was?

"He told me that you and your mother are still taking that yacht trip to St. Thomas in a few days."

"Yeah!" Her smile broadened into a grin. "Mommy said we already made plans. Even though Daddy can't come with us, we might as well go. Plus, it'll be the last vacation Mom and I can take together before the wedding. You know . . . girl time. It'll be a great stress reliever!"

"But what about your father?"

"Oh, he'll be fine, pumpkin!" She pressed a few buttons. The *thump-thump-thump* of her feet picked up the pace again. "We have a . . . nurse sticking around . . . to watch him. No reason . . . for *all* of us to be . . . stuck at home," she said between huffs of breath as she jogged.

She then put the earplug back into her ear and started to hum to the music. The treadmill let out a few beeps. Her jog suddenly increased to a run.

Xavier stared at her like he was looking at a stranger. He couldn't fathom how his fiancée could be so oblivious. Her father was seriously ill and here she was more concerned about enjoying "girl time" with her mother and relieving stress in St. Thomas. Who the hell was this woman?

"The same woman who refused to reschedule her wedding to make sure her ailing father was present because it would interfere with her 'vision,' " a voice in his head chided. But Constance's vision was obviously more than just a little skewed. As her fiancé, Xavier had to set her straight.

He walked around the treadmill, reached over and pressed the red button underneath the digital screen, bringing the tread to an abrupt stop. Constance had to grab the handrails to keep from flying off the back.

"*Hey!*" she shouted, ripping out her earplugs. She jumped down and glared up at him. "Why'd you do that? I could have hurt myself!"

"I did it because I need you to listen to me and stop fucking running for five goddamn seconds!"

Her mouth fell open in shock. "How . . . how *dare* you curse at me?" she sputtered. "What's gotten into you?"

"No, what's gotten into *you*? Your father is dying, Constance! How do you not get that?"

"He's not dying!" she yelled. "Don't say that!"

"It's true! And he needs you and your mother *here*," Xavier said, pointing down at the floor, "with him! Not on some deck putting on sunscreen or on a fucking beach drinking margaritas!"

She slowly shook her head in astonishment. "I cannot believe you're talking to me like this, Xavier!"

"And I can't believe that I have to! Don't you realize how selfish you're being? How callous this is? He's your father, God damn it!" he exploded. "You were pissed at your dad when he lectured you about being more self-reliant and responsible, but he was right!"

Instead of being chastened by his words, she seemed

to get angrier. Constance crossed her arms over her sweaty chest.

"Xavier Hughes, you either apologize to me *right* now for speaking to me like this, or you can get out of my house! I mean it!"

His jaw clenched. His father had been ripped away from him in a matter of minutes! He hadn't had time to prepare. Constance had days, maybe weeks to spend with her father and treasure these last precious moments, and she didn't care enough to stay. She cared more about her vacation.

"Fine," Xavier said as he turned. "I'll leave, because I'm sure as hell not apologizing."

He walked toward the workout room's entrance, leaving his fiancée gaping.

Maybe his mother and Dawn had been right about Constance after all. All these years he thought Constance was oblivious to things and other people because she was overprotected and innocently naïve. Now he realized it was just because she was hopelessly self-involved. In fact, she was so self-involved that she took him and even her dying father for granted.

And he had pushed Dawn away because he thought it was the right thing to do. He had fallen in love with her and had sacrificed those emotions for his loyalty to Constance, for a woman he now doubted deserved that loyalty.

Chapter 21

"Mama, are you ready?" Cynthia called as one of the maids shut the door behind her.

She stepped through the richly decorated entryway, with its mahogany furniture and lush velvet curtains. She was immediately hit with the overwhelming fragrance of hyacinth bouquets in the glass vases that dotted the side tables inside the foyer and along the echoing corridor. Cynthia glanced at her gold watch and then into one of the sitting rooms. Her mother wasn't there, making Cynthia mumble loudly to herself.

Where the hell is she?

Again, Cynthia would be going alone with her mother to one of Yolanda's wedding appointments. Lauren was busy at work. Stephanie was now too exhausted from her pregnancy to climb out of bed—except to go to the bathroom or grab a carton of her favorite Fudge Ripple ice cream from the downstairs freezer. And Dawn had called at the last minute to say she couldn't make it because her father had taken a turn for the worse, was now on bed rest, and she had to visit him.

"Mama, we have to leave now if we're going to make your last fitting!" Cynthia shouted. "Mama, where—"

She paused near the entryway of the dimly lit library. She saw her mother sitting at her writing desk near one of the windows. The older woman was wearing her cashmere wool coat. Her black Chanel purse sat on the tabletop beside her. She was staring down at a sheet of paper.

"Mama, I've been calling you and calling you," Cynthia said as she walked across the Persian carpet toward Yolanda. "Did you hear me?" As she drew closer and saw the perturbed expression on her mother's face, she frowned. "What's wrong?"

Yolanda slowly looked away from the note and gazed up at Cynthia, shaking her head. "I just don't know what to make of this."

"Make of what?"

Yolanda handed her the sheet of paper. The note was written on a legal notepad sheet in blue ink with wild handwriting worthy of any doctor, but Cynthia could still read its loopy scroll:

> *As you can sermise from my letter I know who you are, heffa, and where you're ass lives! Stay away from my man or you will find you're gold diggin' ass 6 FEET UNDER! I'm not fakin! TRY ME!*

Cynthia lowered the letter after she finished reading it. "Oh, my God! Mama, it's a death threat!"

"I *know* it's a death threat, honey," Yolanda replied dryly, rising from her Queen Anne chair. She reached for her gloves, which sat beside her purse. "And a death threat with atrocious spelling and horrible grammar, at that."

"Mama, how can you possibly joke about this? This crazy person just threatened to put you six feet under!"

"Do I look like I'm joking?" Yolanda asked, raising

her finely arched eyebrows. "Because I'm not! I swear, this Beatrice woman will not let up. I am really starting to get tired of her foolishness."

Cynthia's frown deepened. "Wait, you . . . you knew about her?"

Yolanda nodded as she tugged on her gloves and draped the strap of her purse over her shoulder. She ruffled her hair, fluffing her curls. "Of course I knew about her! She isn't exactly inconspicuous with how she's been carrying on. She follows me *every*where! That woman has all the subtlety of a buffalo charging across the Great Plains."

Cynthia stared at her mother in disbelief. This whole time she thought she had been protecting her mother by keeping Beatrice a secret, and Yolanda had known about Beatrice all along.

"So what are you going to do?"

"What I've always planned to do! Marry Reggie."

"I'm talking about what are you going to do about Beatrice, Mama? You have to show this note to the cops. Hell, take out a restraining order while you're at it! She's taken it past just following you to the hairdresser's and the grocery store! Now she's—"

"I will do no such thing! If I call the police and tell them what's happening, then I'll have to tell Reggie. What if he wants to call off the wedding?" She grimaced as if the thought left a bad taste in her mouth. "He's been acting strange enough as it is."

Cynthia dropped a hand to her hip and tossed the note back onto the writing desk. "Mama, now I know you're joking! Are you honestly going to risk your life just to marry a man?"

"*Just to marry a man?*" Yolanda's red lips tightened. "Cindy, do you realize how broke I was before Reggie and I started dating? Before he started paying my bills?"

Cynthia nodded tiredly. "Yes, I do, Mama. We all knew how broke you were! But—"

"So broke that I was selling my furniture to antique stores! So broke that I thought I was going to have to put up your childhood home for sale! So broke that I was calling old boyfriends that I hadn't spoken to in decades and asking them for money! And some of them were so smug about it. Oh, they couldn't get enough of it . . . ol' Yolanda Gibbons begging for money like some grubby panhandler!" She ruefully shook her head. "Do you know how humiliating that was? I'm not going back to that—absolutely, positively not!"

"I'm not asking you to go back to it!"

Cynthia of all people knew what it was like to treasure the financial security that a rich man could bring, but it certainly wasn't worth dying over! She had thought she could handle this, but it was apparent that things were quickly spiraling out of control.

"I'm just saying that Beatrice doesn't seem like she's going to let up *or* back down. She's actually getting worse! I'd hate for you to go to sleep one night and wake up with that crazy behemoth standing over you with a knife at your throat!"

Yolanda waved her hand as she walked across the room toward the open doorway. "Oh, don't be ridiculous, Cindy! I have a state-of-the-art alarm system all around this property. She couldn't make it across the front lawn, let alone into my bedroom to stab me in my sleep!"

Cynthia clenched her hands into fists. Damn, this was frustrating! Why couldn't her mother understand how serious this was? Instead, Yolanda had a glib response to every legitimate point Cynthia believed she was making.

"OK, so she can't get you here, but what about when

you drive around Chesterton, Mama?" Cynthia cried. "What about when—"

"Cindy," her mother began, "I really don't want to talk about this nonsense anymore. That woman is not going to scare me off from what I want, and I want Reginald Whitfield III's ring on my finger. We have an appointment to make and"—she paused to point at the ticking grandfather clock in the corner of the spacious library—"it looks like we're going to be late."

Cynthia knew it was useless to continue this argument with her mother. It was obvious Yolanda's mind was set. "Fine, Mama," she muttered.

For the rest of that day, during the drive to the fitting, even during the appointment, Cynthia kept making furtive glances into her rearview mirror and over her shoulder, wondering if she would find Beatrice or her Grand Marquis there. While her mom flitted around, laughing with the seamstress and rambling on and on about her wedding details, Cynthia kept having visions of Beatrice bursting through the bridal shop glass doors and charging toward them "like a buffalo across the Great Plains" with a butcher knife in her hand.

It had Cynthia on edge the whole afternoon. She jumped at every sudden sound. She almost punched the poor salesgirl who tapped her on the shoulder to ask her if she wanted water or tea. By the time Cynthia dropped off her mother and drove back home, her sense of unease hadn't waned. Something bad was going to happen. She could sense it, and her mother refused to do anything to prevent it!

Cynthia was at a loss for how to change her mother's mind. Maybe her sisters would have better luck. She called Lauren first and rolled her eyes when she got her voicemail. She called Stephanie next.

"Hey, this is Keith." Stephanie's man answered on the second ring in his deep baritone.

"Hi, Keith, can you put my sister on the phone?" Cynthia asked as she stepped out of her high heels and walked barefoot over the cold tile into her kitchen. She opened the stainless steel refrigerator door and peered at the shelves.

She had been so tense that she hadn't been able to eat anything during lunch with her mother.

"Baby, can you come wash my back?" she could hear Stephanie shout in the background. "Please!"

Keith sighed gravely on the line while Cynthia laughed to herself as she took out a loaf of bread and some turkey deli meat. Keith Hendricks was supposed to be this hard-nosed, über-masculine detective, but now he was basically playing handmaiden to a belligerent pregnant woman.

From sexy PI to Stephanie's bitch, Cynthia thought sardonically.

"Can Steph call you back?" Keith asked hurriedly. "She just got into the bath."

"And don't forget to bring my new loofah!" Stephanie yelled.

Cynthia pursed her lips in annoyance. She opened one of her overhead cabinets and pulled out a plate. "Well, can you put her on the phone anyway? It's kind of—"

"*Keith!* Where are you?" Stephanie barked.

"Look, as soon as Steph's done, I'll have her call you, all right? I swear."

"Keith!" Stephanie screeched.

"Gotta go," he said before abruptly hanging up the phone.

Cynthia stared at her phone receiver, completely flabbergasted. "Did he just hang up on me?"

She knew Dawn said she was going to see her father,

but she figured it was worth a try calling her too. Besides, the Allens weren't the only ones dealing with a family crisis right now!

She dialed Dawn's number and listened to the line ring.

"Come on, Dawn," she mumbled as she glared at the ceiling. "Pick up. Pick up. Pick up!"

Chapter 22

Dawn glanced down at her iPhone to see that her sister Cynthia was calling her. Just as she was about to answer the call, the door to her father's mansion swung open. She stepped inside and a minute later handed off her coat and gloves to Carl, her father's housekeeper. She gazed hesitantly at the stairs leading to the east and west wings.

"Would you like me to take that too?" Carl asked, reaching for the large bouquet of roses and calla lilies she clutched in her arms. "I can have someone put it in water and a vase for you."

Dawn quickly shook her head. "No. No, I'd . . . I'd like to give these to my father myself, if that's okay."

The tall older man nodded. "Of course. I'll take you to him directly."

She started to walk toward the stairs, expecting to be led to one of the upstairs bedrooms since her father had told her he was now on bed rest, but instead Carl turned and walked toward one of the side corridors.

She frowned. "He isn't in bed?"

Carl shook his head. "No, I'm afraid he isn't, ma'am."

They walked down a series of halls and finally

emerged onto a stone portico leading to the back of the Windhill Downs grounds. Dawn found her father sitting in a wheelchair, bundled in a coat and blankets, staring off into the distance. A plump, perturbed-looking black woman in a long puffy pink coat and green scrubs was sitting on a stone bench beside him. Dawn assumed she was his nurse.

She wondered where Constance and Raquel were. The mansion had seemed awfully quiet when she entered, and now she knew they weren't with Herbert either.

Carl, who had been holding Dawn's coat and gloves the entire time, offered them to her. "You'll need these."

She walked onto the portico seconds later, pulling her coat collar tightly around her neck with one hand and holding the bouquet in the other.

"Herb," she said, noticing that when she spoke, a gust of mist went into the air because it was so cold outside. "Herb? What on earth are you doing out here? It's freezing! You should be inside in bed."

He looked up at her and grinned. "Well, this is a pleasant surprise. Why didn't you tell me you'd be stopping by today?"

Though his expression was jolly, he looked ghastly. The cancer was taking its toll on him. His face was gaunt. His eyes were sunken. His pink lips were chapped and cracked. The coat that he wore dwarfed him. He looked like he had lost at least fifteen pounds since she had last seen him a couple weeks ago.

"Hortense," he said, turning to his nurse, "meet my daughter, Dawn."

The irritated expression didn't leave the woman's face, but she nodded and mumbled a "Hello."

"Dawn can take over from here," Herbert said. "I know you're cold. You can go back inside."

"But I'm *supposed* to stay with you at all times, Mr. Allen," the nurse insisted in a Caribbean lilt.

"Yes, I know, even when I have to relieve myself," he said with a roll of the eyes. "But I believe I can be out of your sight for a mere fifteen minutes *with* supervision, can't I?"

"I'll take care of him," Dawn promised. "We won't be out here much longer. He should be in bed. I know."

The nurse gazed at her warily for several seconds before finally rising from the bench and following Carl through the glass doors.

"I brought you flowers," Dawn said, handing the bouquet to him.

"Thank you. They're lovely, sweetheart."

He sounded hoarse. He was also breathing harder than she would have liked. She watched as he gazed down at the flowers before setting them on his blanket-covered lap.

"You know, you should be going inside too," Dawn said as she sat down beside him.

He shook his head. "No, I shouldn't. I refuse to spend my last dying days cooped up in a stuffy bedroom."

He pointed to the wintry landscape in front of him. The trees were bare but the setting sun shone through the branches, creating a beautiful tableau of shadows on the remaining snow on the ground. Shades of orange, purple, and blue were splashed across the horizon.

"*This* is what I want to see when I take my last breath," he whispered.

Dawn reached out to him and placed her hand on top of his own. "Don't talk like that. Please?"

"Don't talk like what?" He turned to her. "Don't admit that I'm dying? But, sweetheart, I *am* dying. I've seen myself in the mirror. I feel my body getting weaker and weaker. There's no denying it."

"Yes, there is. You'll get better."

He has to, Dawn thought stubbornly. She had just gotten to know him. He couldn't die now, not when they were still building a relationship, not when there were so many talks for them to have and moments for them to share.

She forced a smile and squeezed her father's hand. "You have to get better. You have a wedding in a couple of months that you're going to attend. Remember? Constance needs you there to walk"—she glanced at his wheelchair—"well, *roll* her down the aisle."

She laughed but her father didn't join her in her laughter. Instead, Herb shook his head solemnly.

"Frankly, I wonder if there is going to be a wedding in May."

"Why do you say that?"

"Because things have changed between them. Xavier and Constance aren't getting along at all. In fact, just a couple of days ago, I heard that Xavier stormed out after arguing with her. It's not like him. He will usually do anything to appease Connie, to make her happy. But that's no longer the case. They haven't spoken to each other since."

Dawn lowered her eyes and stared guiltily at her lap. She hoped she wasn't the cause of that argument. Though she was heartbroken by Xavier's rejection and his insistence that she needed to be exorcised from his life, she knew—in the end—his decision was for the best. She couldn't take the emotional roller coaster anymore. Constance had laid claim to Xavier a long time ago. She was the woman he wanted, not Dawn, a twice-over divorcée with a bad reputation who wasn't sure if she was ready to commit to a relationship anyway. Though Constance was spoiled and not the smartest woman, she was perky, pure, and beautiful; she was the perfect woman for a conservative corporate climber like Xavier to have on his arm—the Black Malibu Barbie to his Ken.

"Couples argue, Herb. Even couples like Constance and Xavier," she urged softly. "That doesn't mean they're breaking up or that the wedding is off. They'll patch things up. You'll see."

"I don't know. It's not just the arguing. I told you something has changed. Their feelings aren't the same. I can tell." He looked away from her and off into the distance again. "I think . . . I think Xavier has fallen in love with someone else."

She frowned, not understanding why her father was saying all of this. "I highly doubt that! Xavier is head over heels in love with Constance. Anyone can see that."

Her father returned his gaze to her. "Remember when I said a while ago that I thought Xavier was a little smitten with you? Now I know it's more than just a little. I think you're the one he's fallen in love with."

Dawn's eyes snapped up from her lap. She stared at her father in horror and genuine disbelief. "With . . . *with me?*"

Xavier wasn't in love with her! There was a steamy attraction between them—yes. Xavier had confessed as much, and Herbert had rightly picked up on that. But Xavier didn't—*couldn't* love her. That was just crazy!

"It's not just my imagination. I noticed it not too long after you started working at the community center . . . how eager he was to see you, how he couldn't stop raving about you, and how he looked at you when he thought no one else was watching. I tried to push those suspicions aside for many reasons." He sighed. "One being that it was pretty unsettling realizing that the man I thought had fallen in love with one of my daughters was now in love with the other. He and Constance have been together since they were teenagers. They're supposed to get married! But I'd hate watching him act out that lie, putting a ring on one woman's finger—even if she is my Connie—while his heart belonged to someone else. I suppose in a way it's my own fault," he said ruefully. "I threw you two together in the first place."

"Herb, I can *assure* you that Xavier isn't"—she paused and swallowed, feeling tears prick her eyes—"that he isn't in love with me. He wants to marry Constance. He knows that they belong together, and he would never do anything to hurt her."

Herb stared at Dawn, staying silent for several seconds. "Yes, I suppose you both would put your love aside if you felt it was the right thing to do, wouldn't you?"

She instantly opened her mouth to lie that she wasn't in love with Xavier, but her father hastily waved his hand.

"Please, don't deny that too. I've also known for a while now that Xavier isn't alone in this. Your feelings for him are just as strong, aren't they?"

One of the tears that Dawn had been holding back spilled onto her cheek. She fussily wiped at it and sniffed. She could blubber so easily now. It was really starting to piss her off.

"You can be honest with me. Are you in love with him?"

Dawn hesitated then slowly nodded. After she did, she looked away, wiping her eyes with the backs of her gloved hands. "I'm sorry. I'm so sorry. You must be so pissed at me right now."

"Why would I be pissed at you?"

"Because you think I ruined everything! And maybe I did. I don't know. Xavier and Constance were the perfect cookie-cutter couple . . . and then a woman like me came into the picture."

Herbert placed a consoling hand on her shoulder, making her feel even worse. She didn't want to be comforted, especially by a man she knew she had disappointed.

"But I swear, I *swear* to you that I didn't come here to hurt anyone or cause anything. I-I came here to get to know you. I wanted to bond with my father. I wasn't trying to come in between them! But I . . . But I guess I do stuff like that without even trying. Maybe it's genetic."

"I really wish you wouldn't talk about yourself that way."

She sniffed again. "I am what I am, Herb. If we're going to accept the truth about you dying, then we need to accept the truth that I'm a gold digger and a home wrecker, but I won't do it this time. It's not past the point of no return with Xavier. Don't worry. Nothing happened between us."

"Except that kiss," the voice in her head whispered, but she ignored it.

"I don't work at the community center anymore. He asked me to quit and I did. He told me how much he cares about Constance—about all of you. He knows what's right. They're going to get married and have a family and they *will* be happy together. You can be sure of that."

"Can I?" Her father tilted his head. "I don't think I can be certain of anything anymore, sweetheart. Not my health. Not the future. Neither can you or Xavier."

"But I walked away! I did what he asked and—"

"You are too smart a woman to think it can be that simple," he said wearily. "Once things start to speed in one direction, it's pretty hard to just . . . just slam on the brakes and suddenly do a U-turn. Life isn't like that, Dawn. What you feel for—"

"What I *feel* is irrelevant," she said firmly. "Herb, I'm a big girl. I know how to suck it up and put all this stuff aside. I can snap back to my senses. Hell, give me a few months and whatever I feel now probably will have faded away by then," she said, though part of her wasn't totally convinced. "I want to focus on *you*, not Xavier. I told you, that's why I came here. I won't let anything get in the way of that."

He squinted at her, searching her face. "You are so strong . . . so resolved."

She chuckled. "Not as strong as you think."

"No, you are. And you're nothing like my Connie. I love her with all my heart . . . but I wish she had more of your will and your fire. You couldn't find two sisters that are more different."

"We grew up very differently."

"Indeed you did. And in some ways, I regret that. You know your mother isn't my favorite person in the world, but she did a better job with you than I could have imagined. Still . . ." He lowered his gaze. His eyes rested on their clasped hands. "I know I failed you. You became the woman that you are because you had to. I should have been there as your father to protect you, to let you know that sometimes it's perfectly acceptable to be vulnerable. I will never forgive myself for that."

"What's past is past, Herb. I won't hold any grudges against you . . . if you won't hold any against me," she whispered.

He looked up at her. "Can you do me a favor?"

"Sure! Name it!"

"Can you call me Dad just . . . just once? I know I haven't earned it. But I'd . . . I'd love to hear you say it."

She grinned, leaned forward, and kissed his weathered, wrinkled cheek. "Of course I can . . . Dad."

They both turned and watched the last of the setting sun. They watched the shadows grow and stretch across the field in front of them, reaching for them eagerly as the night descended.

Dawn pulled her hand out of Herb's grasp and petted his shoulder. "It's getting dark. I think it's about time we head back inside, don't you?" She stood from the bench and gave one last look at his property, admiring its serenity. "So why don't we . . ."

Dawn's words died on her lips when she looked down to find her father clenching the arms of his wheelchair. His eyes were squeezed shut so tightly and he gritted his teeth so hard that the veins along his temples were bulging. The bouquet of flowers she had given him tumbled to the stone portico as he hunched forward.

"*Dad?*" She fell to her knees beside him, feeling the cold stone on her knees and shins. She rubbed his arm. "What's wrong?"

He didn't respond but instead continued to grit his teeth.

"Damn it, talk to me! Can you breathe? Are you in pain? Tell me what's wrong!"

"Get . . . the . . . Get Hortense," he finally rasped.

Dawn instantly rose to her feet. She ran toward the glass doors, yelling for help.

Chapter 23

Xavier raced across the parking lot and through the hospital's automatic doors. He looked frantically around him, not knowing where to go first. He shot past the shuttered gift shop, then beelined to the front desk where a woman in green scrubs sat.

"Excuse me," he said to her. The woman slowly looked up from the clipboard on her desk. "I'm here to see Herbert Allen. He was admitted this evening. I'm not sure—"

"Xavier?" someone called from behind him.

He turned and found Dawn sitting in the hospital waiting area.

He spotted her instantly, though at least ten other people sat in the room with her. As usual, she seemed out of place in her drab surroundings with her vibrantly colored silk top and wool skirt, silver bangle bracelet and chic bob. She looked like a bird of paradise or a rare orchid among a group of potted house ferns. She was sitting in a far-off corner of the waiting room, near the windows facing the emergency entrance. Their gazes met and he could see that her eyes were red, like she had been crying.

Xavier strode toward her. As he did, any thoughts of

Constance and their wedding disappeared. At that moment his sole focus was Dawn. Xavier wanted to quickly close the gap between them, wrap her in his arms, and kiss her like he had at the community center. He wanted to hold her and get all the lines of pain and worry to leave her comely face. But her body stiffened as he drew closer and her full lips tightened. She hastily erected an invisible wall between them, shutting him out.

He could understand why. He was the one who said he needed distance, and she was giving him exactly what he asked.

"So I guess Carl told you what happened," she said flatly.

He took the seat beside her and nodded. "He knows to call me if anything goes wrong."

But you *should have called me, Dawn—not the housekeeper, and I'm pissed that you didn't,* Xavier wanted to say, but bit back those words.

"Are you here by yourself?" he asked instead.

"My sisters came through about an hour ago, but they had to get back home." Dawn wiped at her nose with a balled-up tissue that looked like it was already covered with mascara and a great deal of her tears. "I asked Carl to tell Constance and Raquel what happened too. They weren't there with Herb when he . . ." Her voice drifted off, like it was too painful to finish. She closed her eyes, waited for a beat, and opened them again. "I have no idea where they are."

"They're away in St. Thomas. They won't be back until the day after tomorrow."

"Well, isn't that nice?" Dawn said bitterly. "Herb's sick in the ICU while his wife and daughter are sunning on a beach in the Caribbean."

"They planned this trip a year ago," Xavier said quietly, quickly coming to his fiancée's defense. He had done it for so long, he now did it as a reflex. "There's no way they could have known that—"

"Stop!" She held up a hand. "Just . . . just stop, OK? Forget I said anything. I'm tired of arguing with you. I'm tired of being angry at them. I'm . . . I'm just tired, Xavier." She dropped her head into her hands. "I've been here for hours waiting to hear news about Herb, and so far, I haven't heard a damn thing! What the hell is happening in there?" Her eyes pooled with tears. "Why won't anyone tell me what's going on? Damn it," she muttered, turning away from him again. She dabbed at her eyes. "I'm so fucking sick and tired of crying!"

Xavier instantly reached out to touch her, but drew back his hand before it rested on her shoulder. He wanted to touch her so badly that his hand itched, but it was obvious she didn't want him to do it. Her body practically radiated the message.

Suddenly, a doctor wearing a white lab coat and blue scrubs walked toward them. He was a short man with a slight build. The doctor's pale, wrinkled face was taut with stress as he frowned. The brown eyes behind the lenses of his wire-framed glasses looked weary. It was hard to believe that Herb's life rested in this diminutive man's hands.

"Hello, I'm Dr. Kennedy. Are you Mr. Allen's daughter?"

Dawn took a deep breath and nodded. "Yeah! I mean, yes . . . yes, I am. I'm Dawn Gibbons."

The doctor glanced at Xavier, who sat silently at her side. "I'm sorry. And you are . . ."

"His son-in-law," she answered quickly, gently patting Xavier on the knee.

Xavier didn't let the opportunity go to waste. He laid his hand over hers and squeezed it reassuringly. He felt her stiffen at his touch, but she didn't pull back.

The doctor nodded at them both. "Well, I wanted to give you an update on Mr. Allen."

"Please tell me he's OK, Dr. Kennedy," Dawn whispered.

"He's in stable condition for now. He was awake, though not very lucid. We've since sedated him. I understand that your father hasn't been responding well to his cancer treatments."

"No," she said softly, lowering her eyes. "No, he hasn't."

"In addition to the adverse side effects to his radiation therapy, like the fatigue he's been experiencing and the shortness of breath, I'm afraid he *is* starting to experience some of the end-stage cancer symptoms."

Xavier squinted. *"Meaning?"*

"Meaning that our priority right now is pain management. I've consulted with his doctor, and at this point, we can't do much more than that for him, but we do want to make him as comfortable as possible."

"Because he's going to die," Dawn finished for the doctor. Her eyes started to water again. "That's why you're making him comfortable, because he's going to die?"

The doctor pursed his lips. "I'm very sorry, Ms. Gibbons."

"He knew his time was near. He told me. I just hoped he was . . . he was wrong." A tear trickled down her cheek and Xavier squeezed her hand again. She took a deep breath.

"Can we go and see him now, Doctor?" Xavier asked.

"Yes, you and your wife can see him, by all means."

"We're not marr—" Dawn stopped herself then glanced at Xavier.

She was going to correct the doctor by telling him she wasn't Xavier's wife, but for some reason, thought better of it. "Umm, th-thank you, D-doctor," she said.

"Just be aware that your father probably won't be able to respond because of the pain meds we gave him. But he can hear you."

She nodded again.

Minutes later, she and Xavier trudged down the hall to Herbert's hospital room. Xavier had always hated the smell of hospitals: the overpowering mix of the antiseptic liquid the staff used to sterilize instruments and spaces, and the lingering scent of sickness that floated from the poor souls inside each room. The couple finally reached Herb's private room and stepped inside. Seeing Herb, Xavier breathed in audibly. Dawn's hand instantly clamped over her mouth and she wept.

The tan curtain around his bed was drawn back. The older man was hooked up to an IV and respirator. A hypnotic beep filled the room though Xavier couldn't determine the source. A washable plastic clipboard was slung over the foot of the bed. Another was attached to the wall with Herbert's name and the name of the nurse who was doing the seven p.m. to seven a.m. shift. She was probably the one who shuffled out of the room with her head bowed when Xavier and Dawn entered.

Xavier found it hard to believe this was the same man who had been smoking cigars and laughing behind his immense office desk a few years ago. This man looked tiny, old, and shriveled. He looked only a foot away from death's door.

Xavier's father, Malcolm, had had the same look more than a decade ago. Xavier remembered his lifeless body slumped back on the passenger seat of his Ford truck, how the last breath had rattled out of Malcolm's chest before he closed his eyes and his mouth went slack. The once-powerful man who had been the compass in Xavier's life, the ground beneath his feet, had suddenly been taken away. As Xavier gazed at Herb, that feeling of loss and anguish overwhelmed him all over again.

Dawn slowly crept to Herb's bed. Her shoulders shook as she sobbed.

"Herb?" she choked.

Herb didn't respond, just as the doctor had warned them he wouldn't. The hypnotic beeping continued. Besides her crying, it was the only sound in the hospital room.

"Herb?" She placed her hand on Herb's and rubbed it. "Herb, if you can hear me, we're okay now. All right?" She wiped at her tears with the back of her free hand. "You *are* worthy of being called my dad. I swear. Whatever happened in the past is forgotten. I forgive you . . . and I love you. You're the first man I ever truly loved."

She leaned down and kissed Herb's forehead. Tears spilled from her eyes onto Herbert's gray, dry skin. "Good-bye, Dad."

Xavier knew she didn't want to be touched, but he couldn't take it anymore. He had been by himself when he lost his father—a teenage boy left sobbing and moaning on the side of the road with no one to comfort him. He wouldn't let her endure the same thing. He walked across the hospital room and gently laid his hands on her shoulders.

She turned to him and shook her head in response. "Please, just leave me alone, OK?"

She shoved him away and swiftly walked across the hospital room and out the door.

* * *

"Dawn, let me drive you home," Xavier called after her as he followed her through the hospital lobby's automatic doors. The instant he stepped outside, he was met by the cold chill of the March evening and Dawn's even colder glare.

"Why the hell are you still here?" she snapped, striding away from him. She tugged on her wool coat. The sound of her high-heeled boots echoed off the cement as she walked. "Didn't you hear me back in the hospital room? What part of 'leave me alone' did you not understand? I don't need you to drive me home! I can drive my goddamn self!"

She shoved her hand into her purse and pulled out her keys, but she was trembling so much they slipped from her fingers and fell to the ground with a clatter.

"Look at you!" He leaned down and grabbed her car keys. "Look at how much you're shaking! You can't drive yourself home!"

"Don't tell me what I can't do!" she shouted, reaching for her keys. But he held them out of her grasp. She reached for them again, but he dropped them into his coat pocket.

"I'm not letting you drive in the state you're in. Herb wouldn't want me to either!"

Her face settled into a scowl. "Fine," she muttered defiantly. "I'll take a cab or call one of my sisters."

"Why are you going to take a cab?" he shouted after her in disbelief as she strode off.

Xavier continued to follow her. She was angry. She was stubborn. She was winding him into a tight ball of frustration, but he wouldn't give up. He couldn't leave her alone—not tonight. He could see she was hurting.

He watched as she reached into her purse again to pull out her cell phone. She started to dial a number.

He grabbed her shoulders and whipped her around to face him.

"Damn it, would you listen to me? Why call your sisters when I'm right here? Let me—"

"Because I don't want you here!" She shoved him away again. "I don't *need* you here! My name isn't Constance! I can take care of myself! So just leave me the fuck alone!"

She continued toward the end of the block. A white cab rounded the corner and she waved her gloved hand to signal it. Xavier's heart leapt into his throat. He ran to where the cab was skidding to a halt in the slush and snow.

He reached Dawn just as she swung open the cab door and began to climb inside. He grabbed her wrist and she looked up at him in surprise then rolled her eyes in aggravation.

"God damn it, Xavier! What do I—"

"I'm not trying to rescue you! I don't want to take you home because I've got a hero complex! I want to be with you! If anyone is with you tonight, I want it to be me!"

Dawn fell silent.

The driver leaned over the seat divider and lowered the passenger-side window. "Hey," he shouted, "lady, are you getting in or what?"

She turned toward the cab driver. "Uh, yeah, I-I am. I just—"

"Constance is my fiancée, and *you're* the one I can't stop thinking about!" Xavier continued, pleading his case, feeling as if it was the most important case in his life. "You make me question the woman I'm with, the life I have, what I want in the future—*all of it!* And yes, I'm a pain in the ass! Yes, I chase after you and then I push you away. I know it doesn't make any sense. But it's because I can't let you go, Dawn!" He looked down at the hand he had firmly wrapped around her wrist as evidence.

"Hey, lady!" the driver bellowed. "In or out?"

She looked at the driver then Xavier. He could see the apprehension on her face. She wasn't sure what to do next.

"Let me take you home," Xavier said, drawing closer. "I know how you feel about your father. I've been through this before. I know it's eating you up inside. You shouldn't be alone. Let me comfort you tonight."

"Comfort?" She loudly swallowed and licked her full lips, unwittingly turning him on even more. He had to use all his willpower not to lean down and kiss her. "You know damn well what you're really asking me. The women in my family have been blamed for ruining plenty of relationships, but I'm not going to get blamed for this one. Go home! You don't know—"

"Yes, I do," he said with a firm nod. "I know I want you. I want you, and nothing's going to change that."

She was wavering. He could see it in her eyes.

"If we go there," Dawn said, "there's no turning back. If you thought you felt guilty before, you have no idea how guilty you'll feel when—"

"I know what I feel. I'm aware of what I'm asking. It's too late to turn back now anyway."

He meant that. It had been slowly evolving over time, but the instant Constance refused to give up going to St. Thomas, knowing how ill her father was, something in their relationship permanently shifted. His mother had been right: Constance was shallow and self-involved as well as ungrateful. If he wasn't sure where his heart and his allegiances were before, he certainly knew at this point. They were with Dawn. She was the woman he cared for and wanted to be with.

Dawn hesitated again.

"Let me take you home," he said.

He felt his chest tighten and his stomach clench as he waited for her answer. If she said no again and got in the cab, he would accept it. He would have to. He would go back to his car and drive to his condo alone.

Xavier watched as she slowly closed the cab door.

"So you don't need a ride, then?" the driver yelled.

"No," Dawn said, meeting Xavier's eyes. "No, I don't."

"Well, shit," the driver muttered before shifting the car into drive and flooring the accelerator.

He pulled off with a screech and a plume of exhaust in his wake, but they didn't notice. They were still gazing at one another.

She grimaced. "Are you sure you want to do this?" she whispered.

"Come on." Xavier tugged her forward. "Let's go."

Chapter 24

Dawn opened her apartment door, felt along the wall in the dark, and flicked the switch on her left, flooding her living room with light. Xavier trailed in behind her. She set her leather purse and her keys on her glass coffee table.

They entered her apartment in silence, just as they had carried out the car ride there. All they wanted to say had already been said. Dawn had exhausted all her arguments to talk Xavier out of this. She had tried to reason with him and tried to do the right thing for once, but he just wouldn't listen. And honestly, she wasn't prepared to put up much of a fight tonight.

Seeing her father like that in his hospital bed had been too much for her to handle. Dawn hadn't felt so helpless and hopeless in her life. She couldn't save her dad or extend the days they had left together. She was losing the man she had just gotten the chance to know. And her mother, who was too wrapped up in her own life and the family rules, would never understand her pain. Her sisters could try, but the sympathy they felt wouldn't come close to what she knew Xavier was feeling. He had lost a father too. He cared for Herb just as much as she did. There was no doubting that. What better person to commiserate with tonight than him?

"But this isn't commiserating," a voice in her head warned. "This is fucking!"

That was true, and despite Xavier's protests that he was walking into this with his eyes wide open, she wondered if he really meant that. She didn't believe her father for one second when he said Xavier was in love with her. Xavier desired her, that's all. And now he felt he could no longer put up a fight against that lust.

In her thirty-seven years, Dawn had slept with more than her fair share of guys who were in serious relationships but had given in to their animal urges. A few had cheated on their wives and girlfriends without even flinching, but others, once they left the bedroom, walked around like they had the scarlet letter "A" branded on their pecs.

She had always shaken her head and laughed at those guys, at their guilt and fickleness. But she knew she wouldn't laugh at Xavier if he felt guilty after this. He was a man with a lot of integrity. He seemed to take his promises very seriously, and he had made a promise to Constance. He had given her an engagement ring. The girl had a right to believe that she was the only woman in his life. How would he feel if he broke that promise to Constance, if he broke his fiancée's heart?

"Stop acting like it's *her* heart that you're worried about," the harsh voice in her head replied. "There's no reason for her to find out about this! They're going to make up after this little tiff between them. They're still going to get married and ride off into the sunset together. *You're* the one who'll get her heart broken!"

Dawn tried to push all those weighty thoughts aside as she took off her coat, but she was having a hard time doing it. She was so nervous that she could barely undo the knot in her belt.

Xavier shut the front door behind him and walked toward her. "You need help with that?" he whispered. He reached for her, letting his hands trail along her waist before slowly undoing the knot.

She trembled at his touch. Her pulse began to race. He hungrily gazed at her as he let the belt fall to her sides. He cupped her face and leaned down, swooping in for a kiss.

"Do you want some coffee?" Dawn suddenly blurted out just before their lips brushed. She abruptly turned away from him, rushed across the room, and hung her coat on a nearby rack.

Xavier frowned. *"Coffee?"*

"Yeah, I could use some." She rubbed her hands together anxiously. "H-h-how about you?"

Dawn didn't wait for his reply. She walked into her kitchen and started opening cabinet doors in search of clean coffee cups. She found two white ceramic mugs and almost dropped them both as she removed them from the shelf. Her hands were shaking so badly.

Damn it, girl, get a grip!

Dawn took a deep breath, gently set the mugs on her countertop, and started to load one of the plastic K-Cups into her coffeemaker when she felt Xavier's hands on her shoulders. She halted. She could feel the heat of his palms through the silk fabric of her shirt, sending a warm tingle up and down her spine. Unlike her hands, his were firm and steady.

"Colombian roast or Nantucket blend?" she squeaked.

He didn't answer her, but instead leaned down and kissed the nape of her neck. Her eyes fluttered closed as his hands slid from her shoulders, down her arms to the front of her blouse. He slowly undid each pearl button, all the while kissing her neck, then her shoulders, and nibbling at her earlobe.

If she felt like her heart was pounding fast before, it was nothing compared to now. It was like her heart was trying to pound its way through her rib cage.

When he opened the last shirt button, he delved inside, pushing aside the lace cup of her bra. He held one of her breasts in his large, warm hand. She leaned back against his chest and moaned.

He teased the nipple with his thumb and forefinger while sliding the hem of her skirt up her legs with a slowness that was almost taunting. When Dawn felt Xavier's other hand slide between the junction of her thighs, she gripped the counter to steady herself. The taunting slowness he had shown before was nothing compared to the torture she was enduring now. His fingers played her like a master musician would his instrument, and she grew wetter and wetter. She eased her legs open to give him more access, to allow him even more play and he pushed aside the waistband of her thong and took full advantage. One hand worked in the slick dampness while the other toyed with her breasts, coaxing her like she was clay, making her moan again and twist and grind against him as she gripped the counter.

Xavier pulled his hands away and roughly turned her around to face him. Her eyes flew open. There was no more hesitation or guilt now.

While he pulled the hem of her blouse out of her skirt and pushed the garment off her shoulders so that it landed on the kitchen's tiled floor, she undid the knot of his tie and began to open the buttons of his shirt. While he undid the clasp of her bra and yanked the straps off her shoulders, she undid his belt buckle and lowered the zipper of his pants. The couple was almost frantic, removing clothes as if they were on a timer, as if their clothes were the last barrier between the need that had been building inside them for months.

They stood topless in her kitchen and Dawn trembled, more due to anticipation than the cold air around her. She gazed at him. She hadn't seen him this naked since that day on the basketball court at the community center. He looked just as good now as he had then—maybe even better. She wanted to rake her nails over his washboard abs, bury her face in the hair on his chest, and inhale his scent.

Just as she was openly admiring him, Xavier was admiring her too. She watched as his eyes slowly trailed over her body, from her brown shoulders to her dark nipples to the leather boots on her feet. She had felt naked before, but not as naked as she felt now. He reached out and held her breasts.

"Damn, you're beautiful," he whispered, making her smile. She kissed him again.

As their tongues danced, he hiked up her skirt and pushed her lace thong down her legs. She stepped out of her underwear and kicked it aside. The thong landed somewhere near the stove.

She looped her arms around his neck and hopped up, wrapping her legs around his waist. Xavier cradled her backside as they kissed. She loved the warm feel of his skin and drank in the intoxicating smell of his aftershave and cologne. The hairs on his chest tickled her nipples and made the nubs even harder.

He shifted her back and sat her on the very edge of the cold granite countertop, shoving aside everything behind her. The ceramic mugs fell to the floor, shattering on impact, making her jump. They were joined by spoons and her sugar shaker.

"Are you sure you're ready for this?" the quiet voice

in her head asked her as Xavier parted her thighs and stood between them. He continued to kiss her as he reached into his back pocket for a condom. "Just like there's no turning back for him, there's no turning back for you either."

Dawn didn't get the chance to consider the thought any further. Seconds later, he entered her with one hard thrust. She cried out against his lips and tightened her hold around his back.

He moved enticingly slowly at first, easing in and out, letting her get used to the feel of him inside her. One of his hands gripped her bottom to steady her while the other held her breast and grazed her nipple as he pumped. After a few minutes, she arched her back and rocked her hips to meet his thrusts, testing his measured control. She felt his grip on her bottom tighten and he plunged deeper. Suddenly, the tempo of their lovemaking increased. The controlled pace disappeared and she was finding it hard staying perched on the edge of the counter. She worried they would both go crashing to the kitchen floor.

Dawn could feel it coming. She started to tremble and her hips started to buck uncontrollably. She still clung to him to steady herself, but she could feel her grip becoming slacker. The vibrations were more pronounced now, undulating all over her. She twisted and squirmed and he thrust even harder. She shouted his name when the spasms overtook her body. Her yells were drowned out by his shouts a few seconds later, which echoed off the kitchen walls and ceiling.

She fell back, hitting her head against one of the overhead cabinets.

"Ow," she muttered, then giggled.

"Damn, are you OK?" he asked with a laugh. He rubbed the back of her head.

Dawn nodded and gazed into his eyes. She felt giddy, happy, and content all at the same time, and this wasn't just postcoital afterglow.

She was helplessly in love with this man and she knew that what they had just done would make things twenty times worse for her. But for now she didn't care.

"Kiss me again to make it all better," she whispered before looping her arms back around his neck and raising her mouth back to his lips.

Dawn slowly opened her eyes the next morning and raised her head from her pillow. She squinted at the bright light peeking through her bedroom blinds and turned to Xavier, who was still sleeping in bed next to her. His forearm was over his eyes. His chest rose and fell with each breath he took. Only half of his body was under the bed sheets and satin comforter. The rest was unabashedly on display in the bright morning sunshine: one large foot, a finely sculpted calf and thigh, and the dark patch of hair around his groin that trailed up the length of his stomach and chest. He looked worn out and frankly, she was too.

Last night, they had been greedy, enjoying every sexual pleasure they could think of that involved two people, lots of stamina, and flexibility to boot. They made their way from the kitchen to her living room, to the shower, and finally, the bedroom. Xavier might usually be reserved, but he certainly wasn't reserved in bed. By the time they fell asleep at four a.m., they were down to their last condom and exhausted. The instant Dawn closed her eyes, she fell blissfully asleep.

The night they had spent together had been amazing, but not just because of the sex. Dawn had never felt that way about a man before, and during the night, Xavier had said things to make her think he cared about her too.

"Of course he did," the voice in her head mocked. "Men will say anything when they're having sex with a woman. He probably would have said he was an alien if you asked him."

Probably, Dawn thought as she looked at Xavier. She reached out for him, wanting to tousle his curls and run her finger along his jaw, but she stopped herself. She pulled her hand back and turned away.

It didn't matter what he said last night. She wouldn't hold it against him. He had said whatever she wanted to hear and done whatever she needed him to do to comfort her. That was it. He had made her feel warm and loved. He had made her forget her pain—at least for a little while. But now in the light of day, Xavier was bound to feel differently. Men always did. It was better to accept it now. Longing for something she couldn't have would only make things worse. Besides, she had her father to worry about.

Dawn slowly eased out of the bed, careful not to wake Xavier. She crept naked across her bedroom floor and grabbed her blue satin robe, which was slung over her desk chair. She put it on, tied the belt around her waist, and tiptoed out of her bedroom into her living room.

She grabbed his suit jacket and went to the kitchen next—only to find that the room looked like it had been hit by a cyclone. Their clothes were everywhere. Broken shards of ceramic cup and sugar were spilled all over the tiled floor. Her bra dangled from the granite countertop. His pants were by the stainless steel refrigerator. She sighed, grabbed a broom and a dust pan, and cleaned up the mess. She then gathered their clothes and carried them back into her bedroom.

Dawn neatly folded his shirt, jacket, and pants over

the back of her desk chair. It was then that Xavier finally started to awaken. He wiped his eyes and opened them. He pushed himself to his elbows and yawned.

He looked just as handsome now—with sleep dusting his eyes, a five o'clock shadow on his face, and bed hair—than he did when he was impeccably groomed and wearing one of his tailored suits. He loudly cracked his back as he stretched.

"Good morning," he said as he cracked his neck and flexed his shoulders.

"Morning," she answered halfheartedly in return. "You sound like you're popping bubble wrap. Do you always make that much noise when you wake up?"

He chuckled. "I don't know. Maybe. You're the first person to comment on it." He stopped stretching. "How'd you sleep?"

"All right, I guess." She turned and grabbed a brush from her vanity dresser top and began to brush her hair, trying her best to put on a stoic front. "How about you?"

"I slept okay. Except . . ." Xavier leaned over the edge of the bed and reached for her, cupping her bottom and grabbing her around the waist, catching her off guard. He dragged her toward him. "I kept having the dirtiest dreams last night." He gave a wicked smile as he slowly pulled pack a panel of her robe and began to slide his hand up the inside of her legs. At his brazen touch, she could feel a familiar dampness budding between her thighs. "Frankly, I couldn't wait to wake up, climb back on top of you, and—"

"You should probably take your shower first," she said, tugging out of his grasp and changing the subject to topics that didn't have quite as much of a physical effect on her. "The hot water isn't always the best in my bathroom. The shower can get cold pretty quickly."

"Then take a shower with me like you did last night. That'll definitely conserve hot water." He reached for her again and she took another step back.

"I don't . . . I don't think that's a good idea."

"What's not a good idea?"

"For us to take a shower together."

"Why not?" He frowned. "What's wrong?"

"Why do you assume something's wrong?" She huffed. "I just . . . I just don't want to take a shower with you. That's all! Don't make a big deal about it."

"I didn't think I *was* making a big deal about it."

"Well, you are."

He eyed her. "Why are you acting like this?"

"I'm not acting like anything!"

He glanced at his clothes, which were neatly folded on her chair, and pointed at them. "Oh, you're not? So why the hell are my clothes sitting over there? *Huh?* Is that what this is all about? You want me to hop in the shower and be on my way? Were you planning to kick me out?"

"I'm not *kicking* you out!" She dropped her brush back to her vanity table top. "I was . . . I was . . ."

"You were what?"

"I was just . . . getting your clothes ready so . . . so they'd be waiting for you when you woke up and wanted to leave."

He glowered at her.

"Don't look at me like that! The night is over! Look out the window. The sun is up! I just thought—"

"You just thought last night was a one-night stand and I'd leave your apartment and do the walk of shame back to my car. Go ahead. You can say it. It's what you thought, right?"

She hesitated. "Look, we had a nice night together,

but you're engaged. You're with Constance. This was just an itch you needed to scratch—that we *both* needed to scratch. It's OK. I know how this works."

"Really?" He threw back the bedsheets and climbed to his feet. He slowly walked toward her and stood naked in front of her. "Explain to me how this works, Dawn."

His handsome face was now clouded over with anger, though she couldn't understand why. She was just trying to give him an easy out, to say that she understood.

"Xavier, I keep telling you that I'm a big girl. I'm not an ingénue at this. You don't have to play games with me."

"I'm not playing games! Everything I said last night—"

"While we were having sex," she muttered dryly.

"Everything I said last night, I meant! I don't care what I was doing when I said it, even if I was having sex! I care about you, Dawn! I *love* you!"

She stilled, wondering if she had heard him correctly. "You love me?"

"Yes! Why the hell else would I be here?"

Damn, her father had been right!

"But what about Constance . . . your engagement?"

He raked his fingers through his hair and sat down on the edge of the bed. He sighed, rested his elbows on his knees and gazed at her bedroom floor. "She and I are going to have a long talk about this when she gets back tomorrow . . . among other things. I'll tell her the truth. There's no way to get around it. The engagement is over. We're over."

At that moment, Xavier looked like the weight of the world was on his broad shoulders.

He shouldn't have to carry this alone, she thought.

Dawn hesitated before walking toward him. She sat down on the bed beside him and gently placed her hand on top of his.

"I know this doesn't mean much coming from a girl like me," she said softly, "but I'm sorry. I didn't mean for this to happen. I swear. I just wanted to get to know my father, not come between you and Constance."

"Don't apologize. You didn't force me to do this. I'm a grown man. I make my own decisions."

"But I could see what was happening and I didn't stop it."

"I didn't stop it either." He took her hand and raised it to his lips. He kissed her knuckles before linking his fingers through hers. "And if I remember correctly, *I* chased you. It wasn't the other way around. You tried to push me away."

"I did . . . a couple of times." She smirked. "But you were so damn persistent."

"I always have been when I really want something." He trailed his finger under her chin and gazed into her eyes. She became lost in those gray pools. "Do you wish now that I had stopped when I had the chance?"

"No," she said, slowly shaking her head, finally admitting the truth aloud.

He leaned forward and kissed her.

Dawn's eyes slowly closed and she kissed him back. *Morning breath be damned!* She didn't care. She was in love with a man and, shockingly, he was in love with her too. The realization still left her stunned.

As they kissed, Dawn felt Xavier fiddling with the belt of her robe, pulling at it insistently like a small child would his mother's skirt. He didn't take his mouth away from her long enough to look down to see what he was doing. She smiled against his lips and untied it for him. He quickly opened her robe and pushed it off her shoulders, letting it fall to the bed. His hands slid from her shoulders to her breasts and one dived even lower, resting in the moist spot between her thighs. Dawn groaned and lay back on the tangled bedsheets, wantonly splaying her legs wide-open and lifting her hips to meet his touch.

She thought she was exhausted from last night and assumed he was too, but they both seemed to have found a new spark of energy. It looked like that last condom would be used after all.

Teasing her with his hands wasn't enough. She soon felt his mouth in the same wet spot. He lashed her with his tongue and Dawn's moaning and groaning only grew louder. Her pelvis bucked even more. She shoved her fingers into his hair, closed her eyes, and shouted out his name when the spasms of her orgasm rocked her. The muscles in her thighs stiffened. Her stomach quivered. Seconds later, she was still catching her breath when she felt him shift and rise from the bed. She opened her eyes and watched, dazed, as he opened the last condom packet that sat on her night table. He sat down on the corner of the bed and she watched as he slowly put it on.

He held out a hand to her. "Come here."

How could she resist? At this point if he asked her to walk over fiery-hot coals, she probably would have done it. She shakily climbed to her feet, slowly walked naked toward him, and stood in front of him.

He slowly slid his hands along the backs of her legs, up her backside and then her hips. He leaned forward and kissed her stomach, then swirled his tongue in her navel. She whimpered.

"Sit down," he whispered.

She straddled him and felt his manhood jutting between her thighs. But instead of entering her, he took one of her dark nipples into his mouth and sucked it. His fingers started to play between her legs again.

With all this stimulation, she thought her body would grow numb to his touch. But it was the opposite. Dawn was almost drunk with pleasure. She grabbed his shoulders and arched her back while he sucked. She loved the rough, sandpaper feel of his beard stubble against her soft skin. When he slid his fingers inside her moist folds, she rocked her hips to meet each stroke, coaxing him in.

She looked down into eyes and saw a raw need lingering in those gray irises. He was as turned on as she was. He wanted the foreplay to end. She could tell. It was sweet of him to hold back, but he didn't have to any longer. She was ready.

Dawn drew his hand away, adjusted her hips, and slowly lowered herself on top of him. This time *he* moaned when he slid inside her.

She rocked her hips again and brought her mouth back to his, nibbling at his lips, sweeping her tongue inside his mouth. He ground beneath her and cupped her bottom, drawing her even closer to him, locking their bodies together as they continued their slow, sensual dance. Then, without warning, Xavier picked up the pace of their lovemaking and she braced herself, gripping his back. She lowered her head and rested it in the crook of his shoulder as he plunged deeper and deeper. He panted against her ear and her whimpers only increased.

She was starting to feel the tremors again. She knew them all too well now. They started at her core, then radiated to every part of her body, from her fingertips to her toes. She shouted out once again, digging her nails into his shoulders.

Simultaneously, Dawn felt Xavier do a series of jerks—both inside her and around her. His muscles tightened and so did his grip, to the point that it almost hurt. He clenched his teeth and let out a slow, guttural groan. It sounded like sheer agony but she knew better.

Another spasm shook his whole body and then he loosened his grip. His hands fell away. She watched as he fell back against the mattress with his arms splayed, like a heavyweight after a knockout punch. He took a long, deep, shuddering breath.

She slumped forward and lay on top of him, their bodies now slick with sweat. She rested her head on his chest and listened to the thrum of his heartbeat as it gradually slowed.

Dawn wished they could stay like this, but they couldn't. She had to go back to the hospital to see her father. She wanted to be there if he opened his eyes, to hold his hand when he took his last breath.

Xavier had his own emotional battle to wage. He was going to break off an engagement only two months before his wedding and break Constance's heart in the process.

Dawn closed her eyes as he wrapped his arms around her. They lay still, enjoying the moment for as long as it lasted.

At least they could lean on each other now. There was that one consolation. They wouldn't have to endure this alone.

Chapter 25

Xavier wished he could say he was riddled with guilt about what he and Dawn had done last night and this morning. He waited for the feeling to overwhelm him, to sweep over him like a slow tide, but that feeling never came. Instead, what he felt was content. He was in love with a beautiful, intelligent woman, and she was in love with him too. Yes, he would have to pay a steep price for it, but he'd deal with the consequences when they came. For now, his major concern was to be there for Dawn.

He stayed with her at the hospital all day, only leaving her side twice: to get them both some badly needed food, and to stop at his condo to retrieve some clothes and more condoms. The only time he felt an inkling of guilt was when he grabbed that little black box. Here the woman was grieving over her dying father, and Xavier was looking forward to the next time she would give him some. Frankly, he doubted *either* of them would be in any mood to have sex after the day they were about to endure, but he grabbed them anyway to be on the safe side.

With clothes and condoms retrieved, he sped back to

the hospital. And for the first time in years, he turned off his cell phone.

Let my calls go to voicemail, he thought. But he didn't do it before leaving the umpteenth message with Constance and Raquel's cell phones telling them that Herb had taken a turn for the worse.

All day, Xavier and Dawn sat at Herb's bedside undisturbed by the outside world, keeping vigil. If Dawn seemed to pull away from Xavier's touch yesterday, today she sought it. She reached for his hand and held it when they sat alone in the hospital room. When the pain got to be too much and she couldn't take watching her ailing father anymore, she would ask Xavier quietly if he could step out of the room with her. They'd walk down the hospital corridor and she'd fall against his chest and sob, sinking into him. He'd hold her until the tears subsided and she was ready to go back.

Xavier's mother noticed the change between them when she came to the hospital later that day to visit Herb and lend her support. She raised her eyebrows in surprise when she stumbled upon the couple mid-embrace as she stepped out of the elevator. Xavier looked up and Dawn turned just as his mother walked toward them. Dawn hastily pulled away from him, like a burglar caught in the act.

"Hi, M-Miss Hughes! It's . . . it's good to see you again," she said between sniffs, wiping her eyes.

"It's good to see you too, hon." His mother reached out to rub Dawn's shoulder. "I wish it was under better circumstances, though. I'm so, *so* sorry to hear about your dad."

"Thank you," Dawn whispered. Tears pooled in her eyes again. "I appreciate that."

His mother didn't hesitate. She instantly stepped forward to hug Dawn.

Xavier saw Dawn tense at first. He knew well now that she had a hard time leaning on or accepting comfort from people who weren't her family, but gradually her shoulders went slack and she hugged his mother back.

Gazing over Dawn's shoulder, Xavier's mother gave him a knowing look, but didn't say anything to him about finding him and Dawn together. Now wasn't the time. She wasn't going to hold her tongue forever, though. When he left the room to get himself and Dawn something to drink, she followed him to the cafeteria and cornered him near one of the vending machines.

"So are you *still* insisting there's nothing going on between you?" his mother asked, crossing her arms over her chest. She fixed him with a stern stare.

He shook his head and looked down at the two water bottles he held in his hands. "No, I'm in love with her."

His mother gaped. "You're *in love* with her?"

He slowly nodded.

"Oh, honey!" She dropped her hand to her chest. "Xavier, *what* are you going to do? You and Constance are supposed to—"

"I'm breaking off the engagement. I'm gonna tell her tomorrow when she gets back from her vacation."

His mother took a deep breath. She looked up at a group of nurses who laughed as they passed them on their way to one of the cafeteria tables with plastic food trays in their hands.

"Well, I wish I could lie and say I'm sorry to hear the news, hon, but I'm not. I just wish you had broken it off with Constance *sooner,* before it got this far."

"Me too," he said softly.

"Just be as gentle as you can with her. No one deserves this type of disappointment or heartache."

"I'll try to be as gentle as possible, Mom, but there's no smooth way to do this."

"I know, hon. I know."

His mother left soon after that, but Xavier and Dawn stayed at the hospital until visiting hours ended. When it was time to leave, she walked toward the hospital bed and kissed Herb's forehead before whispering a good-bye. Xavier wrapped an arm around Dawn and gently guided her out of the hospital room, though he could feel her dragging her feet, watching as the nurses adjusted the tubing from his IV bags.

"Let them do their work," he leaned down and whispered into her ear. "He's in good hands."

She gave one last despondent glance over her shoulder at her father, clenched her jaw, and nodded. She linked an arm around Xavier's waist. "OK. Let's go home."

They went back to her apartment, and though he thought Dawn wouldn't be interested in making love, she was. But this time, the sex wasn't as sizzling and fast as it had been earlier that morning or the night before. It was slow and deliberate, though just as sensual—maybe even more so. They lay silently in bed together gazing at the ceiling a few hours later. She was lost in thought, and he diligently tried to put off thoughts of what he would have to do tomorrow, but couldn't.

No matter how you slice it, this is not gonna be easy, he told himself. *This is as dirty as it gets.*

He would try to keep his promise to his mother to be as gentle as possible, but it had to be done.

Xavier tugged up the zipper of his jeans. His hair was still damp from the shower, and because he had forgotten to pack a razor along with all the other stuff he grabbed from his condo yesterday, his five o'clock shadow was now officially a beard. He pulled his blue cable-knit sweater over his head and shoved his arms through the sleeves just as Dawn roused awake.

She slowly opened her eyes and rolled onto her side, revealing her tantalizing breasts and flat stomach. He didn't really need that distraction right now. She watched him as he dressed.

"Are you leaving already?" she murmured drowsily, wiping her eyelids with the heels of her palms.

"Yeah, Constance and Raquel should be back by now. I was going to head over there."

"Oh." Dawn looked stricken by his words. She slowly sat upright and pulled her bed sheets up over her chest. "So you're gonna go through with it, then?"

"I have to. I may be a cheater now, but I refuse to be a liar too. The longer I let her walk around with that engagement ring on her finger, the more I look like a fraud. I'm not doing it anymore."

Dawn closed her eyes and lowered her head. "I am *so* sorry about this, Xavier."

"Why do you keep saying that?" He walked toward the bed, cradled her chin, and gently raised it so that her eyes met his. "Are you sorry about the people I'm going to hurt, or sorry that we'll be together?"

"You know I mean the former. I *want* to be with you, more than I can say." She sighed. "It's just . . . I've been the other woman before, but never in a situation like this. *This* is different."

He lowered his mouth to hers and kissed her. She kissed him back just as passionately, cupping her hand around the base of his neck, drawing him close. He would need the memory of this kiss to fortify him today. Regretfully, he slowly drew his mouth away from hers.

"If it makes you feel any better, if it wasn't you, it would have been something else," he said, stepping back from her. "Or if nothing else stopped me from doing it, I could have found myself married to Constance and then woken up one day wondering what the hell I did with my life, wondering why I was in a sham of a marriage."

She shook her head. "No, it doesn't make me feel any better, but I get what you're saying. I'll head back to the hospital. Just . . . just call me when you can. If my phone isn't on, leave a message."

Call me when it's done, the look in her eyes said.

He nodded before taking one last glance at her and walking out of her bedroom.

Less than an hour later, Xavier pulled into the winding driveway at Windhill Downs. He drew to a stop and parked behind a Lincoln Town Car and a transport van. The two drivers were unloading mounds of suitcases and trunks, dragging the luggage and making sweat pour from their foreheads even though it was about fifty degrees outside. They carried the bags up the steps and through the front door, which was standing open.

Xavier pulled his key out of the ignition and took a deep breath.

Let's just do this, he thought as he opened his car door and climbed out.

When he walked inside the mansion a few seconds later, he found Raquel standing in a sea of suitcases that her maids were either rummaging through or carrying upstairs for her.

"Be careful with that!" she shouted at one of the women. "It has all my shoes!"

"Yes, ma'am," the young woman said, bowing her dark head apologetically.

Raquel frowned with stern disapproval. When she

turned and saw Xavier walking toward her, her face instantly brightened.

"Xavier! What are you doing here? I didn't know you were coming today!" She strode toward him across the travertine tiles and air-kissed both his cheeks. She leaned back and squinted up at his face. "What a scruffy beard! I hope you shave it soon . . . definitely before the wedding."

He opened his mouth to answer her, but Raquel continued to ramble, cutting him off before he could.

"Eager to see your fiancée, are you? I told Connie not to worry about the little quarrel you two had," she whispered in his ear. "Distance makes the heart grow fonder, I said. Well, she will be happy to see you too! We had so much fun in St. Thomas and I know she wants to share all the details! I wish you could have come with us! The beaches were absolutely stunning, Xavier, just mesmerizing! We took so many pictures of—"

"Did you get my voicemails?" he asked, cutting her off. "Any of my texts?"

"Your texts?" She started at him blankly. "Oh! You mean the messages about Herb!" She waved her hands. "Of course we did, darling! We're heading to the hospital as soon as we finish unpacking. I told Connie if we put off unpacking until tomorrow, the house would be in complete chaos. Once that's done, we'll go straight to the hospital." She patted his shoulder. "Don't worry."

Herb was on his deathbed, yet Raquel thought unloading two hundred pounds of clothes and tourist keepsakes was more important? Now Xavier knew where Constance got it from.

"Connie's upstairs in her bedroom, by the way," Raquel said, flicking her fingers toward the stairwell. She glanced at the door where the two burly drivers stood waiting. "If you'll excuse me, Xavier, I have to tip these gentlemen."

She then sashayed away with her high heels clicking.

Xavier climbed the stairs to the east wing and found Constance's bedroom door halfway open. He pushed it open farther and saw her standing in the center of the spacious, bright bubblegum-pink room, unloading one of her Louis Vuitton suitcases. He gently knocked and she turned toward her doorway. When she saw him, she dropped the shirt she had been holding and ran across the room with arms outstretched.

"Pumpkin!" She wrapped him in her embrace. "I'm so happy to see you! You didn't tell me you were on your way here!"

"I wasn't sure if you guys had gotten back already." He sighed. "Look, Constance, we need to talk. I—"

She raised a finger and pressed it to his lips, silencing him and raising his frustration.

"No, I know what you want to talk about. You want to talk about our argument before I left for St. Thomas." She lowered her finger and nodded. "I've had some time to think about it, and I want you to know that as far as I'm concerned, it didn't happen. I know you've been busy at work. You're probably under a lot of pressure with your job and the wedding preparations. That's probably why you acted that way." She tilted her head. "But I forgive you, pumpkin."

Xavier frowned. *She forgives me?* He wasn't aware that he needed to be forgiven, at least not for that.

"Let's just go back to the way things were." Constance scratched his chin. "Speaking of the way things were . . . Pumpkin, what's with the beard? I hope you're not planning to wear that to the wedding! What about our pictures? You can't . . ."

Her voice drifted off when he tugged her arm from around his neck, her hand from his face, and took a step back from her.

She stared up at him. "What's wrong?"

He stepped around her and walked farther inside her bedroom, wondering where to start.

"Pumpkin, what's wrong?" she asked again. "You're . . . you're starting to scare me."

"We can't get married," he blurted out.

There. I said it. I finally said it!

Constance stared at him. "Wha-what?"

"We can't get married, Constance. I have to call it off."

"Please, tell me you're joking," she whispered.

He slowly shook his head. "It's not a joke."

"It *has* to be a joke! This is . . . this is just . . . Is this about our argument? Because I told you that I—"

"This has nothing to do with that. Our issues are bigger than that! It wouldn't be right for us to go ahead with the wedding."

The dumbfounded expression didn't leave her face as she stood silent, staring at him. "Who are you?" she asked, sounding dazed. "I swear I don't know you anymore! Because the Xavier Hughes I know wouldn't do this to me. He wouldn't tell me *seven weeks* before I'm supposed to walk down the aisle with him that he's breaking up with me! Not after we sent out invitations to three hundred people and booked florists and a band and . . . He wouldn't humiliate me like that!"

"I'm sorry. I'm not trying to humiliate you. I'm only trying to—"

"*You're sorry?*" she shrieked. Tears started to spill onto her cheeks. "You're sorry? Well, that's just great!" She clenched her fists at her sides. "I knew it! I knew something was going on with you! It's not just work, is it? You've been acting strange for months now! But I had no idea it was this bad! What happened? Why are you doing this to me?"

"I've been feeling this way for a while. I just didn't know how to tell you."

"Is there someone else?" she asked, searching his face.

He clenched his jaw. He hadn't planned to tell her the part about Dawn—at least not this early. He knew Constance would find out about his relationship with her sister soon enough, but he didn't want to deliver that blow today. She was still staggering from the emotional punch he had already dealt her.

"There *is* someone else, isn't there?" she persisted when he didn't answer her. "Xavier, are you . . . are you cheating on me?"

I may be a cheater, he told himself again. *But I'm not going to be a liar too.*

He had to tell her.

Xavier sighed. "Constance, please understand that neither of us meant for this to happen. I didn't want to hurt you. But yes, I'm in love with someone else."

Her eyes went wide. He took a deep breath and closed his eyes, unable to look at her stricken face anymore.

"I've fallen in love with—"

"Oh, my God!" Raquel shouted. "Oh, my God!"

Xavier opened his eyes. He turned at the sound of Raquel's racing footsteps as she climbed the stairs to the second floor two at a time. She skidded to a halt in front of Constance's bedroom door, almost slipping in her high heels on the marble floors.

She hadn't heard them all the way downstairs, had she?

"Oh, my God!" Raquel pointed frantically at the cell phone in her hand. "It's the hospital! Herb is . . . Herb is dead. Oh, my God, my husband is dead! They tried . . ." She paused and sniffed. "They tried to resuscitate him. He went into cardiac arrest but . . ." Her voice trailed off as she broke into tears.

Constance rushed toward her mother and the women fell into each other's arms. Constance sobbed uncontrollably.

Xavier stood and watched them, not knowing what to do next. The blood drained from his head. He felt absolutely numb. *Herb is dead?* His mentor, his surrogate father, had died.

Chapter 26

"Dawn, are you OK, honey?" Lauren asked.

Dawn blinked her reddened eyes and turned to look at her youngest sister. "Huh?"

The skies were a gloomy gray and the air was thick with a cold mist that made Dawn shudder and pull her black wool coat more tightly around her. The graveyard looked just as bleak with its leafless trees; mud-laden earth; shallow, murky puddles; and granite headstones and crypts. Inside, Dawn felt as dull and dark as her surroundings. She'd never felt sadness and grief this bad in her life.

"I said, 'Are you OK?' The burial is about to start. Do you think you can make it?" Lauren shut her car door and gazed at her worriedly.

"Yes, I can make it. Of course."

Despite her assurances, the worried expression didn't leave her little sister's face. "Well, why don't you take my hand anyway," Lauren said, linking her fingers through Dawn's. "We'll walk there together."

"We *all* will," Cynthia said before shutting the door behind her, stepping forward, walking up to Dawn's other side, and looping her arm around Dawn's shoulder.

The trio trudged up the grassy hill toward the burial site, following the stream of mourners who had all come to pay their last respects to Herbert Allen.

Dawn was glad that she had her sisters to lean on today. Stephanie couldn't make it because she was past her due date and didn't want to chance going into labor at a funeral, but Lauren and Cynthia had come to show their support.

Though Dawn had tried to remain stoic throughout the funeral and the car ride to the burial site, there were several times when she had broken down weeping. Her sisters had held her while she cried and shielded her from the conspicuous stares and whispers of the other mourners. It seemed that second only to Herbert Allen himself, Herbert Allen's illegitimate daughter was the person of interest for all those who attended the funeral. Word had obviously gotten around about who Dawn was.

She didn't want to bring any drama. Dawn had tried to stay in the background and not bring attention to herself, though Cynthia had argued during the funeral that she should take her rightful place up front in the first pew with Raquel and Constance—and not in the far back near the sanctuary doors.

"Hell, you're just as much family as *they* are!" Cynthia had whispered fiercely.

But Dawn had shaken her head and raised her finger to her lips to silence her eldest sister's angry mutterings as the eulogy began. She didn't want to make a scene. She would sit there only if she had been explicitly invited, but that never happened. Not only had her stepmother and sister not invited her, they seemed to make a concerted effort to ignore her. She soon figured out it wasn't her imagination. Cynthia pointed out repeatedly how they were slighting her.

"I don't see your name in here," Cynthia had whispered as the reverend began his sermon. She had flipped open the funeral program. "You're nowhere in here!"

"Shh!" Lauren had said while glowering at Cynthia. "Not here, not now," she had mouthed silently.

Cynthia had ignored her and pointed down at one of the program's pages. " 'Herbert Allen is survived by his *darling* wife, Raquel Allen,' " she read with a roll of the eyes, " 'and his *beautiful* daughter, Constance Marie Allen.' I mean . . . Where the hell is Dawn in here?" She had made a big production of flipping the pages again, even turning the program upside down before slapping it onto her lap. "Hell, even the *florist* got a shout out! They couldn't remember to include his other daughter? That little detail escaped them?"

"Quiet down!" Lauren had snapped.

Instead, Cynthia had crossed her arms over her chest. "Hell no! This is bullshit, some straight-up *bullshit* and you know it, Laurie!"

Listening to her sisters argue, Dawn had to agree with Cynthia. She was sure the omission of her name from the program and from the glowing obits that had appeared in several of the local papers wasn't an accident. She knew it wasn't because of her affair with Xavier. He said he hadn't had the chance to tell Constance the truth. Whatever hostility her sister and stepmother had toward her was rooted in something else, but she didn't have the heart to work up any anger at the Allen family today. Whatever sting she felt from their dismissal was nothing compared to the pain she felt seeing her father in that casket, knowing that she had been there when he took his last breath and had watched, paralyzed, as the nurses and doctors tried valiantly to save him but failed.

The only thing that she hadn't been able to block out today was how Xavier was behaving. Anyone at the funeral would be hard-pressed to believe she and Xavier were lovers. He had only nodded to her politely when he and Constance entered the church and then quickly escorted his former fiancée toward their pew. Constance had literally leaned on him as they walked toward the front of the church.

"Is that Xavier?" Cynthia had whispered as he and Constance walked down the center aisle.

Dawn had nodded in reply.

"The sexy lawyer you've got a thing for?" Cynthia had pressed. "Well, by the looks of it, you didn't work the Gibbons charm on him. That woman is practically *glued* to him!"

Lauren slapped her sister's thigh in admonishment.

Dawn had been too annoyed with her sister to explain the real status of her relationship with Xavier. He claimed that he was only playing a role that Constance had asked him to play. He said Constance was angry that he was leaving her, but it was more important to her to save face and pretend they were still a couple. She hadn't even broken the news to her mother yet for fear of devastating Raquel further. The widow was already shaken by the loss of her husband, Xavier had explained. Constance and Xavier agreed they wouldn't make the announcement that their engagement was off until *after* the funeral. The exact date of when that would happen was still up in the air.

But even with this explanation, Dawn didn't feel right. With Xavier and Constance continuing to pretend to be the happy couple, that put Dawn firmly in the role of "the other woman." She had taken on that role before in her life, but didn't think she would be doing it again under these circumstances. And though she was trying diligently not to be fazed by the whole farce, watching Xavier walk arm-in-arm with Constance while he ignored her truly hurt.

In fact, Constance and Xavier were playing the part so well, Dawn wondered if the love he claimed he no longer felt for Constance had really disappeared. Had he really intended to tell Constance the truth about their affair? What would stop Constance and Xavier from getting back together in the end?

"It's your own fault," a voice in her head admonished as she watched the couple. "You broke the family rules by sleeping with your sister's man. Now look where it got you!"

As the mourners reached the crest of the hill in the cemetery, the three Gibbons girls took their place among the throng who surrounded the casket. They stood on the outskirts of the black tent as a light rain began to fall. Dawn lifted the netting over the brim of her hat. She spotted Raquel, Constance, and Xavier toward the front, closest to the casket and the wide array of sumptuous funeral flowers. Leslie Ann, Xavier's mother, stood on the other side of Xavier, weeping quietly and wiping her nose with a tissue.

When the reverend began to read his final prayer, Xavier raised his bowed head. Dawn watched as he scanned the crowd. When his eyes reached her, their gazes locked. She saw something in those gray irises that made her momentarily forget about her grief and disappointment. The familiar feeling of love and yearning swept over her, sending a surge of warmth through her chest, but the feeling abruptly ended when he suddenly broke their mutual gaze to attend to Constance. His ex-fiancée dropped her head onto his shoulder again and burst into tears as the casket was slowly lowered. Xavier wrapped an arm around her and held her close. He whispered something into her ear. Seeing them being so intimate, Dawn had to look away.

"Let's go," she said to her sisters as Raquel stepped forward and tossed a red rose onto the descending casket.

"You sure?" Lauren whispered.

Dawn nodded, giving one last forlorn glance at Xavier, then at her father's casket. "I'm sure. I've paid my respects. Let's go." She then turned around and stepped from under the tent into the drizzle. Her sisters exchanged a look then followed her.

Soon after, a stream of people began making their way from the funeral site back to their cars. The walk downhill over the wet grass and mud was slippery, so Dawn, Lauren, and Cynthia walked slowly, holding one another's hands for steady footing.

"*Dawn?* Dawn!"

Dawn stopped and turned to find Xavier striding toward her.

"Dawn, wait up!"

She was half tempted to turn back around and keep walking, but instead she pasted on a bland expression. "Yes?"

He stopped in front of her and glanced at her sisters. He extended his hand for a shake. "Hi, I'm Xavier Hughes. I'm engaged to—"

"Oh, we know who you are," Cynthia said dryly. "I'm Cynthia, Dawn's big sister, and this is our little sister, Lauren."

Lauren stepped forward and shook his hand. "Pleased to meet you."

"And you." He then focused on Dawn again. "Can I speak with you . . . privately?"

Dawn shook her head. "We were just leaving. I don't—"

"Please? It'll only take a few minutes."

There was desperation not only in his voice, but in the expression on his face. She didn't know why he was doing this now, especially since they were supposed to be pretending that nothing was going on between them.

She pursed her lips and turned to her sisters. "Can you give us a sec?"

"Sure. We'll be waiting for you at the car," Lauren said. She took Cynthia's hand, tugging their nosy sister away none too subtly. That didn't stop Cynthia from giving one last glance at Xavier.

He started to walk toward a deserted spot of the cemetery and motioned for Dawn with a tilt of his head to follow him. Dawn rolled her eyes and trailed after him, though it was hard since her heels kept sinking into the mushy turf and she kept sliding. Xavier noticed her distress and instantly reached for her. She waved his hand away.

"I've got it," she muttered irritably. She didn't want his help and she certainly didn't want his hands on her—not with the way he could make her feel.

"How are you doing?" he asked softly seconds later. "I didn't get the chance to talk to you today."

"How do you think I'm doing, Xavier? I just watched my father being put in the ground."

He grimaced. "You're right. That was a stupid question. I'm sorry. I knew today would be painful for you. I wish . . . I wish I could be more supportive . . . you know, standing there beside you."

"Well, you have a role to play." She crossed her arms

over her chest. "You warned me how this would go down. Wouldn't want you to break character, now would we?" she mumbled sarcastically.

"Maybe I could come to your place later, after I make sure Constance and Raquel are OK."

Of course, Dawn thought bitterly. *Roll around in the sheets with me before you head back to your girlfriend.*

"I'll stop by and—"

"That isn't necessary."

"I *know* it's not necessary." He looked and sounded frustrated. "I'm not doing it because it's necessary. I'm doing it because I want to be with you!"

He said that, but did he mean it? She wasn't so sure anymore. She wanted his companionship. She wanted nothing more than to be wrapped in his arms and to lie naked in bed beside him, but it seemed every time she dealt with Xavier, she was the one left feeling heartbroken and empty in the end.

How the hell had she gone from the old, self-assured Dawn to the insecure, emotional wreck she was now? What had happened to her?

Dawn shook her head. "Not tonight. I'd rather . . . I'd rather be alone."

"Alone?" He took a step toward her. "Is something wrong? Are you pissed at me? Look, I told you why I'm doing this! I can't—"

"Nothing's wrong. I'm just sad and exhausted, that's all," she lied, shrugging off his hand. "I'd rather be by myself tonight."

He wavered then slowly nodded. "Then I guess I'll give you a call tomorrow. I'll check on you then."

"Sure," she said, but she had no intention of taking his phone call. She couldn't choose to stop grieving over her father, but she could choose to end things with Xavier. This pain had to stop.

Dawn turned around and headed toward her sisters, who patiently waited for her on the gravel-covered shoulder near her BMW. She didn't look back—in more ways than one.

Chapter 27

Xavier sat in the leather seat of the Lincoln Town Car and glared out the tinted window. The driver had pulled away from the graveyard more than twenty minutes ago, but Xavier barely noticed. His thoughts were too heavy. He was still mourning the loss of his mentor, and now he had Dawn's standoffishness to contend with.

Not being able to leave the funeral with her but instead having to watch her walk away was one of the hardest things he had ever done. She should be crying on *his* shoulder, but instead she rushed toward her sisters and acted as if she couldn't get away from him fast enough.

He wished he could make her understand why he was bothering with this pretense that he and Constance were still together, but truth be told, he wasn't totally convinced why he was doing it either. He thought he was doing it out of respect for Herb. He had not wanted to humiliate the Allen family or tarnish Herb's legacy by bringing drama to the funeral. He and Constance would simply pretend to be a couple for a few more days. No big deal, *right?* But he had highly underestimated how much that move would hurt Dawn. Though she claimed it didn't matter to her, he could tell differently.

Damn it, what have I done? he thought tiredly while running his hand over his face.

"Thank God that's over," Raquel muttered, breaking the silence that had permeated the car ride.

She and Constance were also being driven back to Windhill Downs in the Town Car.

Raquel took off her fur-lined hat, set it on her lap, and began to finger-comb her auburn hair back into place. "The sermon went a bit long, but all in all, I thought it went well."

Constance sniffed quietly beside Xavier and raised a tissue to her eyes. "Daddy would have liked it. He always liked Reverend Wilson's sermons."

"Yes, it went well overall," Raquel said again distractedly like she hadn't heard Constance. She tilted her head and pursed her lips. "Well, it would have been perfect if Dawn could have spared us a bit of scandal today, but I should have known she would come to the funeral."

Constance nodded in agreement. "It was a little embarrassing."

"More than a little, darling! More than a little!"

Xavier, who had been trying to ignore their conversation up until this point, suddenly turned from the window. "What was embarrassing about it?" He frowned. "Why shouldn't Dawn have come?"

"Because she's already accomplished what she came here for," Raquel said bitterly, glaring at the younger man. "There was no need for her to rub it in, walking around gloating the way she did."

"What are you talking about?" he asked, feeling the first surge of anger. "She wasn't gloating! She was there crying just like everyone else."

Raquel snorted with contempt. "Please, Xavier, don't be so naïve. I saw past her façade! While she was pretending to cry over my husband, she was probably secretly laughing about the millions she's going to inherit thanks to the manipulations that she did behind the scenes, talking poor Herb into adding her to his will. But I've got a rude awakening for her," Raquel said in a low, menacing voice as she pointed her finger at Xavier. "I'm not just going to . . . to *roll over* and let her take my husband's money! She's in for a fight!"

Herbert had mentioned to Xavier that he was exploring the possibility of changing his will so that some of his money and estate would go to Dawn. Because Xavier was his future son-in-law at the time, he had recused himself from involvement with the will in order to avoid accusations of manipulation like the ones Raquel was throwing around now. He'd never found out if Herb had actually gone through with modifying the will. Judging from Raquel's fiery tirade, it looked like Herb had.

"I mean, we don't even know for sure if she *is* his daughter, with the reputation her mother has! That woman will sleep with any man who she thinks has money," Raquel sniffed. She twisted her red lips in disgust. "She's no better than a prostitute!"

"So what are you suggesting . . . that Dawn should have to take a DNA test?" Xavier asked.

"That . . . and I think her background as a money hunter should be presented in court. If that doesn't work, maybe we can even leak it to the newspapers if this new will goes forward."

He gazed at Raquel in disbelief. "You would actually do that? You would humiliate her like this?"

Raquel raised her nose into the air. Her green eyes narrowed. "If it means protecting my husband's legacy, Xavier, yes, I will do what needs to be done."

The sedan suddenly lurched to a stop. A few seconds

later the driver opened the door. Raquel scooted across the leather seat and stepped out of the car first, looking every bit as cold and imperial as an old English queen who was about to send someone to the stockade. Constance immediately followed her mother.

Xavier stayed slumped in his seat, now shell-shocked by what he had just heard. Raquel was going to war over the will and would drag Dawn's and Dawn's mother's names through the mud to win the battle.

He couldn't let that happen.

Xavier suddenly leapt out of the car and ran after Constance. She was climbing the steps to the mansion's French doors, through which her mother had already disappeared.

"Constance!" he called after her as she quickly climbed the stone stairs. "Constance!"

He grabbed her shoulders and whipped her around to face him just as she reached the last step.

"Constance, you can't be OK with this shit! Don't let your mother do this!"

Constance fixed him with a steely glare and pulled out of his grasp. "Why shouldn't I? Mommy's right. We don't even know for sure if Dawn *is* Daddy's daughter. If she wants access to his millions, the conniving bitch should have to prove she's related to him."

"Conniving bitch?" He slowly shook his head, not understanding why these words were coming out of Constance's mouth. What garbage had her mother dumped into her head? He knew the two women didn't particularly like each other, but this seemed especially venomous.

"But she doesn't want his money! She probably doesn't even know he changed his will. She's grieving the loss of her father just like you are!"

Constance didn't look convinced.

"Please don't turn against your own sister like this, not over an inheritance. It's not worth it! And Herb wouldn't want you to treat your sister this way!"

Constance squinted. "You mean the same sister who's been sneaking around fucking my fiancé?"

Xavier's mouth clamped shut. His face drained of all color.

"You mean *that* sister?" Constance taunted. "Is that the sister I shouldn't turn against?"

He closed his eyes. *How the hell did she find out?*

"Constance, I'm so . . . We didn't want—"

"Save it!" she snarled. "You must think I'm the stupidest girl in the world, Xavier! Did you honestly think I wouldn't figure out what was going on? I know what type of woman she is! You wouldn't give me all the details, so I had someone do a background check on her on my own."

He gaped, now struck speechless as he watched his ex-fiancée morph into a woman he had never seen before.

"She's nothing more than a whore! But I never, ever thought I had to worry about her being around you. *Not* trustworthy Xavier, *not* the man who looks down on people who don't keep promises and aren't of their word—not *that* Xavier! No, he would never betray me and sneak around with a woman who claims to be my sister!"

Her words cut deep. She was calling him out for the dog that he was, and he couldn't disagree with her.

"You know, Byron was right about you all along," she said, dropping her hand to her hip. "He knew you were a total hypocrite from the beginning! I just didn't believe him!"

"*Byron?* What does Byron have to do with this?"

Constance gave an impish smile. "You aren't the only one who has secrets, Xavier," she whispered.

Secrets? The truth finally dawned on him. His face went from pale to bright red.

"You've . . . you've been cheating with Byron?"

"It's not cheating!" Constance snapped. She adjusted her leather gloves. "He and I were hooking up before he even got married. I was with him *first* and he wanted to marry me, but I knew that Daddy would never go for it. He could barely tolerate Byron, but he thought the sun shined out of your ass," she said with a contemptuous curl in her lip. "Plus, you were cute, smart, and success-ful. It wasn't like it was a big sacrifice to marry you. But Byron and I didn't see a reason not to continue what we were already doing *just* because we were with other people! He married Kelly. I would marry you. And we'd both continue to have our fun on the side."

Xavier stared at his ex-fiancée in disbelief. Here he had been agonizing for months and feeling like he had committed the ultimate betrayal, while Constance had been sneaking around for *years* with one of the men he most despised—that asshole Byron Lattisaw.

No wonder she's rarely interested in sex, Xavier thought. It was hard to fake passion with one man when you had just climbed out of the bed of another.

"So I was the pushover? I was the sucker you were going to pretend to be in love with. Meanwhile, you're running off fucking that piece of shit, Byron Lattisaw?"

"He's not a piece of shit!"

"He *is* a piece a shit! He got an accountant pregnant in our office, lied to her, and told her that he was going to marry her. Then he tried to cover it up. That selfish ass-hole was going to have the company foot a two-million-dollar paternity bill!"

"If she's stupid enough to believe that he would marry a woman like her, then that's her fault, isn't it?" Constance argued. "Besides, you're one to talk! If he's a piece of shit, so are you! *You* cheated on me with Dawn! You and Byron are no different!"

Xavier slowly shook his head and turned around, feeling nauseous. The truth crashed around him like falling skyscrapers, like the tumbling sky. Everything between him and Constance had been a lie—one big, horrible lie. He thought he had been pretending for the past few days that they were a happy couple, when she had been pretending the same thing since the beginning of their relationship.

"Where are you going?" she yelled as he walked away from her. "God damn it, we made a deal! You said you'd pretend we're still together!"

"Until after the funeral . . . and the funeral is over." He kept walking. "Find yourself another sucker."

Chapter 28

"Well, good of you to finally show up!" Cynthia exclaimed as her sisters Dawn and Lauren walked through the doorway of the room adjacent to their mother's spacious makeshift bridal suite at Glenn Dale mansion.

The duo was more than twenty minutes late. Their mother's wedding was slated to start in less than an hour and Cynthia had been glancing at her watch every five minutes wondering where the hell her sisters were.

"Cindy, don't start," Lauren warned as she adjusted the front of her silk bridesmaid gown and beelined for the four bouquets of yellow roses, white calla lilies, and pink peonies. The flowers sat in a straight line on the white macramé tablecloth on an oak table facing the floor-to-ceiling windows. Lauren took one bouquet then handed another to Dawn, who was still hurriedly taking off her coat.

"Little Cris was colicky, kept me up all night, and I didn't get to sleep until around three a.m.," Lauren explained. "I am dead on my feet. And Dawn's having a pretty rough week herself. *Remember?*"

Cynthia pursed her lips and nodded grudgingly. She had been so preoccupied with her mother, last-minute wedding details, and making sure security was prepared just in case the groom's crazy ex made an appearance that she had totally forgotten about Dawn's whole ordeal.

Dawn had attended her father's funeral last week only to receive notice in the mail a few days later from one of Raquel Allen's lawyers that the widow was challenging his will in probate court. Dawn didn't understand why that had anything to do with her until she read further that Raquel was alleging that Dawn had exerted "undue influence" on Herbert Allen before his death, taking advantage of a sick, elderly man's weakness and talking him into adding her to the will. Raquel was also challenging Herbert's paternity, insisting that Dawn prove she was his daughter.

When Dawn had told Cynthia about the letter, Cynthia had been so furious she couldn't see straight.

"Why that pinched-faced, redheaded *bitch!* Does she know who she's messing with? Obviously, she doesn't!" Cynthia had shouted as she paced back and forth in Dawn's living room. "Well, you're gonna get a lawyer too. I know a good one, Dawn, who kicks ass and takes names! There is no way she's going to push you around and—"

"I'm going to tell the lawyer that I forfeit," Dawn had said quietly with her head bowed as she sat on her couch.

Cynthia had stopped pacing to stare at her sister. "That you forfeit? Forfeit what?"

"My inheritance. If Raquel wants to challenge it, so be it. I'm not going to fight her in court over this."

"*What?* But you're just as much an heir as that Constance chick! You were his daughter too!"

"Cindy," Dawn had said with a loud sigh, "I told you in the beginning that I went into this to build a relationship with my father. That's why I agreed to meet him in the first place. It wasn't to get an inheritance. I'm not going to fight over money that I don't even want."

Cynthia had gazed at her sister as if Dawn's body had been taken over by some alien life form. She had no idea what had gotten into her. Dawn Gibbons was turning down millions of dollars—millions of dollars that were rightfully hers?

What the hell is going on here?

Cynthia had crossed her arms over her chest and cocked an eyebrow. "And you're sure this has nothing to do with your disappointment over Prince Charming? Things not working out with Xavier isn't clouding your judgment, is it?"

Dawn's sad eyes suddenly went chilly. She glared at her older sister. "This has nothing to do with him," she had said before rising from the couch, gathering her coffee cup, and walking toward her kitchen.

"You say that but—"

"I've made my decision, Cindy," Dawn had said, letting Cynthia know by her tone that was the end of discussion.

Now, two days later, Cynthia watched as Dawn tossed her coat onto a settee and took the bouquet Lauren handed to her. Cynthia still wondered what had gotten into her sister to make her throw away a fortune like this.

"So you're still going to give up your inheritance?" Cynthia asked.

Dawn nodded as she smoothed the front of her gown. It was an identical pale yellow to Lauren's and Cynthia's bridesmaid dresses, but was a different style and cut. Dawn's dress was a slinky sheath that accented her lean, tall frame. Lauren's dress had a halter top and flared at the waist before ending at her sleek, brown calves. Cynthia's was strapless with a split that hit her almost mid-thigh, matching her sultry personality.

"I called the lawyer yesterday," Dawn said. "He hasn't gotten back to me yet."

Cynthia slowly shook her head. "I still think you're making a big mistake."

"I know what you think, and frankly, I don't care," Dawn snapped.

Lauren held up her hands. "OK . . . OK, guys. Let's not argue. Not today. We can save it until after the wedding."

"I need a chair . . . *now!*" Stephanie yelled as she burst through the doorway. She waddled across the hardwood floors and flopped into a leather wingback chair. She plopped her feet on a footstool and let out a long, ragged breath. "God, that feels good! My back and hips are killing me!"

"Still haven't popped yet?" Dawn asked with a laugh.

"No," Stephanie grumbled, blowing away a lock of hair that had fallen into her eyes. "But if this little girl doesn't make an appearance by the end of the week, the doc says he's just going to induce. I don't care at this point. I'm ready for this to be over!"

Cynthia glared at Stephanie's shoes. "What the hell is that on your feet?"

"*On my feet?* You mean my Keds?" Stephanie asked, rubbing her ample belly and wiggling her canvas sneakers. "My feet are swollen. They're the only shoes that fit. I tried everything—my Louboutins, my Manolos, *and* my Jimmy Choos. I couldn't squeeze into them. What do you expect me to do?"

"You can't wear Keds to a wedding!"

"Says who?" Stephanie countered.

"Says me!" Cynthia argued.

"Cindy," Lauren interjected, "Steph's nine-plus months pregnant. The world won't come to an end if she shows up to the wedding in Keds. I'm sure everyone will understand."

"I don't care if they understand!" Cynthia shouted with hazel eyes blazing. She balled her fists at her sides. "Our clothes and shoes are supposed to be coordinated! I gave you guys a list of what to wear, and that list didn't include goddamn Keds! Pale yellow heels that are two inches or higher. That's what I said!"

"Calm the hell down," Dawn muttered. "You can't possibly be this pissed about Keds. What is this *really* about?"

"I'll tell you what this is about!" Cynthia shouted, finally unable to hold in her rising frustration at all her sisters anymore. "This is about the fact that I've been busting my ass trying to make this wedding perfect for Mama, agonizing over every little detail and organizing everything even though Mama and Reggie wouldn't make one damn decision! And now this psycho stalker is trying to break them up! Now I have that to worry about too!"

Her sisters stared in amazement at her outburst.

"And none of you—not *one* of you has been of any help! You've been too busy playing house with your new baby and millionaire hubby," Cynthia shouted, staring angrily at Lauren. "Or you're too busy being pregnant!" She turned to Stephanie. "Or falling *in love!*" she scoffed at Dawn. "Meanwhile, this whole fucking wedding has been hanging on by a thread and I'm the only one holding it together!"

"What on earth is all the shouting about?" Yolanda Gibbons asked irritably as she swung open an adjoining door. She stood in her robe and bedroom slippers with her hand on her hip. "The makeup artist and hair-dresser could hear you all carrying on like when you were bickering little girls! The guests might hear you too!"

"Sorry, Mama," they all murmured in unison.

"Now, one of you come in here and help me get into my gown. No one in here can figure out the clasps." Yolanda fixed them with a stern gaze. "I'm already running late."

"All right. I'll do it," Cynthia said tiredly, walking toward the opened French door.

"No, *I'll* do it," Lauren insisted, grabbing her sister's arm. "You stay here and take a breather," she whispered before scurrying toward their mother.

Cynthia watched as Lauren shut the door behind her. Cynthia slowly walked to a velvet medallion couch and sat down before dropping her head into her hands.

"Cindy, I'm sorry you've been carrying the burden of this by yourself," Dawn said softly seconds later.

"I needed you guys and you've all been MIA," Cynthia mumbled behind her hands.

"I know. That's why I'm apologizing. We didn't mean to—"

"I hate to interrupt, but can someone give me a back rub?" Stephanie whimpered.

Dawn sighed. "Scoot forward," she ordered Stephanie before sitting on the wingback chair's armrest. Stephanie obeyed her command and Dawn began to massage her sister's lower back. She turned back toward Cynthia. "Look, I know it's been trying, but don't let it overwhelm you. What wedding doesn't come with its share of drama? What else in our lives doesn't?"

"I just can't take any more of this," Cynthia muttered. "This is *too much* drama! I mean, why can't it just be a simple wedding? Who the hell has to get a security team for their nuptials to make sure no one walks in with a butcher knife to take out the bride?"

"So I guess this stalker thing has gotten out of hand, then," Dawn said.

"Way out of hand! It's gotten so crazy that even I couldn't hide it from Mama anymore."

"Really? But Mama doesn't seem upset by it," Dawn said. "She's acting as if everything is fine."

"Of course she is! She's this close to her jackpot! She isn't going to let this Beatrice chick intimidate her. And you know me. I don't intimidate easily either. But I swear to you, this woman is crazy, with a capital 'C!' She made a *death threat!*"

"A death threat?" Dawn murmured.

"Yeah, I know! And Mama won't even report it to the police!"

"Well, we'll *all* keep an eye out for crazy today," Dawn said. "Hopefully, after the wedding, Mama can get a restraining order. Until then, we'll just have to stay on our toes."

Cynthia sighed again.

An hour later and *eighteen minutes* behind schedule, the Gibbons girls lined up near the doors to one of Glenn Dale's sitting rooms where the ceremony was about to take place. At the sound of violins playing the first notes of Pachelbel's Canon in D major, Lauren stepped through the doorway, smiling. Stephanie waddled in after her, followed by Dawn. Cynthia brought up the rear, being the eldest sister and the maid of honor.

As she walked inside, she surveyed the room. The flowers were as she ordered after haranguing the florist for several days to make sure the proper freesias were brought in from Ecuador. The decorator had kept the decorations minimalist and tasteful. The reverend and Reginald stood on the raised stage that she had brought in especially for the wedding.

About sixty or so people sat in the gilded Chiavari chairs on each side of the red-carpeted aisle. Cynthia spotted several familiar faces in the crowd. Most were friends of her mothers and a few were business associates of Reginald.

A minute later, the music the string duo was playing changed and her mother stood in the doorway, looking splendid in her off-white empire-waist gown, sparkling lace bolero jacket, and hat-style short tulle veil. Her bouquet was a more luxurious version of her daughters' bouquets. Everyone rose to their feet.

Yolanda slowly walked up the aisle alone, smiling at Reginald. He gazed proudly at his bride. His rotund chest puffed out another inch.

When Yolanda reached the front, she took Reginald's hand. The music ceased and the room fell silent.

"You may all take your seats," the reverend rumbled.

Cynthia breathed a sigh of relief, happy that everything seemed to be going so smoothly.

"Dearly beloved," the reverend began, "we are gathered here today, in the sight of God and this company, to witness and celebrate one of life's greatest blessings. We are here to recognize and bless the union of"—he stared down at the sheet of paper hidden inside his Bible—". . . of Yolanda Gibbons Hirschfield Banks Esposito Thomas Parsons." He looked up in awe after saying all her last names. "And, uh, Reginald Whitfield III."

The tenseness in Cynthia's muscles finally began to ease and she settled into the ceremony.

"Reggie!" a voice boomed from the entryway minutes later.

A hush fell over the room. Even the reverend—who

had been droning on during introductions about the sacredness of marriage and a wife's sanctified duty to obey her husband, drawing droll eye rolls from many of the women in attendance—suddenly fell silent.

Cynthia went stark still when she heard the shout, knowing instantly who had caused the disturbance.

Oh, God, Cynthia thought with desperation. *How the hell did she get in here?*

Cynthia had at least three guards posted at the door who had cost Reginald a pretty penny. She had ordered them to do a full surveillance of the room and the first floor. How had this nutcase managed to make it through the front door, let alone to the ceremony?

Reginald better ask for his goddamn money back, Cynthia thought indignantly.

"Reggie, you know you hear me!" Beatrice shouted, stomping up the center aisle with arms swinging, sounding like a rhino making its way to a watering hole.

Yolanda's mouth fell open as she watched Beatrice approach while Reggie went bug-eyed with terror.

Cynthia turned to find Beatrice wearing a brown uniform that one of the groundskeepers would wear, except Beatrice's large frame was barely contained in the tight cotton fabric. Her large bosoms burst over the top of the zippered front.

So that's how the bitch got in, Cynthia realized. She wondered if there was some poor gardener knocked unconscious somewhere on Glenn Dale's grounds, wearing only his T-shirt and boxers.

Cynthia watched as Beatrice came to a halt only a few feet away from the bride, groom, and the rest of the bridal party. Beatrice yanked off the brown baseball cap that was partially hiding her face.

"Reggie, what the hell do you think you're doing?" Beatrice bellowed with her hands on her hips.

"Now, Bea," Reginald said, holding up his hands, "don't cause a scene!"

"Don't cause a scene? *Don't cause a scene?*" she screeched. Her head looked like it was about to explode. "You told me last night while we were in bed together that you loved me."

Cynthia's eyes widened with shock. So did her mother's. *In bed together?*

"And yet here you are, about to marry this . . . this two-bit heffa! You said we would be together until the day we died, Reggie!"

"Hey!" Dawn shouted. "Don't call my mama a two-bit heffa!"

"Yeah!" Stephanie yelled, holding her aching back while glaring at Beatrice.

"Enough of this bullshit," Cynthia muttered and stepped forward. "Security! Where the hell is security?"

Two burly men in suits suddenly galloped into the room, looking confused.

Cynthia slowly shook her head in exasperation, then snapped her fingers at the guards and pointed at Beatrice. "Do your damn jobs and remove this crazy bitch from the premises—*now!* Or I'll have to take care of her myself!"

As the men stepped forward, Beatrice shoved her hand into the collar of her T-shirt and began to rifle around in her bra.

What the hell is she doing now?

Seconds later, Beatrice removed her hand from her bosom, revealing a petite .38 revolver. A few people gasped. Several shouted in alarm.

Cynthia felt as if she was going to pee her pants. She was at a loss for what to do next. Her worst nightmare had manifested in full living color.

"Stand back!" Beatrice turned and barked at the guards. "Stand right there!"

The men came to an abrupt stop. Panicked wedding guests, making their way toward the doors, halted.

Beatrice turned back around toward the front of the room. Tears ran down her plump cheeks, giving her raccoon eyes and smudging her foundation.

"How could you do this?" she sobbed. "How could you do this to me, Reggie? You know how much I love you!"

"Baby," he said softly. "Put the gun down. We can talk about this if you put the gun down."

Cynthia noticed out of the corner of her eye Stephanie's man, Keith, lean toward her brother-in-law, Crisanto, and whisper something into his ear. They both stood in the audience only a few feet away from Beatrice, who was still ranting. Cris nodded and a second later, Keith started to ease toward the aisle. Cris followed him.

Cynthia frowned. *What the hell are they doing?*

"Beatrice . . . baby . . . I swear to you, if you—"

"Don't you swear a damn thing to me, you lying, cheating S-O-B! I'm telling you now, if you expect me to play second fiddle to this heffa, you've got another thing comin'!"

With a trembling hand, Beatrice raised her arm and pointed the gun at Yolanda.

"It's not happening, Reggie. I'll kill her and kill you rather than let that happen," she said flatly.

"Oh, my God!" Yolanda gasped, taking a step back and dropping her lush bouquet to the stage.

"Damn it, do something!" Cynthia shouted to the guards, who seemed to be virtually frozen in ice near the doors. "Don't just stand there! *Do* something!" she squealed.

But the guards didn't do a damn thing. Cynthia could feel panic make the bile rise in her throat as Beatrice stopped trembling.

"Say good-bye to your heffa, Reggie," Beatrice ordered.

Cynthia closed her eyes, preparing herself for the boom of gunfire, but instead she heard Beatrice scream and then a loud thump, followed by more shouting. Cynthia slowly opened one eye, then the other to find that Cris had tackled Beatrice. The fat woman now whimpered and writhed underneath the former NFL player. Meanwhile, Keith had one hand firmly pressed against the back of Beatrice's head, shoving her face into the red wedding carpet, while the other hand wrenched the revolver away from her.

"Got it!" Keith shouted. He opened the revolver's chamber and dumped the bullets onto the floor. "Everything's OK, everybody. It's under control."

Cynthia dropped her hand to her chest and let out a long breath of relief.

So men can be useful after all.

"No, everything is *not* OK!" Lauren suddenly shouted.

Oh, Lord, what next? Cynthia turned to her sister. "What? What the hell happened now?"

Her eyes settled on Lauren, who was clutching Stephanie's hand. Meanwhile Stephanie was holding up the hem of her gown, revealing the dreaded Keds. She also was standing in a puddle of water.

"Steph's water broke," Lauren said. Her doe eyes were wide with alarm.

With that statement, all hell broke loose.

Chapter 29

"I know that I'm supposed to sound utterly sophisticated and blasé about this, but can I just say that I am *so excited?*" Madison McGuire gushed. "I feel like I could do cartwheels!" She paused. "Well, I would, if it wouldn't throw out my back."

Dawn laughed as they strolled across the hardwood floors.

Gallery staff and contractors darted around the two women in a frantic effort to prepare for tomorrow night's premiere exhibit. The sound of drilling and hammering filled the massive room as workers hung the last few paintings and Lucite plaques on the walls. Tables were being set up along the front where the platters of hors d'oeuvres and wine would be served.

The gallery had been renovated slightly since Maddie had purchased it from Martin Sawyer months ago. She had removed some of the more extreme and off-putting industrial touches, but the space still had a huge presence that Dawn admired. Any lingering doubts Dawn might have had about leaving Templeton Gallery disappeared while she walked through this new space.

"You should be excited," Dawn said. "Tomorrow is

the first official showing at your gallery. It'll be a big night."

"My gallery! *My* gallery!" Maddie shouted, clasping her hands together as she gazed around the exhibition hall in awe. "Oh, it's just surreal! A small-town girl like me having her own gallery? Who would have thought . . ." Her voice trailed off. She turned to Dawn, still grinning. When she saw Dawn's intensely focused expression, she frowned. "But you don't look excited. Is something wrong?"

Dawn looked up from her iPad, where she had typed her to-do list for the day. She had just added another item to the list. "No, nothing's wrong. It's just . . . Well, my job is to make sure that everything runs smoothly so that the gallery's first showing goes off without a hitch. Unfortunately, that means dealing with a lot of last-minute details that can include a lot of hassles. I don't usually get excited until the actual exhibit night."

"Oh," Maddie said, looking deflated.

And frankly, Dawn wanted to add, but couldn't, *I haven't been able to work up much enthusiasm for anything lately.*

Emotionally she was still exhausted by the events of the last few days.

First, it was her father's death. Then she heard news that her stepmother wanted to cut her out of the will. *Then* she had made the heartbreaking decision to sever all ties with Xavier. Dawn thought she couldn't possibly handle any more upheaval in her life—until that whole fiasco at her mother's wedding. Being held at gunpoint by one of the groom's crazy lovers hadn't been fun. But thanks to Keith and Cris's quick thinking, no one had gotten hurt—well, no one except Beatrice, that is. Being tackled by a former NFL player wasn't pretty. When Beatrice was finally dragged away by police, she had several bruises and a bad case of rug burn on her face to show for it.

Of course, as Beatrice was being shoved into the back of a sheriff's office patrol car, Stephanie was being driven away at high speed to the local hospital. She delivered her baby girl later that night after much pushing and screaming and *lots* of cursing at poor, beleaguered Keith. Zoe Hendricks entered the world at 8:58 p.m. weighing seven pounds, eight ounces. Stephanie said Zoe seemed to take more after her father in temperament since so far her little angel seemed tranquil and content, though Dawn bet only time would tell if Zoe would grow up to be a spitfire like her mother. *No one* who had Gibbons DNA had ever been described as "tranquil." Dawn suspected that Zoe would bring her own mix of drama to the Gibbons clan when her time came.

You can bet on it, Dawn now thought with a smirk as she and Maddie approached her office door.

"I don't know why I didn't realize you were so busy, Dawn! And look at me blathering on and on to you," Maddie said, looking flustered.

"You weren't 'blathering'! Besides, I can always make time in my schedule for you. You *own* this gallery, Maddie. Remember that! This is your baby, and if you want to talk to your gallery director or ask questions, you have every right to."

"You're right. But even a gallery director needs some peace and quiet to get things done." She patted Dawn on the shoulder and turned. "I'll let you get back to work. See you at the exhibit tomorrow night!"

Dawn waved. "See you!"

She watched Maddie head back down the hall. Dawn sighed and stepped into her office, going over her to-do list again. It would all get done. She knew it would. She just wished she didn't feel so down. Her dark mood made each day seem longer and each task seem harder.

"Gotta get out of this funk, girl," she mumbled to herself before pulling out her office chair and sitting down behind her glass-top desk.

But she didn't know how. She was still mourning the loss of her father *and* the end of her short-lived romance with Xavier.

She glanced at the photograph of Herb that she now kept on her desk. It was a quick digital shot she had taken of him with her camera phone during one of their "dates." He had been smiling and waving at the camera as he raised a cup of coffee to his lips.

Dawn ran her finger over the picture frame and gave a forlorn smile. She missed her father. She missed him dearly. She wished she could talk to him now and share her doubts and misgivings. She wished she could ask him if she'd made the right decision when it came to Xavier.

But I don't have him here now, she thought, pulling her hand away from the picture frame.

She had to trust her own instinct on this one, and her instinct said to put as much distance between Xavier and herself as possible.

With that, she returned her attention to the stack of contracts on her desk, pushing her sadness and heartache aside for now.

"Dawn, are you busy?" Kevin asked an hour later.

She had asked him to come with her to Sawyer Gallery when she quit the Templeton. "Like I would ever let you leave me behind," he had joked before also turning in his resignation.

He gently knocked on her office door and pushed it open now. "You have someone out here who'd like to speak with you if you have some time."

"No more busy than usual," Dawn grumbled with a frown as she tore her eyes away from her laptop screen. "Is it about tomorrow night's exhibit?" Her shoulders fell. "God, don't tell me it's the florist or the caterer coming in with some issue. I don't think I can take it, Kev!"

He shook his blond head. "No, it's not the florist or the caterer."

"OK, well, at least there's that. Send them in, I guess."

Kevin nodded.

"Oh, and Kev," she whispered.

He paused. "Yeah?"

"Pop back in my office in like . . . fifteen minutes and make up a lie about how you really, *really* need me out on the exhibit floor. I don't want to get sucked into a long conversation. I've got too much to do today."

Kevin nodded again, pushed the door open, and stepped into the hall. She heard him mumble something to someone in the hallway. Dawn busied herself with neatly arranging the stacks of papers on her desk. When she looked up and saw who was walking into her office with his head bowed, heat flared along her cheeks, chest, and neck. Her heartbeat accelerated.

Well, speak of the devil, she thought.

"Hey," Xavier greeted her softly as Kevin shut the door behind him, leaving them alone.

Xavier wasn't wearing a suit today. Instead, he wore dark jeans and a powder blue button-down shirt that was open at the collar. His curly hair looked a little shaggier than usual and he sported a five o'clock shadow. But despite his disheveled appearance, Xavier still looked handsome. He reminded her of what he looked like when she woke up next to him the morning after they spent their first night together. He reminded her of the heartache and disappointment she had experienced days later at the funeral when he acted as if she meant nothing to him.

"What are you doing here?" she asked.

She hoped her voice didn't betray how shaky she felt on the inside, because her skin, muscles, and bones felt like a quivering mass of Jell-O.

"I told you that I was going to check on you," he answered, slowly walking toward her desk. "You haven't returned any of my phone calls, so I just decided to come and see you myself. I went to Templeton and the receptionist told me that I could find you here."

"Well, you shouldn't have come." She rose from the chair and glared at him. "I don't want to talk to you. I'd hoped you would take me ignoring your messages as a hint. But I guess not." She stepped around her desk, giving him a wide berth as she walked toward her door. "Now I'll just have to skip the hints, be a straight-up bitch, and tell you to leave."

"I quit my job at Allen Enterprises," he blurted out, making her pause.

He quit? Why the hell did he quit?

"Sorry to hear that," she muttered blandly, pretending to have little interest in his announcement. She turned the door handle.

"I cut off all contact with Constance and Raquel too . . . especially after I found out that they're planning to cut you out of Herb's will."

"*Really?*" she said as she swung the door open. "Well, you didn't have to do that on my account."

He raised his hand and promptly slammed the door shut, making her stare at him in shock.

"Yes, I did," he said. "It's the least I owe you." She watched his Adam's apple bob as he swallowed. "Look,

Dawn, I know I hurt you. And I know you're angry at me. It's well deserved. But I just want to—"

"Do what? *Apologize?*" she choked, trying to hold back her tears. She took a step back from him when he started to reach out for her. "Is that what you're about to say? Is that what you came here to do?" She closed her eyes and shook her head. "Frankly, I've had enough of your apologies. They don't mean a damn thing if you're just going to do it again."

He cringed. "I never meant to hurt you, and I'm *not* going to do it again!"

"That's what you say now!" she chided as she opened her eyes and began to cry. "You always say that! But you can't please everybody, Xavier. When are you going to figure that shit out? When you're torn between disappointing other people or hurting me, your choice has always been clear, hasn't it? Well, you don't have to make that choice anymore. I've pulled myself out of consideration. So for the last time, go back to Constance! Make up with her and—"

"I'm not going back to Constance! I told you. I've cut off all contact with her! There's nothing between us anymore."

"*Nothing between you?* I *saw* you two together at the funeral! I saw how—"

"You didn't see anything! What you saw was an act! I don't want to marry her and Constance doesn't want to marry me. She never did! The whole time we've been together, she's been fucking some other guy! She was *pretending* that she loved me to save face, to impress her father!"

Dawn paused again. She stared at him in amazement. *Constance cheated on Xavier?* "Bullshit," she whispered.

"No, it's not bullshit! She told me herself, and I was just as shocked as you are. The Constance that I knew—that I've dated since I was nineteen years old—would never do that. But I guess I never really knew her." He raised a hand to Dawn's cheek, wiped at one of her tears, and caressed her. "I never really knew myself either, Dawn. Because if I did, I would have ended it with Constance the moment I met you. What I felt for her is no comparison to how I feel when I'm around you."

Her heart started to flutter at his words and his touch, but she ignored it, reminding herself that she had been sucked in by his captivating spell before and it had only led to disappointment.

"So things fell apart with Constance and . . . and now you've come here to collect the consolation prize?" she asked bitterly. "Is that it?"

"You're no consolation prize." He cupped her other cheek, and despite the alarm bells that went off in her head, she didn't pull away. She gazed into his eyes, feeling herself sinking faster than the *Titanic* into those gray pools. "You're the *ultimate* prize, Dawn. You're the woman who's right for me. You're the one I want to be with . . . to spend my life with, if you'll have me."

She was falling for it. The stone fort she had erected around her heart was being torn down piece by piece again despite her best efforts.

"You talk a good game," she whispered, "but—"

"I'm not talking game. I'm not lying to you, and you know it. We should be together. You feel it, just like I do."

And she did. Despite everything, she wanted him and it made her feel weak and vulnerable, which was everything she had been taught all her life never to be.

"Don't do this to me again," she said desperately, feeling the tears tumble down her cheeks more profusely now. She licked her lips as she trembled, unable to keep up her cold front any longer. "Please, don't do this to me, Xavier. I can't . . . I can't take this. Not again. I know I come off as strong, but I'm not always! I can't—"

Xavier silenced her by bringing his mouth to hers. He moved his lips against her lips, coaxing them open, urging her to kiss him back. He wrapped his arms around her waist and pulled her tightly against him so that their bodies were plastered together and she couldn't get away from him even if she tried.

"I love you," he whispered. "I want you and I love you."

With that, the last wall fell.

Dawn kissed him back, tentatively at first but then more vigorously, until they were both panting and drinking in one another. She felt herself being pressed against her office wall. Her head grazed one of the paintings' frames. Her shoulder bumped her metal shelf and several books and catalogs tumbled to the floor, but she barely noticed. With his tongue in her mouth and his hands on her body again, the world around her faded.

"Damn, I missed you," he murmured before hungrily kissing her again. She whimpered in response.

She felt his hand reach up to caress her breast and she shuddered. When he began to fiddle with the buttons of her blouse, she let him, even helping him to undo a few. When her shirt was open and her bra was bared, Xavier lowered his mouth to her collarbone. She loved the dual sensation of his wet tongue and the rough bristles of his chin and cheek on her skin. He switched his focus to the swell of her breasts over her bra, kissing them both and nipping at her.

"Oh, God," she groaned breathlessly as her eyes fluttered closed. A dampness formed between her thighs.

When he kissed her again, fisting his hands in her

hair, she blindly reached for the zipper of his jeans. At that moment, she didn't care that they were in her office and that only a few feet away gallery staff and contractors were preparing the exhibit floor space for tomorrow night's show. She wanted Xavier. She wanted him inside her and she wouldn't feel whole again until he was.

He must have felt the same, because he shimmied up the hem of her pencil skirt until it was around her waist. He shoved his hand into the front of her thong, needing the wetness on his fingers.

"Dawn," Kevin said as he knocked gently on her office door. "Hey, Dawn," he said again, pushing the door open, "sorry to interrupt, but you're needed on the— *Oh, shit!*"

At the sound of Kevin's voice, Dawn opened her eyes, popping out of her lust-filled haze. Xavier jumped back from her. She turned toward the doorway, closing her shirt and shoving down her skirt. Meanwhile, Xavier raised the zipper of his jeans.

"Sorry, Dawn!" Kevin's face went beet red. He flapped his arms helplessly. "I didn't mean to . . . you know . . . I thought you said to—"

"Um, no, it's . . . it's OK, Kev." She reached up to smooth her disheveled hair but then realized that her shirt only popped open again when she did that. She brought down her arms and clenched the front of her blouse closed. "Mr. Hughes and I were just . . . just about done. I'll be out soon."

"Oh, don't rush on my account!" Kevin said with a grin. "I can take care of everything out here."

"Th-thanks, Kev."

He nodded and began to close the door, but paused to give her a saucy wink before shutting the door completely behind him.

"Good Lord, that was embarrassing!" Dawn said, dropping her face into her hands.

Xavier chuckled. "Oh, come on. It wasn't that bad. He seemed to find it amusing!"

She looked up at him, astonished. "*Wasn't that bad?* My assistant caught you with your hand shoved down the front of my crotch. I'm surprised *you're* not embarrassed." She squinted, eyeing him more carefully. "In fact, why *aren't* you embarrassed? The prim-and-proper Xavier Hughes that I know would go rushing out to apologize."

He shrugged. "I guess the events of the last couple of months have forced the old Xavier Hughes to pull that stick out of his ass."

She redid the buttons on her top. "He wasn't *that* bad."

"I was a self-righteous, judgmental know-it-all. Admit it."

She held up her index finger and thumb. "Just a little."

"But I'm not anymore." He grabbed her shoulders, making her drop her hands to her sides. "I've been humbled and I'm prepared to beg you to take me back . . . to love me again. If it means making an ass out of myself doing it, I will."

"I don't want you to beg or make an ass out of yourself, Xavier. That's not—"

"I will if it'll work." He rubbed her shoulders. "This past week without you, not seeing you or hearing from you, has been the shittiest I've had in a long time."

"It has been for me too," she admitted softly.

"The way that we met wasn't the greatest. Point taken. But frankly, I don't care anymore. If I had to do it all over again, I would. I want to be with you! Just . . . just give me a second chance, Dawn, I swear I won't—"

She placed a hand on his lips, stopping him midsentence. "So this is what it's like to be with a lawyer. You're really set on pleading your case, aren't you? You think if you keep talking that you're going to convince me?"

He tugged her hand away from his lips and held it against his chest. "I figured if I keep talking, it doesn't give you a chance to say no," he answered honestly.

She snorted. "And that's where you have me wrong, Xavier."

He grimaced.

"Because I wasn't going to say no."

Xavier suddenly broke into a smile, looking every bit like a boy who had just wandered into his perfect idea of heaven. His elation at having her back made a warmth surge in her chest. He loved her and he wanted her: a straitlaced, no-nonsense guy like him had fallen for a woman like her, and she hadn't used any of the Gibbons family arsenal of wiles to seduce him.

Wonders never cease, she thought.

He leaned forward to kiss her again.

"No!" she said, shoving her hand against his chest, holding him back. She laughed. "No more of that! This is my office and a place of business, Mr. Hughes. I just started working for this gallery a few weeks ago. I'm not trying to get fired this soon for inappropriate behavior!"

"I see." He looked a little crestfallen, but quickly recovered. "Well, how about we save that inappropriate behavior for tonight, then? I'll make you dinner at my place and—"

"Have me for dessert?" she finished for him.

"Exactly!" A twinkle returned to his gray eyes. "Are you sure I can't get just one . . . just *one* more kiss before I leave?"

She pursed her lips, pretending to consider his question for several seconds. She sighed dramatically. "Well, all right. I guess you—"

She didn't get a chance to finish. He wrapped her in his arms and kissed her, knocking the breath out of her.

Epilogue

"I think I'm more anxious tonight than I've *ever* been for any exhibit," Dawn said as she wrung her hands. She nervously looked around Sawyer Gallery, watching as the throng of people mingled over hors d'oeuvres and champagne while ogling the paintings on the wall.

She then jumped in surprise when she felt someone wrap an arm around her waist. She looked up to find Xavier smiling down at her.

"Calm down," he urged, turning her around to face him. He kissed her and she felt herself relax a little. "Don't be so worried."

It was funny that he was the one uttering those words, considering only seven months ago *he* had been the one who looked tense when he set foot in her gallery. Now he looked like the image of cool in his jeans, T-shirt, and fashionable sport coat. She rarely saw him in his staid business suits anymore now that he no longer worked as general counsel at Allen Enterprises and had become the new director at the community center. He had even talked about donating a few of his old getups to Goodwill.

"How can I not be worried?" Dawn asked him,

glancing over her shoulder at the room again. "There's a lot riding on tonight."

Maddie had been kind enough to let Dawn use the space for a fund-raiser for the community center. Dawn had some of the more talented art students at the center contribute pieces to the exhibit. She also had asked (and begged) a few local artists to do the same. She'd even contributed one of her own works. The proceeds from the art sales would go toward getting laptops for a new computer lab for the kids.

A few of those kids were in attendance tonight, mingling with the rest of the exhibit patrons. Tanisha, the girl whom Dawn had coaxed into skating at the ice-skating rink, was here with her mother. For the special occasion, Tanisha wore a purple and black taffeta dress and her braids in ringlets. She stood proudly in front of one of her canvases talking to a curious patron while her mother beamed as she stood at Tanisha's side.

Dawn smiled at Tanisha then squinted as she gazed across the exhibit hall, eyeing what looked like an empty champagne glass sitting on one of the sculpture podiums.

"Are you kidding me? I can't believe some people!" She started to walk toward the offending glass. "I swear if you want something done right, you have to—"

Xavier followed her gaze and grabbed her arm before she could go stomping off. "It's all right," he said softly. "Look."

He pointed to one of the waiters, who grabbed the glass and placed it on his silver tray already filled with dirty glasses and used napkins.

"See," Xavier said, rubbing her shoulders, "everything's covered. It's one of the few times when everything is going as it should. No drama." He grinned. "Take a deep breath and just enjoy the night."

Dawn slowly exhaled. Xavier was right. Considering what they had been through in the past several months, she should treasure these blissful moments.

At least she was no longer warring with the Allens, though truth be told, that war had been mostly one-sided. Raquel, who had already been furious at Dawn, went on a rampage when she found out that Xavier had left Constance to run away with Constance's older half sister. Raquel went forward with her smear campaign and pushed even harder to have Dawn prove that she was Herbert's legitimate daughter.

When Raquel started attacking both Dawn *and* Yolanda publicly, Dawn decided she couldn't take it anymore. To attack her was one thing. To attack her mama was something completely different. Gibbons girls didn't go out like that! To keep Xavier out of it, she got a lawyer on her own—the one that Cynthia recommended who could "kick ass and take names." The lawyer immediately submitted a motion to the court that if Dawn had to prove she was Herbert's legitimate daughter, so did Constance. Dawn would therefore submit to a blood test if her sister *also* did one. Dawn wasn't sure of the purpose of that tactic, since Constance was obviously Herb's daughter, but her lawyer said to trust him.

"I don't get paid this much money to waste your time, sweetheart," he had proclaimed before propping his Cole Haans up on his office desk.

Shockingly, the lawyer had been right. Raquel immediately withdrew her challenge to the will and her request that Dawn submit to a blood test. That only left folks to wonder whether Yolanda was the only one who "got around" and whether Beautiful Constance was really an Allen after all.

"What's that old saying? Mama's baby, daddy's maybe," the lawyer had said over the phone with a chuckle when he told Dawn that the will would proceed according to Herb's wishes.

After all creditors were paid, the lawyers took their cut, and money was bequeathed to the charities that Herb requested, his surviving relatives—Raquel, Constance, and Dawn—would split the remaining fortune. Though Dawn now stood a strong chance of being a millionaire thanks to her father's death, she would much rather her father be alive than have his money. She wondered if her half sister Constance felt the same.

Speaking of Constance, the last Dawn and Xavier had heard was that she had moved out of Windhill Downs . . . and moved in with that self-entitled asshole Byron Lattisaw. Now that Byron was going through a nasty divorce from his wife since his affair with Monique Spencer had come to light, the two formerly secret lovers were free to come out into the open. Despite finding out that Constance had been cheating on him with Byron during their entire relationship, Xavier no longer held malice toward them.

"I refuse to carry around that baggage with me," Xavier had confessed to Dawn one night while they lay in bed. "I want to focus on what I have going on now . . . on us."

Though he had to admit, he openly speculated how rosy a future Constance and Byron faced now that Byron might have to dole out a big divorce settlement to his wife and pay a lot of child support to his baby mama. But word around town was that he and Constance were engaged.

While their engagement was on, it looked like Yolanda's engagement to Reginald was officially off. Their relationship had never really recovered after that near shooting at the almost-wedding in March.

Beatrice was behind bars, but Yolanda said she didn't want to have to worry about another one of Reginald's old girlfriends or side pieces coming after her with a pistol or any other weapon. Reginald seemed heartbroken, but accepted the breakup.

Dawn secretly suspected that her mother calling off the engagement had less to do with fear for her life and more to do with the fact that her mortgage was paid off and almost all her outstanding debts were settled. She could afford, emotionally and financially, to let Reginald go. But Dawn didn't feel too sorry for Reginald. She doubted a rich widower like him would stay single for long.

As for finding her own rich man, Dawn had officially retired from the hustle, to Cynthia's great disappointment.

"Another one bites the dust," Cynthia had muttered with a droll roll of her eyes when Xavier came to his first Saturday Gibbons family brunch.

But it wasn't just her inheritance that influenced her decision. She was truly in love with Xavier. Plus, after thirty-seven years, two husbands, and numerous rich boyfriends, she wasn't interested in the chase anymore.

"Are you OK now?" Xavier asked, breaking into the bubble of her thoughts.

Dawn dropped her head to his broad shoulder and smiled. "Yeah, I'm fine. Taking a deep breath helped a lot. Thanks."

"No problem," he said, rubbing her back again. His gaze drifted over her shoulder as he looked around the hall. "It's amazing that you did this. The kids will really appreciate it."

"No, what they'll appreciate is those damn laptops."
She laughed. "But if we don't raise enough money
tonight, I've got a few millions coming my way. I'll be
happy to spend some of it on computers."

"Herb would be proud of what you're doing," he
whispered in her ear, making her eyes glisten. She instantly choked up.

"Damn it!" She slapped his arm then flapped her
hands in front of her eyes. "Don't get me started! I'm
going to mess up my mascara."

"Well, he *would* be proud. Doing stuff like this is a
good way to continue his legacy. He was definitely a
giver."

She nodded sadly. "He was, wasn't he? I hope I can
do his legacy justice."

"You can . . . in more ways than one," Xavier said
cryptically as he brushed back a lock of her hair, making
her frown.

"What do you mean?"

He tilted his head and slyly pursed his lips. "Well, I'd
bet he'd love for the Allen genes to go on another gener-
ation."

Dawn cocked a finely arched eyebrow.

"And you keep reminding me how old you are . . . and
frankly, you aren't getting any younger," he continued.

She yanked his arm from around her waist. "Neither
is my uterus, which practically needs a walker at my
age, by the way."

"Oh, come on, Dawn, your uterus isn't geriatric!
And you're great with kids! Wouldn't you like one of
your own?"

"What I'd like is a drink," she said as she walked
away from him toward the waiting arms of a martini.

"I can see it now," he shouted after her with laughter

in his voice, drawing amused stares from those around him. "You waddling through the gallery. Pudding stains on the exhibits!"

"Shut up," she mouthed. She then gave one last menacing glare at him before turning back around and grinning ear to ear.

ANOTHER WOMAN'S MAN

Shelly Ellis

ABOUT THIS GUIDE

The suggested questions that follow are included to enhance your group's reading of this book.

DISCUSSION QUESTIONS

1. Do you think Dawn is right to be hesitant about agreeing to get to know her father better? Should she accept his explanation for why he stayed away from her for so long?

2. Constance wants Xavier to do some research on Dawn. Is she right to be wary of her sister?

3. Dawn doesn't want to tell her mother that she's started a relationship with her father. Do you believe her explanation for feeling this way?

4. Should Xavier have had lunch with Dawn's ex-husband? Did he cross a line?

5. Cynthia says that Dawn should have no allegiance to Constance or Herbert because they're not really her family. What is Cynthia's rationale for this, and do you agree?

6. The more Xavier is around Dawn, the more he can feel his attraction toward her grow. In a similar situation, would you put more distance between you and a future in-law, or is that unrealistic?

7. Did Herbert make the right decision in how he handled the situation with Byron Lattisaw? Should he have shown more support for the son of family friends?

8. Yolanda says she isn't going to allow threats to keep her from marrying her man because she doesn't want to go back to the way things were before she met her fiancé, Reggie. Facing a similar dilemma between threats and livelihood, what decision would you make?

9. Xavier's behavior during the funeral hurts Dawn badly. Do you think she's impractical in her expectations of how he should have behaved?

10. Is Constance right when she says that Xavier is no better than Byron Lattisaw?

11. Dawn decides to forgive Xavier for how he treated her. Would you do the same?

Don't miss the second book in the Gibbons
Gold Digger series

The Player & the Game

On sale now!

Chapter 1

(Unwritten) **Rule No. 3 of the Gibbons Family Handbook:** *Never give a man your heart—and definitely never give him your money.*

Busy, busy, busy, Stephanie Gibbons thought as she hurried toward her silver BMW that was parallel parked in the reserved space near her office. Her stilettos clicked on the sidewalk as she walked. Her short, pleated skirt swayed around her hips and supple, brown legs with each stride.

She shouldn't have gone to the nail salon before lunch, but her French manicure had been badly in need of a touch-up. Unfortunately, that slight detour had thrown off the entire day's schedule and now she was running ten minutes late for the open house.

The spring day was unseasonably warm, but it was tempered by a light breeze that blew steadily, making the newly grown leaves flutter on the numerous maples lining Main Street in downtown Chesterton, her hometown. The breeze now lifted Stephanie's hair from her shoulders and raised her already dangerously short skirt even higher.

She adjusted the realtor name tag near her suit jacket lapel, casually ran her fingers through her long tresses, and reached into her purse. She pulled out her cell phone and quickly dialed her assistant's number. Thankfully, the young woman picked up on the second ring.

"Carrie, honey, I'm running late . . . Yes, I know . . . Are you already at the open house?" Stephanie asked distractedly as she dug for her keys in her purse's depths. "Are any buyers there yet? . . . OK, OK, don't freak out. . . . Yes, just take over for now. Put out a plate of cookies and set the music on low. I'll be there in fifteen minutes . . . I know . . . I have every confidence in you. See you soon."

She hung up.

With car keys finally retrieved, Stephanie pressed the remote button to open her car doors. The car beeped. The headlights flashed. She jogged to the driver's-side door and opened it. As she started to climb inside the vehicle, she had the distinct feeling of being watched.

Stephanie paused to look up, only to find a man standing twenty feet away from her. He casually leaned against the brick front of one of the many shops on Main Street. He was partially hidden by the shadows of an overhead awning.

He looked like one of many jobless men you would find wandering the streets midday, hanging out in front of stores because they had little else to do and nowhere else to go. Except this bored vagrant was a lot more attractive than the ones she was used to seeing. He also was distinct from the other vagrants in town because she had seen him several times today and earlier this week.

Stephanie had spotted him when she walked into the nail salon and again as she left, absently waving her nails as they dried. He had been sitting in the driver's seat of a tired-looking Ford Explorer in the lot across the street from the salon. Though he hadn't said anything to her or even looked up at her as she walked back to her car, she had the feeling he had been waiting for her.

She had seen him also on Wednesday, strolling along the sidewalk while she had been on her date with her new boyfriend, Isaac. The man had walked past the restaurant's storefront window where she and Isaac had been sitting and enjoying their candlelit dinner. When Stephanie looked up from her menu and glanced out the window, her eyes locked with the stroller's. The mystery man abruptly broke their mutual gaze and kept walking. He disappeared at the end of the block.

The mystery man had a face that was hard to forget—sensual, hooded dark eyes, a full mouth, and a rock-hard chin. He stood at about six feet with a muscular build. Today, he was wearing a plain white T-shirt and wrinkled jeans. Though his short hair was neatly trimmed, he had thick beard stubble on his chin and dark-skinned cheeks.

"Are you following me?" Stephanie called to him, her open house now forgotten.

He blinked in surprise. "What?" He pointed at his chest. "You mean me?"

"Yes, I mean you!" She placed a hand on her hip. "Are you following me? Why do I keep seeing you around?"

He chuckled softly. "Why would I be following you? Lady, I'm just standing here."

He wasn't just standing there. She sensed it.

"Well, this is a small town. Loitering is illegal in Chesterton. You could get arrested!"

"It's illegal to stand in front of a building?" Laughter was in his voice. He slowly shook his head. "We're still in

America, right? Last time I checked, I was well within my rights to stand here, honey. Besides, I'm not panhandling. I'm just enjoying the warm sunshine." His face broke into a charming, dimpled smile that would have made most women's knees weak. "Is that a crime?"

Stephanie narrowed her eyes at him warily.

She didn't like him or his condescending tone. He was attractive, but something emanated from him that made her . . . uncomfortable. It made her heartbeat quicken and her palms sweat. She wasn't used to reacting to men this way. Usually her emotions were firmly in control around them, but they weren't around this guy. She didn't like him one bit.

"If . . . if I catch you standing here when I get back, I'll . . . I'll call the cops," she said weakly.

At that, he raised an eyebrow. "You do that," he challenged, casually licking his lips and shoving his hands into his jean pockets. Defiantly, he slumped against the brick building again.

Stephanie took a deep breath, willing her heart to slow its rapid pace. She climbed into her car and shut the driver's-side door behind her with a slam. She shifted the car into drive and pulled off, watching him in her rearview mirror until she reached the end of the block. He was still standing in front of the building, still leaning under the shadows of the awning, still looking smug as she drove to the end of Main Street and made a right.

Finally, she lost sight of him.

"Shit," Keith Hendricks muttered through clenched teeth as he pushed himself away from the brick building once he saw the taillights of Stephanie Gibbons's BMW disappear.

"Shit," he uttered again as he strode across the street

to his SUV, pausing to let a Volkswagen Beetle drive by.

Though he had played it cool in front of her, he had started to sweat the instant Stephanie's eyes had shifted toward him.

He was getting sloppy. He had decided to get out of his car and walk near her office to try to get a better vantage point, to see if her boyfriend, Isaac, was going to meet her here today. But Keith hadn't counted on her noticing him standing there. More importantly, she had noticed *and* recognized him from the other occasions that he thought he had been discreetly tailing her and Isaac. It had been a mistake, a rookie mistake that wasn't worthy of the four years he had spent as a private investigator.

"You messin' up, boy," he said to himself as he opened his car door, climbed inside, and plopped on the leather seat. He shut the door behind him and inserted his key into the ignition.

But he had to admit he was out of practice. This was his first real case in months.

He had been eager to accept this one, to sink his teeth into something meaty. He had been tired of the busy work that had filled his days for the past few months. Stokowski and Hendricks Private Investigators had been going through a bit of a dry spell lately. With the exception of this con artist case, they had been doing nothing but process serving for months, delivering summonses and subpoenas. When Keith left the ATF to start the PI business with retired cop and family friend Mike Stokowski four years ago, process serving wasn't exactly the exciting work he had had in mind. He had hoped things would pick up soon. Now they finally were, but this case had been complicated.

He had finally located Reggie Butler, also known as Tony Walker, *now* known as Isaac Beardan. The con artist and Casanova had left a trail of heartbreak and several empty bank accounts along the Eastern Seaboard. Each time Isaac moved on to his next con, he changed his name, his look slightly, and his story. It made him a hard guy to find.

One of the most recent victims from whom Isaac had stolen thirty thousand dollars' worth of jewelry had hired Stokowski and Hendricks PI to track him down. Keith had traced the smooth-talking bastard here, to the small town of Chesterton. Keith still wasn't sure though if Isaac worked alone on his cons. He didn't know what role his girlfriend, Stephanie Gibbons, played in it—if any. Hell, maybe Isaac had selected her as his next victim.

"Don't worry about her," a voice in Keith's head urged as he pulled onto the roadway. "You finished your part of the case. You found him. You've got photos . . . documentation. The police can track him down now and press charges. That's all that matters."

But was that all that mattered? Should he warn the new girlfriend about Isaac?

An image of her suddenly came to mind: her pretty cinnamon-hued face; the limber legs like a seasoned dancer's that were on full display underneath her flowing, pleated skirt; and her full, red, glossy lips. He remembered the stubborn glare she had given him too, trying her best to intimidate him but failing miserably.

"If you tell her the truth, she'll tell Isaac," a voice in his head warned. "It'll put him on the run again. The authorities will never be able to track him down."

Keith frowned as he started the drive back to his hotel. It was true. Isaac would know he had been found and only move on to the next place and start a new con. No, Keith couldn't tell her the truth about Isaac. He had worked too hard on the case to throw it all away now.

"Maybe she'll figure out he's full of shit by herself," Keith murmured as he gazed out the car's windshield.

But he knew that wasn't likely. Isaac was well practiced at this game. He was a champion player. Keith doubted Stephanie Gibbons would be any different than any of the other saps Isaac had swindled.